THE JOURNAL OF A THOUSAND YEARS

THE GLASS LIBRARY, BOOK #6

C.J. ARCHER

WWW.CJARCHER.COM

CHAPTER 1

LONDON, 1920

The long, sweltering summer surrendered to a damp autumn the day the calendar changed to September. The cooler weather was welcome for those of us who couldn't afford to leave London. The city had become an oven throughout most of August, and anyone who could retreat to the seaside or country did so. Except for Gabe Glass, that is. His family owned an estate, and with his parents away, the manor was available for his use, but he chose to stay in London. My friend Daisy suggested I was the reason behind his decision.

"He wants to be where *you* are, Sylvia," she said as we walked along Bond Street. The end of the drizzling rain meant we could finally lower our umbrellas and walk arm in arm. "It's clear to everyone that he stayed in the city because of you."

Gone were the days where I'd dismiss the suggestion, or change the subject, or deny my feelings for Gabe. I no longer even blushed when someone mentioned his affection for me. Ever since we'd kissed outside the drawing room of his Mayfair townhouse almost a week ago, I'd accepted that we couldn't deny our feelings for each other any more than we could stop breathing.

Nevertheless, I wasn't so self-absorbed as to think I was the only reason he remained in London. He wanted to flush out the person who'd tried to kidnap him. That same person had also stabbed him and conducted tests to study his reactions. The most recent test had involved us being shot at. Gabe's magic responded by slowing time, ensuring we all survived. Despite his friends' attempts to squirrel him away to the countryside, Gabe was determined to stay and capture whoever was responsible for disrupting his life.

I didn't mention any of that to Daisy. She was only partly listening as she gazed upon the wares displayed in the shop windows. At first, I thought she was envious of the expensive jewelry and exclusive hat designs, but then I realized she was studying them with a creative eye. She'd recently declared she was going to become a fashion designer, although her conviction had already begun to waver as she realized she didn't like to sew, and all her best designs were inadvertently copied from magazines.

I also didn't mention Gabe's troubles because that would remind her of Alex, and thinking of him would make her melancholy. I'd yet to discover what had happened between them, but I suspected it had something to do with introducing him to her parents.

Daisy stopped abruptly in front of the window of The Home Emporium, a shop that sold soft furnishings and housewares. "Oh, look at that."

I followed her gaze to the black velvet cushions embroidered with a bold geometric pattern in gold arranged on a chaise longue. I couldn't see the price, but I knew from a past visit to the shop that only the very wealthy could afford their items. Despite her privileged upbringing as the daughter of a lord, Daisy wasn't well-off. The money she'd inherited from her grandparents had almost run out, hence her need for employment. Unfortunately, daughters of noblemen weren't equipped with many employable skills. Daisy's keen sense of the modern woman's style might benefit her, however.

"It's very smart," I said, "but it won't suit your flat." Daisy's furniture was a mixed ensemble of pieces from her parents' home that they no longer wanted, and things she'd bought cheaply. There was no cohesion to the collection, yet somehow it all worked together.

"Not the chaise or the cushions, although they are terribly *chic*." She pointed at a card propped up against one of the cushions. "I'm referring to that. Look at what it says."

"*Wanted: a respectable, steady young woman, about twenty-three years of age, as a shop assistant. She must have a pleasant disposition and good appearance*," I read. "Are you giving up on fashion, Daisy?"

"I think so, yes. While I adore clothes, I'm no designer."

I watched her studying the chaise longue and cushions, and the small table lamp beside it with a slender brass base and domed shade. Her gaze held wonder as she took in every detail. "Perhaps you're not a designer of clothes, but of furnishings."

Her head whipped around, and she blinked at me. "Do you think so? I do love The Home Emporium. I often go in just to browse and imagine how I would use a particular piece in a particular room."

"There you are then. Plus, that advertisement has your name all over it."

She studied it again. "I am twenty-three. And I'm from a respectable family and have a pleasant disposition."

"Not to mention that your appearance is better than good. Although I don't know why appearance matters for a shop assistant."

Daisy pouted. "The ad asks for someone steady, and I have a rather fickle nature."

"Nonsense. When it comes to the things you love, you are as steady as they come, and I know you love furnishings. Besides, you have an excellent eye for putting a room together. The position was made for you, Daisy. Go inside and apply."

I gave her a little shove in the direction of the door, then waited for her to return a few minutes later.

She emerged, beaming. "I begin tomorrow."

I hugged her. "There now, doesn't it feel right?"

"Yes. Yes, it does."

I hooked my arm through hers and we continued our walk to Petra Conway's stationery shop. "It's good to see you smiling again, Daisy. I've been worried about you. It's not like you to be gloomy for so long."

A stoop of her shoulders accompanied her sigh. "I'm sorry I've been a bore. It's my family, you see. I always knew they were snobs, but now I've realized how horrid my parents truly are."

"What happened? What did they say when they met Alex?"

"Nothing. That's the whole problem. They treated him as though he was a groom or footman escorting me. They barely even looked at him, let alone spoke to him."

I hugged her arm. "What will you do?"

"As I see it, I have two choices. If I want to speak to my parents ever again, I must stop seeing Alex. And if I want to be with Alex, I'll lose them. The choice is simple, really. Alex is my future. I'd do anything to be with him and make him happy. If Mother and Father can't accept him, I won't return to their home."

She said it with such conviction that I believed her. I also believed she'd fallen deeply in love with Alex, and he with her. She would protect that love with every fiber of her being.

We arrived at Petra's shop a few minutes before she was due to close for the day. To my surprise, her one and only customer was Huon Barratt. The graphite magician and ink magician did not get along. Their magic disciplines were in competition with one another, not to mention that their personalities clashed. Where Petra, the graphite magician, was sensible, Huon treated each day as if it would be his last. He threw wild parties that continued past dawn. He drank until he forgot where he was, and cared little about finding work, earning money, and settling down. While the carefree and careless attitude had been in evidence before the war, apparently his wartime experiences, coupled with the loss of his beloved uncle, had plunged him into a downward spiral that seemed to have no end.

Huon's story was typical of many men who'd come back from the war. It had altered them, but the changes manifested in different ways. Some couldn't cope in society and had to be hospitalized, others turned inward and serious, like Gabe, while some preferred to drown their awful memories in alcohol and excess, like Huon. I couldn't blame Huon for his recklessness, after what he'd been through. I only hoped he could find a way to climb out of the pit he'd fallen into.

Indeed, I suspected he'd discovered a way out recently. He'd begun a business where he used his magic to write and read invisible messages for anyone who hired him. We had been his first client after he'd transcribed some ledgers for us that had been written in invisible ink. His skill had helped solve a decades-old mystery.

Although the new business venture had certainly helped focus Huon, there was a part of me that suspected reconnecting with Petra had made him *want* to change. Not that either of them would admit it.

"What are you doing here?" I asked him.

He slouched against the shop counter, his ankles crossed and one elbow resting on the countertop near the cash register. Despite the casual pose, he looked like every other gentleman in the city with his neatly pressed clothes, polished shoes and smooth jawline. It was a far cry from the unwashed, unshaven man I'd first met months ago.

Huon jerked his head at Petra, standing behind the counter with a stiff back and a rumpled brow. "I've come to warn her."

Petra rolled her eyes. "Don't listen to him. He's being obnoxious, as usual." She gave his shoulder a shove. "He was just leaving."

Huon straightened but didn't walk off. Although his lips didn't so much as twitch with a smile, his eyes twinkled. Huon in a mischievous mood could lead to all sorts of mayhem. No wonder Petra looked worried.

"Warn her about what?" Daisy asked.

"I'm going to call on her mother and tell her we're in love."

"We are not in love!" Petra exploded.

Huon took her rebuttal in his stride. "First of all, you can't speak for me. I am in love with you, Petra, and there's nothing to be done about it except follow my heart and declare myself. Secondly, you think you don't love me, but you do. You just don't want to admit it because you're worried what people will think."

"They will think I'm doolally, and I quite agree. It's the only explanation for what happened between us."

My interest piqued even further. "What happened? Did you kiss again?" Last time they'd kissed, Petra claimed it had been a drunken mistake. This time, she flushed scarlet and wouldn't look at anyone. Nor did she deny it.

Huon winked at Daisy and me. "A gentleman never tells. Suffice it to say, Petra wants to be with me as much as I want to be with her, only she doesn't like to admit it because of the graphite and ink rivalry."

"Oooh," Daisy cooed. "Your love story is as intriguing as *Romeo and Juliet*." She wrinkled her nose. "Hopefully the ending won't be as tragic."

Huon clicked his fingers. "Yes! We are the magical equivalent of Shakespeare's star-crossed lovers. Don't worry, fair Daisy. Our story won't be a tragedy. It will see the uniting of the two feuding households and an end of the ancient grudge. Love will conquer all."

Petra made a sound of disgust in her throat. "Do shut up, Huon, or I'll throw up my lunch."

He simply smiled at her, revealing dimples that made him even more handsome. "I'll shut up when you agree that you like being with me, that I fulfill your life as much as you fulfill mine, and that I complement you in ways you never realized needed complementing." He turned to face her fully and lowered his voice to a seductive rumble. "I see your face when I close my eyes, and you're the first thought I have when I wake up. Every decision I make, I ask myself what would you do. The change you've seen in me these last few weeks is because of you. You bring out the best in me, Petra, and if I want to continue to be the best version of myself, I *must* have you in my life. So, I won't give up easily. If I give up on you, it'll be like giving up on myself." He leaned across the counter and touched her chin. It had dropped a little further with every sentence he uttered, parting her lips until her mouth formed an O. "You are very beautiful, especially when you're not trying to be."

She snapped her mouth shut and moved out of his reach. "You are quite simply the most *impossible* man I have ever met. Do not call on my mother, Huon. It's far too soon."

Huon's smile teased wider. "You're right. It is too soon in our relationship. But at least you're acknowledging that we have a relationship."

She bristled. "I am not!"

He looked at Daisy and me for confirmation. I shrugged, not wanting to get involved.

Daisy gave Petra a sympathetic look. "I'm afraid that's how it came across. Don't feel horrid. Any woman would find him hard to resist after that speech."

Petra crossed her arms but seemed to have run out of steam. She stayed silent.

Huon picked up his hat from the countertop. "She found me hard to resist before the speech. She just doesn't want to admit it." He slapped the hat on his head. "Good day, ladies. Enjoy your evening. I will be home tonight, just in case you'd like to call on me to discuss anything." This last sentence he said to Petra.

She was having none of it. "If I do call on you, it will only be to tell you that I think you're an arrogant idiot."

He touched the brim of his hat in farewell. "I look forward to your visit." He sauntered out of the shop.

Once the door closed behind him, Petra uncrossed her arms and buried her face in her hands. "Oh, lord. What am I going to do?"

"Call on him, of course," Daisy said. "I take it you two…"

"Kissed?" I offered.

Petra lowered her hands and slumped against the counter. "It went a little further than kissing last night."

I gasped. "Were you drunk again?"

"No," she said on a groan. "I wish I was, but there's no excuse. I can't stay away from him, even though I tell myself I should."

"Why should you?" Daisy asked. "Perhaps you're meant to be together."

"I should stay away because we're wrong for each other. Not only are we very different people, but our families would also never approve. You're right, Daisy. There are similarities to *Romeo and Juliet* about our story, and we all know that didn't end well."

"Petra," I chided. "Huon clearly adores you, and you're obviously a good influence on him. Why not explore where a relationship with him will lead? Perhaps your families will surprise you. Perhaps you'll surprise yourself."

She groaned again. "Why are relationships so difficult? They shouldn't be. They should be easy. I like things to be easy."

Daisy slumped against the counter, too, with another heartfelt sigh. "You took the words right out of my mouth."

* * *

IT WAS difficult to concentrate on work the following day. Gabe visited the Glass Library and although he wasn't there specifically to see me, I was all too aware of his presence. Whenever I passed the first-floor nook where he sat in an armchair, reading, I couldn't help flicking a glance his way. I was drawn to him. I was no more capable of *not* staring as a bee was of not buzzing around a blossom.

As if Gabe was aware of me, too, he looked up whenever I passed. He smiled. I smiled back.

Alex sat opposite Gabe but did not look up from his book except to write notes on a notepad balanced on his knee. He was engrossed in their research. The two men were studying texts in an attempt to learn something about Gabe's magical ability. He could alter time by slowing it down or speeding it up, but only to save his own life or that of someone he cared about, and it wasn't something he could control. Unlike magicians who used spells, Gabe's magic simply activated when required. He'd always thought himself artless until he went to war and found his life in danger almost every day. His mother's powerful watchmaker's magic had become mutated within him as the result of an incident she'd experienced while pregnant.

Yet despite her power and her magical connections, she couldn't give Gabe the answers he sought. He hoped ancient texts could. He and Alex were searching the library's books, scrolls and other documents for any reference to mutated magic similar to his.

It was an area the military had an interest in, too. Mr. Jakes from Military Intelligence had come to the Glass Library a few months ago in search of relevant texts. He'd since claimed to have no interest in Gabe anymore, but some of us believed he was behind the recent kidnapping attempts.

Alex was always with Gabe nowadays, acting as bodyguard wherever his friend went. Gabe's second bodyguard, his father's cousin Willie, was usually with them, but she was absent this time. She loathed reading anything more in-depth than *The Daily*

Mirror, so had arranged to meet a friend instead. In her words, reading books from the Glass Library's collection was "more boring than listening to a lecture about watching paint dry." Her absence made for a peaceful morning.

I entered the stacks in search of a book requested by a patron, only to see Professor Nash emerge from the hidden door that led to his flat. He carried a leather-bound notebook in one hand. I recognized it as the book in which he was writing the rough draft of his memoir.

I nodded at it. "Are the words flowing today?"

He stared down at the notebook clutched in both hands, then folded it against his chest, as if afraid of dropping it. "Slowly, Sylvia. Very slowly."

I watched him shuffle past, bald head bowed, his thin shoulders more stooped than usual. He seemed less cheerful of late. His smiles were wan, when he smiled at all, and there was a sense of heaviness about him that hadn't been there months ago. I knew he missed his friend, Oscar Barratt, but I wondered if a part of him had held out hope that he'd walk through the door. Unlike the professor, Oscar hadn't returned to England when war broke out, and instead continued to the Arabian Desert, where he met his end. I wasn't sure of the details, but I did know that the professor missed him terribly. It seemed that writing his memoir was stirring up memories that made the pain of losing Oscar more acute.

I retrieved the book I needed from the shelves and returned to the ground floor reading nook where the patron was poring over another text at the desk. We chatted for a while about his area of interest—cotton magic. Although paper magic descended from cotton magic, I didn't tell him I was a paper magician. Very few people knew. I wasn't yet sure what I thought about it, and until I did, I wanted to keep it to myself.

When the patron left, I went to check on Gabe and Alex's progress. Although their stack of books had shrunk as they completed their review and set them aside, neither had made many notes.

"No luck?" I asked, peering over Gabe's shoulder.

"Not really," he said. "I found one reference to a mutation, but that only came about after a carpentry magician ingested a herbal concoction over several years. He wasn't born that way."

He sounded so forlorn that I wanted to comfort him. I was still reluctant to show much affection toward him in front of others for fear of backlash, particularly from Willie, so I simply gave his shoulder a reassuring squeeze.

He reached up and placed his hand over mine, tucking his fingers underneath. We exchanged small smiles that said more than either of us had yet to express in words.

I looked to Alex, but he didn't notice. "Alex? Have you discovered anything?"

"Hmmm?" He blinked at me. "Sorry, I wasn't listening. My mind was elsewhere."

"With Daisy perhaps?"

"With the meeting we had with her parents."

I would have probed further to ascertain his opinion of the event, but the professor appeared at the top of the stairs with three visitors in tow. I smiled at the Hendry sisters, genuinely pleased to see them. They smiled back, even Myrtle, the most serious of the trio. I invited them to sit on the sofa while I took the armchair Alex vacated.

Mere days after learning that I was most likely related to the Hendry family, I was still somewhat shy around them. That was perhaps because I wasn't sure how I was related to them. I could be a distant relative, or I could be their niece. If their brother, Melville, a man they didn't like, who had caused trouble for Gabe's parents years ago, turned out to be my father, then any relationship we'd built would be on shaky foundations.

It would also affect my relationship with Gabe. Although he claimed not to care, Willie cared very much. Gabe's parents would also be anxious if my presence attracted Melville Hendry back into their lives.

According to his sisters, however, it was unlikely I was Melville's daughter. He didn't like women, and so wouldn't have done what was necessary to produce children. That didn't mean he couldn't, just that it went against his nature.

We exchanged the obligatory pleasantries before Myrtle came to the reason for their visit. "Do you recall that we said we'd contact our extended family and ask if anyone was aware of a brother, uncle or cousin who may have fathered you?"

"I do. Those must have been awkward telephone calls."

Rosina, the pluckiest of the sisters and the only paper magician among them, chuckled. "We offended a number of elderly aunts. One even hung up on me."

"That's because you called her son a philanderer," Myrtle pointed out.

"He was, as his mother knows all too well."

My interest was piqued the moment she mentioned philanderer. "Could it be him? What was he like?"

If he were a monster, then he was a likely candidate. My mother had been fleeing from someone all her life. Since she refused to tell my brother and me anything about our father, it made sense that he was the reason for her constant fear of discovery. I'd come to terms with the fact my father could turn out to be an awful person. I was at a point where I simply wanted to know, no matter the outcome.

It was Naomi, the gentle-natured youngest sister who answered me. "My dear Sylvia, it's not possible. He died before you were born. We hadn't been aware until his mother informed Rosina."

I splayed my fingers across my lap, releasing some tension. I'd not been aware how tightly wound I'd been ever since they'd arrived. "So…are there any candidates?"

Once again, Myrtle the no-nonsense eldest sibling, answered.

"Not that we've found. There is a surprising lack of men in our family tree."

"They're all rather a weak lot," Rosina added.

"Weak paper magicians?" I asked.

"Weak in character. It seems to be a flaw in the male line."

"Rosina," Naomi chided. "Melville wasn't weak. He was... different. He didn't fit into the world's view of how he ought to think and act. That's why he became so—"

"Cruel?"

"Introverted."

"His crimes weren't the result of his introversion," Rosina pointed out, somewhat hotly. "They were the result of a corrupted mind and had nothing to do with whether he preferred men to women."

Naomi blushed at the mention of her brother's homosexuality, turning her ruddy cheeks even pinker. She was the homeliest of the three, and the only spinster. She lived with Myrtle and Myrtle's husband, next door to Rosina, a widow, and Rosina's two adult children. Whenever I looked for similarities between myself and these women, I always felt I was most like Naomi, somewhat reserved and a peacemaker. Although Gabe had once pointed out that I wasn't all that shy, merely cautious with people I didn't know well, he did agree that I liked to settle disputes rather than inflame them.

Myrtle told Rosina to quieten her voice. "Don't talk about Melville's predilections in public. People will talk."

Rosina rolled her eyes.

Myrtle noticed but chose to ignore her. She turned to me. "Disregarding Melville's dislike of women, I'm beginning to think he is your father, Sylvia."

I glanced at Gabe, seated in the other armchair, to gauge his reaction, but a newcomer ascending the staircase caught his attention. He rose, as did Alex who'd been perching on the edge of the desk, when they saw the visitor was a woman.

"I hope I'm not interrupting," Evaline Peterson said.

The paper magician, aged in her forties, was most certainly not my relative. We looked nothing alike. She was tall and thin, and came across as officious and prim at first, but I'd since discovered she was good-natured. Despite agreeing that we weren't related, she and her brother, Walter, had taken me under their wing when they discovered I was a paper magician with no family. They'd enjoyed teaching me their spell to strengthen paper, which they used on cards and paper they manufactured for exclusive clients. I'd introduced the Hendry sisters to Walter and Evaline Peterson mere days ago. It was hard to imagine that the two paper magician families had never met, but the Hendrys weren't involved in manufacturing. Two of the sisters were even artless.

"I couldn't help overhearing as I came up the stairs," Evaline said. "You were talking about Sylvia's father."

"There's a possibility it could be our brother," Myrtle told her. "He's been missing a number of years, however, so we could be clutching at straws."

"She does look like all three of you." For someone usually so stiff and reserved, Evaline brought an air of excitement with her that had us all waiting eagerly for her next words. "That's why I'm here. Ever since meeting the three of you, I've been thinking how much you look like one of our employees. His name isn't Hendry, and he isn't a magician, but the similarity nagged at me so much that I couldn't rest until I mentioned him to you. I thought perhaps you could come and meet him, thinking he might be a cousin, but hearing you mention your brother, well… might it be him living under an assumed name?"

My heart seemed to suddenly stop.

"What name does he go by?" Gabe asked.

"Maxwell Cooper."

"Cooper!" Alex bellowed. He turned wide eyes onto me.

Gabe reached across the gap between us and took my hand in his. "It can't be a coincidence."

"Do you know him, Sylvia?" Rosina asked. "How are you connected to this Cooper fellow?"

I blinked at Gabe, appealing to him to explain since I seemed unable to form the words. My tongue was thick in my mouth, my throat tight.

He offered a reassuring smile. Without taking his gaze off me, he answered Rosina. "Sylvia's mother's last known address was a house in Wimbledon. Her neighbor knew her as Marianne Cooper."

CHAPTER 2

The connections snapped together like magnets.

Although I knew my mother as Alice Ashe, we'd discovered she was really Marianne Folgate, the only child of a silver magician from Ipswich, who himself descended from a lineage of magicians that was suspected to be the last of its kind. Gabe's parents had met Marianne years ago when she was living in Wimbledon. When Gabe and I visited that house recently, we'd learned that Marianne had been known as Mrs. Cooper while living there, and that the man she lived with was most likely her husband. The house they rented was owned by Lord Coyle, but Coyle's widow had sold it after his death.

It couldn't be a coincidence that a man named Cooper worked at the Petersons' paper factory and that he resembled the Hendry sisters, and me. It was precisely the place in which a paper magician would feel comfortable.

Yet Evaline claimed he wasn't a magician, and we knew that Melville Hendry was. My initial thrill dampened a little. Perhaps they weren't the same man. Having the Hendry sisters meet him, and confirm or deny if he was their brother, would resolve the issue once and for all.

I wasn't the only one with that idea. All three sisters

suddenly stood together, as if they'd been raised up by strings pulled in unison. They'd never seemed more alike.

"Is he at work now?" Rosina asked, at the same time Naomi said, "Can we meet him?"

Myrtle was more cautious, her tone less enthusiastic. "Did you mention us to him?" she asked Evaline.

"Yes, just before coming here. I asked him if he was related to the Hendry family. I thought he might be a cousin on your mother's side, hence the different name." Evaline frowned. "He looked shocked at first, but that quickly vanished. He told me he's not related to any Hendrys, then reminded me that he's not a magician. I told him he might have relatives he didn't know about, including a young paper magician." She nodded at me.

Myrtle's lips pressed together. "If it is Melville, he won't want to see us. He has probably disappeared again."

"He has worked for us for years. He won't leave without giving notice."

Myrtle remained unconvinced. "If our brother doesn't want to be found, he'll go to great lengths to disappear."

Gabe made an excellent and intriguing point, however. "If he didn't want to be found, he wouldn't have used the same name he was once known by—Cooper. He would have chosen something entirely different."

We decided to travel to the factory. Gabe's Vauxhall Prince Henry was parked on the adjoining street near the end of Crooked Lane, but we couldn't all fit. Alex searched the vicinity for a taxi, or perhaps he was checking there were no suspicious looking characters lurking nearby, waiting for an opportunity to kidnap Gabe.

I asked Evaline about her previous visit to the Glass Library. She wasn't a person who called on someone without a reason, and that time had seemed odd, although I'd dismissed it as a friendly gesture. Now, I wondered if she'd had a purpose, after all. "Last time you were here, you suspected your employee was related to me, didn't you?"

Her sharp features softened. "I wanted to study you, Sylvia. While you look a little like him, he's a man in his sixties and you're a woman in your twenties. In fact, you look more like Rosina than Mr. Cooper. But that day, I wanted to study your mannerisms to compare them to his. That's when I noticed you talk like him. It's the way your mouth moves, I think. I can't quite explain it, but there is a resemblance that goes beyond obvious physical similarities."

The thought of seeing those similarities in person soon, and comparing myself to the man who could be my father, made me feel somewhat weak-kneed. I moved closer to Gabe in case I needed to hold on to something solid.

"We should wait for Willie," Alex said, as he signaled to a taxi that had just turned into the street. "She doesn't like you wandering around without her."

Gabe checked to see that we were out of earshot of the others. "*You're* here to protect me."

"She has something I don't. A gun," he added when Gabe arched his brows.

"She could be hours. I think the airman she met with is more than a friend."

Willie's interest in both men and women was the reason I wasn't shocked when I'd learned about Melville Hendry's homosexuality. But I had thought Willie was monogamous. "Has something happened between her and Nurse Tilda?"

"She told me to mind my own business this morning when I asked," Gabe said. "I value my life, so didn't press her."

The taxi pulled over and Alex opened the door for the three sisters. Once they were on their way, he invited Evaline to travel with us in the Vauxhall.

Thirty minutes later, we alighted at the main gate to the Petersons' paper factory on Bethnal Green Road. The sky was murkier here, thanks to the smoke spewing from the chimneys, and the air felt cloying. A lorry drove slowly through the gate and headed up the street, most likely on its way to deliver paper around the city. The Petersons supplied small stationery shops like Petra's, as well as large institutions, including the Bank of England. It was a lucrative business, and one that I'd been accused of coveting for myself when I was attempting to discover if Walter and Evaline's father was also my father. Neither sibling had accused me. It was their long-time employee who'd suspected I was a fortune hunter.

It suddenly occurred to me that *he* could be the fellow Evaline wanted us to meet. I didn't know his name, but there was a resemblance between him and the three sisters.

Evaline asked us to wait for her in her brother's large office in the administration building while she went in search of Mr. Cooper. The Hendry sisters sat, but I couldn't settle. Gabe and Alex's good manners meant they wouldn't sit unless I did, so the three of us stood by the window that overlooked the courtyard surrounded on three sides by buildings. That's how we saw Evaline striding towards us with her brother. There was no sign of a third person.

I smiled at Walter when he greeted me and listened as Gabe introduced him to the Hendry sisters. I didn't really hear the conversation, however. I had the strange sensation of being outside the scene, as if I were standing in the wings watching a play being performed on stage. I knew before Evaline spoke that the man known as Cooper couldn't be found.

"He said he was feeling unwell and went home early," Walter added. "It's unlike Cooper to be ill. He rarely takes time off." The frown looked unnatural on the usually cheerful man.

Evaline paced the floor, her hand pressed to her chest. "I mentioned the Hendry family to him this morning in all innocence. I thought he was a distant relative. I never suspected he was a Hendry himself, but now it seems as though I triggered his flight." She stopped in front of me. "I am so sorry, Sylvia."

Walter shook his finger at her. "We don't know for certain if that's why he left. I'm prepared to give him the benefit of the doubt. Cooper has been a loyal employee and a solid worker for a number of years."

"None of that matters if he's trying to remain hidden," Gabe said.

Rosina clicked her tongue in irritation, while Myrtle muttered, "Typical Melville," under her breath.

"We don't know if Mr. Cooper is Melville," Naomi reminded her sisters.

"He must be, or why avoid this encounter?" Myrtle turned to Evaline. "You say you mentioned we three to him, and told him about Sylvia, too?"

"I simply told him he might have a relative who was a young paper magician. I didn't mention her name, nor that she's searching for her father."

Walter threw doubt over the idea that I was Mr. Cooper's daughter. "He had one son, who I believe died, although I'm not entirely sure, now that I come to think about it." He frowned. "He rarely speaks about family."

"Because he was avoiding us," Rosina muttered with a bitter edge.

Naomi looked sheepish. "We didn't get along with Melville," she told the Petersons. "Not when we were children, and certainly not as adults. He avoided us, and we him, then he disappeared altogether."

I rubbed my arms as a chill rippled through me. He didn't get along with his sisters, and I suspected my mother didn't like my father. Indeed, she was most likely afraid of him. It was too much of a coincidence.

Walter strode toward the door. "We have Cooper's address on file. I'll send someone to check on him."

"We'll go," Gabe said.

Walter hesitated before nodding. He left to speak to his assistant in the outer office and returned moments later with a large photograph. "My assistant reminded me of this. It was hanging out there on the wall." He showed it to the Hendry sisters. "It was taken a few months after war was declared. When we realized a lot of our men would enlist, we had a photograph taken of all the staff."

Evaline peered over Naomi's shoulder. "We lost some young men in the war, then the influenza outbreak took more." She pointed to a figure in the photograph which had been taken in the courtyard. "There. That's Cooper."

Rosina and Naomi squinted at the photograph while Myrtle removed a pair of spectacles from her bag.

"That's him!" Rosina cried. "That's Melville."

"Are you sure?" Naomi asked.

Myrtle took the photograph from Walter and inspected it. "That's him. Older, yes, but it's definitely him."

Walter removed a magnifying glass from his desk drawer and handed it to Naomi. "When did you last see your brother?"

"In 1891," Myrtle said.

"That's not a year many of us who lived through it will forget."

Gabe and Alex exchanged knowing glances. It was the year Gabe's parents had set in motion the emergence of magicians from the shadows. Laws had been implemented to prevent their persecution, but it had taken time for the situation to settle. With the well-made products of magicians flooding the market, and with their more efficient practices, they'd quickly asserted themselves as the makers of superior merchandise. Artless manufacturers and craftsmen had suffered, leading to tensions in London and elsewhere. Those artless who hadn't repositioned themselves as producers of lower quality products and priced accordingly had gone out of business, causing further resentment.

Naomi peered through the magnifying glass at the photograph. "Oh, yes, I see him now. That's Melville. He lost most of his hair." She handed the magnifying glass to Rosina.

"So he did." Rosina sounded satisfied to see her brother suffer in that small way.

I asked to see the photograph and Naomi handed it to me.

She pointed at Melville, standing in the front row of what must be a hundred employees. I didn't need the magnifying glass to recognize him.

It was the man I'd spoken to on a few occasions, the one who accused me of coveting a share of the Peterson fortune. He'd come across as cantankerous and rude.

"It doesn't confirm whether he's your father," Myrtle told me with a gentleness I'd not experienced from her before. "It just confirms that Cooper is Melville."

When I didn't respond, Gabe answered. "Sylvia's mother was known as Marianne Cooper at one point. The man she lived with in 1891 was also known as Cooper, so we believe they were married, although that may not necessarily be the case. If the paper magician Melville Hendry disappeared around that same time, and reappeared as Cooper here at the factory, and Sylvia's mother was also known as Cooper and Sylvia's father is a paper magician…" His eyes became hooded as he looked at me, his voice gentled. "Then it stands to reason that Melville is her father."

The evidence was compelling. No one could deny it. No one did. A weighty silence filled the office, as oppressive as the smoky air outside.

Until Naomi broke it. She blinked back tears as she took my hands in hers. "We have another niece. Isn't it wonderful, sisters?"

Rosina threw her arms around me and hugged me fiercely. "My children have cousins. *And* you're a magician, too. How I've longed for another in the family. Both of my children are artless."

My eyes filled with unshed tears, so I closed them. When I could be sure I wouldn't cry, I reopened them. Myrtle filled my vision as she hugged me, too. "Welcome to the family, Sylvia. It's lovely to have you."

Finding three aunts and two cousins was everything I'd hoped for. More. It made the trials of my complicated past less bitter. I didn't even mind having a man nobody liked as my father if his connection to these women meant I had a lovely family.

When Myrtle pulled away, I caught Gabe smiling at me over the top of her head. His fingers briefly touched mine in a featherlight flutter before slipping away.

Alex clapped me on the shoulder. "You'll have to telephone Daisy to give her the good news. She'll be thrilled for you. As am I."

I found I couldn't speak to thank him, as tight as my throat was, so I simply nodded and smiled instead.

Walter had slipped out of the office, but now returned with a piece of paper. He handed it to Gabe. "Cooper's address. Are you sure you don't want me to come?"

Gabe shook his head, but it was Myrtle who answered. "It's now a family matter, but thank you for all your help. Before we go…" She glanced at her sisters. "Before we go, can you tell us what you know about our brother? It's been decades since we saw him, so perhaps he has changed."

"He's a good employee. He works hard and is prepared to put in extra time when necessary. The others respect him, but I think that could be because they fear him a little, which is not entirely a bad thing for a foreman."

"I mean on a more personal level. What was he like?"

Walter shrugged. "I can't say I know him well. He's always respectful to me and Evaline."

"Speak for yourself," his sister said. "He was often curt when he had to deal with me. I got the distinct impression he resented the times he had to answer to me instead of you. Particularly in the early days, when I first came to work here. Our father was still alive then, and he praised Mr. Cooper for his strong work ethic, but to me, Cooper was rather rude. I think he thought I wasn't up to it. It took years before I felt as though he respected me as a magician and a manager."

"Because you're a woman," Rosina added with certainty.

"You had to work extra hard to prove yourself to him. He treated Myrtle and Naomi abominably because they were artless, and he was little better with me. He was a much stronger magician than me, you see. When we were young, he'd taunt me. He called me weak and pathetic whenever I performed magic. He tore up my origami creations and left little pieces of them around for me to find to prove that my magic didn't last as long as his and wasn't as strong."

"He wasn't always like that," Myrtle said. "When we were small children, he was a normal brother. It wasn't until he was thirteen or fourteen that he changed."

It was an age that a lot of youths changed, both physically and emotionally. It was a trying time for some. Probably even more trying for a boy who realized he was unlike others in a way society wouldn't allow. But that was no excuse for his cruelty.

"He never performed magic here at the factory?" Gabe asked.

Walter shook his head. "Not that we know of. Evaline and I are the only ones who use spells on our luxury paper line."

"When did he start working here?"

Walter looked to Evaline, but she merely shrugged. "I'd have to check his file," he said.

Gabe asked him to do so.

Walter returned a few minutes later with a document that he handed to Gabe. "February 1898."

Alex peered over Gabe's shoulder at the file. "The troubles between artless and magicians had largely ended by then. He must have thought himself safe."

Gabe agreed. "The police would have stopped actively searching for him. If he kept his head down and didn't make any trouble, no one would find him."

"Not even his sisters," Myrtle muttered.

Gabe tapped his finger on the document. "He used the name Cooper here, the same name he was using in 1891 when he was involved with Lord Coyle. It was a risk not to change it again. So why didn't he? Why keep using a name that linked him to the past?"

Alex pointed to the address on the document. "Let's see if he's home and ask him."

* * *

ALTHOUGH ALEX DIDN'T SPEAK during the short drive to Melville Hendry's flat, I could tell he was anxious. He constantly checked the surroundings and drove as quickly as he could through the traffic. Fortunately, he'd given the driver of the Hendry sisters' taxi the address so they didn't have to keep up.

Gabe regarded Alex narrowly but didn't comment on his friend's speed. He kept a watchful eye on our surroundings, too, as we alighted from the Vauxhall. I couldn't see anyone suspicious, but Alex's caution worried me.

While we waited for the sisters to arrive, we spoke to the landlady. She informed us that Mr. Cooper was at work at the paper factory.

"We've just come from there," Gabe told her. "He left early. He hasn't returned home?"

The matronly woman wrung her plump hands together. "I don't think so, but I've been out myself, so he may have come back while I wasn't here. I'll knock on his door."

We waited somewhat impatiently while she headed upstairs. She returned a few minutes later, shaking her head. "There's no answer."

"We should go in and check," Gabe said.

"What if he's not there?" She looked Gabe and Alex over, biting on her lower lip. "It wouldn't be right to let strangers in without his permission."

It was fortuitous that the Hendry women arrived at that moment. Gabe introduced them as Mr. Cooper's sisters, and me as another young relative, all of whom were concerned that her tenant had left work feeling unwell. Our physical resemblance to

Mr. Cooper must have swayed her. She went to fetch the spare key, then invited us to follow her up the stairs.

His room contained a bed, narrow wardrobe, and washbasin on a stand on one side, and a table with a portable stove on the other. The copper kettle on the stove was cool to the touch, and the blue-and-white teacup beside it was clean. A wooden chair was tucked under the table, and a plate and bowl in the same blue-and-white pattern as the cup and saucer were placed neatly on a shelf by the window. The jars lined up on the second shelf proved to contain exactly what their neat handwritten labels stated—sugar, tea, and other non-perishable essentials. The only other furniture was a comfortable-looking armchair positioned by the fireplace, separating the room into a sleeping half and a dining half.

The rug under the armchair was small but good quality, as were the armchair and crockery. They weren't the type of things left behind when a resident moved, so I suspected he'd simply gone out to avoid seeing his sisters.

Gabe didn't agree. "All his clothes are gone." He went to close the empty wardrobe door, but Myrtle wanted to take a look, so he left her to it while he checked the small cupboard under the washstand. It was also empty. "There's no shaving equipment or other personal items. He left."

"But he hasn't paid me this month's rent!" the landlady cried.

"I'm sorry, but it doesn't look like he plans to return."

She clicked her tongue and muttered something under her breath.

I checked the name of the manufacturer on the base of the saucer. I recognized it. "This is magician-made. The set would have cost quite a lot. Surely he wouldn't just leave it behind. The armchair, too, is good quality and worth taking to his new place of residence. Are the stove and kettle his?"

The landlady wasn't listening. Her matronly manner had disappeared beneath the huffing and puffing of her fury.

Gabe inspected the plate and bowl. "They may be magician-made, but the bowl is chipped." He fingered the jagged edge. "It's also probably part of a larger set, or it was, once. My guess is that this was made years ago, and when the magic wore out, it got damaged. The owner probably threw it away or gave it to Hendry."

"Or he stole it," the landlady muttered.

Naomi bristled, but it was Rosina who stood up for her brother. "Melville wasn't a thief."

"Who's Melville? My tenant's name was Maxwell. Maxwell Cooper."

"He went by more than one name," Gabe told her.

The landlady wagged a finger at Rosina. "As his sisters, you are responsible for the rent he owed."

Rosina crossed her arms. "We're estranged."

Gabe removed a banknote from his pocket. "Will this cover your lost rent?"

The landlady tucked it into her apron pocket.

Myrtle slammed the wardrobe door closed. She shook her head at her sisters. "He must have taken it with him."

"What are you looking for?" I asked.

"A journal that's been in our family for a long time. It disappeared along with Melville years ago."

"It belongs to all of us," Rosina added. "It has been handed down to the strongest male magician of each generation, so I suppose he felt he had a right to it." She sighed. "All that history, just gone."

Naomi took her sister's hand. "Not gone. I'm sure he's taking good care of it. And when we find him, we'll tell him about the strongest magician in the next generation. She may not be male, but she certainly ought to have it." She gave me a small smile.

Alex had been giving the room a more thorough search while we spoke. He'd checked under the bed and inside the jars. He'd lifted the rug and felt about for loose floorboards. He found nothing of interest until he checked the back of the armchair cushion. He removed a scrap of paper, no larger than a postage stamp, and handed it to Gabe. "He was in Ipswich."

Gabe read the scrap then handed it to me. It was part of a train ticket with the word Ipswich clearly visible. It must have fallen out of Melville's pocket when he sat in the armchair.

Recently we'd learned that the silver corner protectors on the Medici Manuscript had been made by a magician in Ipswich. Since my brother, James, believed he was a silver magician, we'd traveled there and learned that Marianne Folgate had been the daughter of the magician who made them. According to a neighbor, she'd left home shortly before her parents died and not been seen since. A photograph of a young Marianne proved she was my mother, the woman I'd known as Alice Ashe.

At each step, we'd learned of another man making the same inquiries, discovering the same things as us. It seemed likely that man was Melville Hendry.

I twisted the slim silver ring on my middle finger, one of the few possessions of my mother's that I'd kept. She'd ensured our safety by moving from city to city, but I wished she'd told James and me why we were always moving, always keeping to ourselves and not putting down roots. It would have made life less confusing.

Although telling one's children they were hiding from their cruel father wouldn't have been an easy conversation for anyone.

The landlady locked the door to Melville's room as we left. Alex led the way downstairs to the entrance hall, most likely to make sure the coast was clear.

"What's he like as a tenant?" Gabe asked the landlady as we followed Alex.

"He kept to himself. I rarely even got a 'good morning' out of him. Nor did my other tenants. I never liked him. Now I know why. I have good instincts."

The Hendry sisters chose not to defend their brother. Rosina and Naomi walked to the waiting taxi, while Myrtle hung back to speak to Gabe. "We'll pay you back Melville's rent just as soon as we can."

"No need," he said.

"We can't let you do that for us."

He gave her one of his charming smiles that no middle-aged lady could resist, even if she was a practical-minded one. "As much as I like you all, I'm doing it for someone else."

"Ah." She smiled at me. "Do let us know if you find him."

We would have watched them drive away, but Alex ushered Gabe to the Vauxhall while Myrtle was still climbing into the taxi. Although both men were usually chivalrous, I was left to my own devices and had to open my own door.

"Were we followed?" I asked as I looked up and down the street.

"It seems so," Gabe said as Alex cranked the engine. Once his friend had slid into the driver's seat, Gabe asked why we were in such a hurry.

"A black vehicle sat behind us for a long time on the way here, but I think I lost him," Alex said.

"Was it following us from the factory? Before?"

Alex hesitated then shook his head. "I can't be sure. I wasn't —" He swore loudly then stamped his foot on the accelerator.

The Vauxhall shot forward to join the traffic. I clamped a hand to my hat to keep it on my head.

Gabe turned around to look past me out of the rear of the vehicle. He swore, too, something he rarely did. "I need a new motorcar."

"Why?" I shouted over the roar of the engine.

"This one isn't fast enough. There *is* someone following, and they're gaining on us. Brace yourself for impact, Sylvia. Hopefully my magic will engage like the last time we were run off the road, but in case it doesn't…"

He didn't finish the sentence. He didn't need to. We all knew an impact with another vehicle could be fatal.

CHAPTER 3

Alex turned the steering wheel sharply, and the Vauxhall careened around a corner, narrowly missing a motorbus that had stopped to pick up passengers. If I hadn't been gripping the door, I would have slid across the seat to the other side.

"He's still with us!" Gabe shouted.

I dared a glance behind us. The bus driver shook his fist, while the driver of a vehicle we cut off bellowed something I couldn't hear. A black motorcar sped along in our wake. At this distance, and with his cap pulled low, I couldn't make out the face of the driver hunched over the steering wheel.

"Hold on!" Alex's instruction was unnecessary. I was already holding on as tightly as I could, to both the door and my hat.

The Vauxhall sped around another corner then immediately turned again. Alex must have known the two turns were close together, but I was quite lost. We were in a part of London I'd never visited.

"He missed the turn," Gabe said. "Good driving."

Alex continued at speed. He made more turns, taking us through busy streets and quiet ones, wide thoroughfares lined with shops and narrow residential lanes edged with neat row houses. We left a trail of angry drivers behind us, but it wasn't until Gabe told him to slow down that Alex finally eased his foot off the pedal.

"We lost him," Gabe said. "Let's take Sylvia back to the library."

Alex's gloved hands readjusted their grip on the wheel. "If he knows you at all, he'll know to find you there. He'll be waiting."

"Then so be it. I can't run forever."

I expected Alex to disagree, but he simply continued to drive, albeit at a more sedate pace.

We were now in an area I recognized as the location of Hobson and Son, the boot-making factory owned by the family of Gabe's former fiancée, Ivy. Driving down the street wasn't the wisest choice for Alex to make. The traffic slowed as we passed the ever-present protestors on the pavement. Former soldiers on crutches or in wheelchairs held placards accusing the Hobsons of greed and demanding an apology and compensation for the boots that failed under the muddy, soggy conditions of the Front. While the majority of boots made at the factory had held up well for the duration of the war, a batch had fallen apart. *All* army-issued boots should have been strengthened by a leather magician's spell, as stipulated in the company's contract with the military, but it seemed that one batch had missed out.

According to the family, both Mr. Hobson and his son, Bertie, were leather magicians, but we'd begun to doubt if Ivy's brother was a magician at all. We'd discovered he'd spent some time at a private clinic that used to treat the artless children of magicians in an attempt to draw the magic out of them. The treatments failed, of course, since artless were born artless. No medical intervention could change that.

Ivy refused to believe that Bertie was artless, and their parents continued to claim he was a magician. They blamed the soldiers for the failure of their boots, putting out statement after statement that they contained magic like all the others. They'd even tried to coerce Gabe, as the son of a powerful magician, to endorse their statements. His refusal had created a rift between him and the Hobsons that was partly responsible for him ending his relationship with Ivy, although Ivy had never quite accepted it was over.

The Hobsons' denial of responsibility had continued even after the recent death of Mr. Hobson. I'd thought the protestors might back down once the head of the company could no longer be held accountable, but their continued presence outside the factory proved they were as determined as ever.

Gabe's head turned as we passed the protestors, keeping his gaze on them. Once they were behind us, he turned again to speak to me in the back seat. "I called on Bertie at the factory yesterday. At least, I tried to. His mother was there and wouldn't let me see him."

"Did you want to tell him to come clean about his artlessness?"

He nodded. "It would be best coming from him rather than me."

"Will you tell Jakes if he doesn't?"

Mr. Jakes had shown an interest in Gabe's unnatural ability to remain unscathed during the war, as well as in the failed Hobson boots. Although we suspected Bertie's artlessness was to blame for the failed batch of boots, we'd not informed Jakes. Gabe was giving Bertie every opportunity to do the right thing himself.

But if the Hobsons continued to deny responsibility, and Jakes found out that they knew the boots failed because they never received the required magic, then they risked the full legal weight of the government descending on them.

Gabe rubbed his jaw. "I'll keep trying to speak privately to Bertie. He needs to understand the consequences of doing nothing."

It sounded easy enough in theory, but getting through Mrs. Hobson to her son would be difficult. She would protect him and the family with all her might.

"You're being too reasonable, Gabe," Alex chided. "The Hobsons don't deserve it. They told a journalist that ridiculous story about you healing yourself magically." It wasn't the only story the newspapers had published about Gabe's incredible feat of survival. One had even speculated something close to the truth.

"They also met with Thurlow," Alex added, almost reluctantly. His reluctance stemmed from his concern that Gabe's obsession with the corrupt bookmaker who'd tried to have us run off the road was consuming him, clouding his judgment.

I didn't quite agree that it was an obsession. A genuine fear, yes, and that fear was justified. Thurlow was ruthless, and he had Gabe in his sights. Witnessing the base criminal meet with two very upright women in Mrs. Hobson and Ivy was not only an unusual sight, it was also baffling. How did they know one another? More importantly, why had they met?

None of the theories we'd come up with painted the Hobsons in a good light.

I hadn't realized how frayed my nerves were until Gabe opened the door to the Glass Library and I entered my sanctuary. I'd never used that term to describe it, but I now realized that's precisely what it was. My little piece of paradise. The library felt more like a home to me than my room at Mrs. Parry's boarding house. I breathed deeply, drawing in the familiar smell of old books. Perhaps it was my magic responding to all of the paper within the books, scrolls, correspondence, and other documents housed across two levels. Or perhaps it was because it was the first place in London where I'd begun to feel like my true self. Whatever the reason, I felt at peace in the library.

That peace was shattered by the fury of one small but fierce middle-aged woman dressed in trousers, waistcoat and man's shirt. "Where have you been? Why didn't you stay here, like I told you?" She didn't wait for an answer. Instead, she pointed a finger at me. "This is your fault!"

I didn't snap back. Her trembling finger was a sign that she'd been sick with worry over Gabe's safety, and that was an emotion I understood well.

She stood in the entrance to the main section of the library, the two black marble columns framing her like a painting. Her arms were at her sides, neither loose nor rigid, and her right hand hovered near her hip. She looked like she was about to draw the gun that I knew to be tucked into the waistband of her trousers. I couldn't entirely dismiss the idea. She certainly seemed angry enough to threaten to shoot someone, most likely me. At least I could be sure it would only be a threat and she wouldn't actually go through with it.

Most likely.

Gabe pushed past her. "I don't need coddling, Willie."

She opened her mouth to offer a retort, but Alex got in first. "But if you do want to coddle him, then you should be here instead of gallivanting off with your latest petting pal."

She stiffened. "The airman and I are friends, nothing more. I'm with Tilda now, and even if I weren't, he's too much like my second husband to tempt me. I loved Davide, but we should never have married."

"Davide was Lord Farnsworth?" I couldn't resist asking. "Why shouldn't you have married him?"

She looked at me like I was stupid. "Because he was a lord. He should have married a proper lady." If any other woman had said it, I'd have thought she was fishing for compliments, but not Willie.

She charged after Gabe and Alex, heading for the reading nook. She still sported a furious expression, so I tried to distract her to save them. "How did you meet the airman?"

"It was during the war."

"Yes, but how exactly did you meet?"

Her pace slowed to an amble. I was surprised to see her sporting a lopsided grin rather than a scowl. "His Sopwith was downed not far from where I was stationed. Stretcher-bearers carried him to my ambulance, and I drove him to a field hospital. When he recovered, he wanted to thank me, so sought me out.

We shared a drink—actually it was several—and have been friends ever since."

"Did he suffer terrible injuries?"

The smile inched wider. "It wasn't as terrible as it sounds. He got shot."

"How is that not terrible?"

"In his left ass cheek."

"Even worse!"

She shrugged. "It's the most padded spot on him, and not an uncommon place for airmen to get shot." The smile slipped, replaced with a frown. "Stop distracting me, Sylvia. This is your fault."

"That your friend was shot in his arse? I don't think so."

She huffed. It was almost a laugh. "There's a word I never thought I'd hear from your prim mouth."

"I am not prim."

She snorted and walked off. She had Alex and Gabe well and truly in her sights again. "What was so important that you had to leave the library without me?"

"We found Sylvia's father," Gabe said.

Willie's jaw dropped. I'd never seen her look more stunned. She recovered quickly, however. "You still shouldn't have left the library without me."

Alex dragged a hand down his face in exasperation. "If you wanted to be his escort, you shouldn't have left."

Willie ignored him. "Was I right? Is it Hendry?"

"It is," I told her.

"We'll need extra security. He's going to come after you, Sylvia." She jabbed a finger in my direction. "Unless Gabe agrees to stay away—"

"I don't," he said, his voice ragged with frustration.

Willie barreled on. "We have to worry about Hendry on top of the kidnapper, and maybe Thurlow, who may or may not be the kidnapper. And Jakes." She removed the gun from her waistband to check the barrel. "Who also may or may not be the kidnapper."

"Put that away," Gabe growled.

"Tea?" Professor Nash's arrival in the reading nook was a welcome distraction. He set down the tray he carried on the desk. "I'd just made it for Willie and me, but when I heard you three enter, I fetched more cups. I thought you might need it."

"You're a marvel." I picked up the teapot and poured. "Sit, Professor. Have a rest." He looked as though he needed the tea more than me. "We have news."

I told Willie and the professor what we'd learned at the Petersons' factory. To my surprise, Willie didn't interject. She seemed riveted, and impatiently ordered me to continue when I paused. "We then went to Maxwell Cooper's lodgings, but he'd vacated it without informing his landlady. He seemed to have left in a hurry."

"I knew it," she muttered into her teacup. "He's no good."

"Given he goes by the name Cooper and Marianne Folgate—my mother—was also once known as Cooper, it seems likely he's my father."

The professor pushed his glasses up his nose. "And you look like the Hendry women. Yes, it does all seem to fit, doesn't it?" He patted my arm. "I'm very pleased for you, Sylvia. It must be a relief to finally know."

"Pleased!" Willie cried. "Relief! Her father's a low-down pigswill who tried to kill me! She shouldn't be happy to be related to that."

Gabe arched his brows pointedly. "We can't choose our relatives. Every family has an undesirable member or two."

If Willie realized he was referring to her, she didn't show it. "He tried to kill your mother, Gabe! Not to mention he was tangled up with Coyle. Does he know about you, Sylvia?"

"Evaline told him about a young paper magician relative who'd just entered the family fold. She didn't say I could be his daughter. She didn't know he was Melville Hendry when she spoke to him this morning."

She blew out a breath. "Good. Hopefully he won't realize and won't come looking for you."

I nodded along. She was right, of course. Melville Hendry had been a danger years ago, and there was no reason to believe he'd changed. He ought to be kept at arm's length.

If only that thought didn't leave me with a heaviness that weighed me down.

* * *

THE FOLLOWING MORNING, I received another visit from the Hendry sisters. They'd been worried about me and wanted to check on my well-being. Although they didn't stay long, their visit almost brought me to tears. Good tears. Happy tears. I'd gone from having no family to being the niece of three kind aunts who took it upon themselves to check on me. I was fortunate indeed.

I had errands to run at lunchtime. After informing Professor Nash that I'd be back in an hour, I grabbed my hat and bag and was about to open the door when it was opened from the other side.

"Mr. Jakes! What are you doing here?"

The debonair gentleman removed his hat and held it to his chest. He gave me a shallow bow. "Good afternoon, Miss Ashe. I've come to see you. May I come in?"

I hesitated then stepped aside. I couldn't very well block his entry. Besides, I was wildly curious about his visit. Why call on me and not Gabe?

I didn't invite him further into the library, but remained by the front desk where I placed my hat and bag. "Are you after a particular book? I'm afraid we've found nothing more on magical mutations." He'd come here before looking for documents on that subject. He believed Gabe's miraculous wartime survival was somehow the result of a mutation of his magic, although Mr. Jakes didn't know how that mutation manifested itself. His theory was close, but in his version, he believed Gabe was born a magician who could control his magic with spells. In truth, Gabe had always believed himself to be artless. His magic only engaged when his life, or the life of someone he cared deeply about, was in danger.

"I came to talk to you." Mr. Jakes' light blue eyes usually sparkled, and he often smiled, which I suspected were his favorite weapons designed to disarm people and lull them into a false sense of security. But not this time. He looked quite serious. "In fact, I want to warn you. You may be in danger."

My pulse quickened. He'd heard about my connection to Melville Hendry extremely quickly, considering the authorities didn't even know Melville was still alive let alone in London.

He wasn't referring to my father, however. "The danger stems from a powerful criminal figure who controls a gang of thugs."

"Do you mean Thurlow?"

"You know of him?"

It was rather satisfying to see that I'd surprised a Military Intelligence officer. "We've met him."

Realization dawned. "At the racetrack. Yes, of course. Then you know how slippery he is."

"We certainly do. Thank you for your warning, but we're already aware of the danger he poses. Rest assured, Gabe is capable of protecting himself, and he has his friends surrounding him at all times."

"It's not Glass who's in danger. My information says you are."

"Me?"

"Thurlow will avoid Glass because of his magical abilities."

"Gabe isn't a magician."

He held up his hand to stop me. "Let's stop pretending. I know he possesses some kind of magical ability. Thurlow knows, too. He witnessed it at the racetrack recently." Mr. Jakes watched me closely.

I crossed my arms and waited for him to go on. If he suspected me of being a weak link who'd blurt out the truth, he was a fool.

"Thurlow has been trying to discover more about Glass's abilities, to no avail. But he believes you are an easier target. Capturing you could force Glass to cooperate."

My skin prickled. Thurlow wasn't the only ruthless element that probably saw me as a way to get to Gabe. Was Mr. Jakes breaking ranks by coming here and warning me? Would the authorities stoop to the same tactic? Or did Mr. Jakes genuinely know Thurlow's plans?

"You seem to know a lot of what Thurlow thinks and suspects. Why is that?"

"I have eyes and ears everywhere."

I didn't doubt it, but something didn't quite make sense. "Thurlow is a criminal, as you pointed out. He operates an illegal bookmaking ring and probably has fingers in other pies. But he's not a threat to national security. So why are Military Intelligence interested in him? Surely his activities are a matter for the police."

Mr. Jakes settled his hat on his head. "I stumbled upon his interest in Glass while investigating another matter."

"Ah, yes. The Hobsons."

I'd managed to surprise him again, but he quickly covered it. "Consider yourself warned, Miss Ashe."

"Wait. Do you know why the Hobsons met with Thurlow?"

"If I did, I wouldn't be able to tell you. Good day."

I watched him walk down the lane then closed the door. Although I believed he was genuinely warning me, I didn't trust that the threat came from Thurlow. Despite Mr. Jakes's assurance that he was no longer interested in Gabe except where he could help with the Hobson and Son boot matter, I suspected Military Intelligence would still like to know how Gabe had survived unscathed for the duration of the war. If they thought there was a way to replicate Gabe's magic, they would try. But first they had to study him, and Gabe refused to be treated like a laboratory specimen.

Would Military Intelligence stoop to kidnap? Would *they* target me to lure Gabe?

I contemplated the various scenarios as I exited the library. The moment the door closed, someone caught me from behind. A hand clamped over my mouth, smothering my scream. My arms were pinned to my sides.

Mr. Jakes had warned me. Now I was paying the price for not heeding it immediately.

CHAPTER 4

"Don't move," whispered a male voice in my ear. It was familiar, but it didn't belong to Thurlow. "I'm going to uncover your mouth so you can answer my questions. Promise not to scream."

I nodded as best I could.

He removed his hand, and I felt a slight relaxation of the arm trapping me. It was my opportunity.

I stamped on his foot. He grunted, and while he was distracted by the pain, I pulled free of his grip. I jabbed my fist into his stomach, hard. He doubled over with a sharp gasp. He was now the perfect height for me to elbow him in the jaw. The blow knocked him to the ground.

I adjusted my hat and pushed my bag's handle up to the crook of my elbow. "My mother taught me those moves."

Melville Hendry rubbed his jaw, eyeing me carefully. When he realized I wasn't going to attack again, his gaze turned cold. He pushed himself to his feet. "I wasn't going to harm you. I just wanted to talk."

"Usually when people want to talk to me, they greet me nicely, not accost me in the street outside my workplace."

He looked up at the library's sign. "Are you the paper magician Miss Peterson told me about?"

"Yes."

"You're a Hendry."

I hesitated. "I've just discovered a family connection. You followed them here, didn't you? You followed the Hendry sisters to the library, hoping they'd lead you to the magician Evaline Peterson mentioned."

He looked me over, paying particular attention to my face. If he saw a resemblance to his sisters, or himself, he gave no indication. "Why did Miss Peterson think *I* was related to the Hendrys?"

"If you hadn't left the factory in a hurry, you could have asked her that question yourself."

His lips thinned. My impertinence clearly annoyed him. "Who gave her the idea that I'm related to the Hendrys? You? Or those three…women?"

Had he seen his sisters arrive at the factory with Gabe and me? Had he been watching the factory, or his lodgings? Or did he simply guess they were involved?

We both wanted answers, but skirting around the truth was getting us nowhere. One of us had to crack the shell before those answers could pour out. "You don't know who I am, do you?" I asked.

His gaze sharpened, studying me again. Did he see the freckles and fair hair of the Hendry family? Or the petite figure and gray eyes of my mother? "I don't care who you are, miss, since you're not who I thought you were. If you can't tell me how Miss Peterson came to assume I was related to the Hendry family, then I have no further business with you." He started to walk off.

"Who did you think I was?" I called after him.

He didn't slow down or turn around.

"Did you think I was a man?" That made him stop. "Did you

think Miss Peterson had in fact met a young *man* who'd just discovered he was a Hendry?"

He looked at me over his shoulder. "Very perceptive, miss. You're right. I didn't trust Miss Peterson's account. I thought she'd heard about you from others. I wanted to check for myself. But I can see you're not who I'm looking for."

It suddenly clicked into place. He had no idea I even existed. He hadn't been looking specifically for my *mother* all these years; she was his only link to the one person he *did* want to find.

"Is it James?" I asked the retreating figure.

He stopped again. From this distance, he looked old and worn out. His shoulders were stooped, his clothes a little too loose on his slim frame. His face half-turned to look at me over his shoulder again. "What did you say?"

"Are you looking for your son, James?"

He whipped around. "How…?" He charged toward me. "Do you know him? Where is he?" His eyes were huge, wild, and he stood a little too close. He must have realized how threatening he appeared because he took a step back. He dragged a hand over his jaw. It shook.

"I'll tell you everything," I said. "But it's not a conversation to have on the street." Crooked Lane may be quiet, but we had much to discuss. "We should go inside." Even as I said it, I realized it was a terrible idea. Melville Hendry could wield paper like weapons using a moving spell, and the library was full of it. "On second thought, let's go to a café instead. There's a French-style one not far from here."

We walked in silence to Le Café De Paris and sat inside. Although it was a pleasant day, and the restaurant had chairs and tables outside, I suspected Melville didn't want to be too conspicuous. I chose a quiet table in the corner and ordered coffee and a pastry from the waitress. Melville didn't want anything.

The moment the waitress was out of earshot, he leaned forward. "Well then? Answer me. How do you know James?"

There was no easy way to tell him, so I just came out with it. "My name is Sylvia Ashe. James was my brother."

He sat back heavily, the breath knocked out of him. He stared at me as an array of emotions flickered across his face, beginning with surprise and ending with sad realization. "'Was?' He's... dead?"

"Three years ago, in the war."

"She let him enlist?"

I bristled. "If by 'she' you mean our mother, she had no choice in the matter. James was in his twenties and his own man. She couldn't stop him. I can assure you, she didn't like it. What mother would? She's dead, too, by the way. Not that you asked. She died of influenza."

That news didn't rock him as much as being told of James's death, but he did acknowledge it with a nod. "That's why Miss Peterson said you were happy to be part of the Hendry family. Because you had no one."

"Your sisters are kind. They've welcomed me with open arms."

The waitress arrived with my coffee and a pastry on a plate. She asked Melville if he still didn't want anything. He dismissed her with a brief shake of his head. He hardly seemed to register her presence.

"Was James a paper magician, too?" he asked.

"I don't think so. If he was a magician, it was probably silver, like our mother. We were both raised as artless."

He huffed and gave a disappointed shake of his head. "You only just discovered your magic?"

"Yes. It's been a long journey that began when I met Gabriel Glass. You remember his family, don't you? You tried to kill his mother."

His gaze lowered to the table. "I can't believe James is gone." His voice was so soft that I barely heard him. "I've been searching for so long...and to discover this..."

If he was a friend, I'd reach across the table and take his hand. But I wasn't ready to feel sympathy for this man. I wasn't sure if I would ever be ready.

He looked up and blinked at me. "You said James was your brother. Half-brother?"

"Why would I be welcomed by the Hendrys if I had a different father to James?"

His gaze took me in anew. "I thought…"

"We have the same parents. You're my father," I clarified as he seemed to be having trouble taking in the news.

"How old are you?"

"Twenty-six. I was born in 1894."

"When she ran away," he murmured.

"Marianne?"

His gaze refocused on me. "She must have been pregnant with you when she left. Perhaps that's why she left."

To protect me, I wanted to say. But I kept the thought to myself. I felt no threat from Melville, seated as we were in a popular café in the middle of London. But if he was as dangerous as everyone claimed, I needed to be careful. "Why were you looking for James?"

"Because he was my son," he said, matter-of-factly. "Marianne shouldn't have taken him from me. She had no right."

"She was afraid of you."

"I wouldn't have hurt James."

"What about her? Or me?"

The lowering of his gaze gave me my answer. "I was different then. I was under the influence of a powerful man."

"Lord Coyle."

He stilled. "Of course, you'd know all about him if you associate with the Glasses. You must know everything."

"Why did you allow Coyle to have such power over you?"

"You think I had a choice? He forced me to do his bidding. He forced your mother and me to have children."

"Why? Was he blackmailing you?" When he didn't respond, I took it as confirmation. According to the file Gabe's parents kept on Melville, Lord Coyle had used his influence to get him out of jail.

He suddenly stood.

I reached over and caught his sleeve. "Wait. Please. I promise I won't ask again about Coyle."

He slowly sat, his gaze wary. "I won't tell you where I'm living now. You know that don't you? I can't afford for the authorities to find me. They'll arrest me."

"I know. I just need to clarify some things." I blew out a measured breath. What could I ask that wouldn't send him fleeing, never to return? "Did you know Marianne Folgate was a silversmith magician?"

He nodded. "That's why we were together. Two strong magical lineages…" His top lip curled with his sneer. "I didn't know her surname, however. Nor did I know where she was from. I didn't find out about the Folgates from Ipswich until recently."

"We have that in common. We were always a step behind you."

"She never told you?"

"She told James and me nothing about our pasts or hers. It's all quite new for me."

"And everyone thinks I was the cruel one. I would have told James everything. Children should know their origins. Children of magicians especially." He drummed his fingers on the table before abruptly stopping. "We never married. You're not legitimate."

The possibility had always been in the back of my mind, so I wasn't shocked. "Did she know your real name was Hendry? Or did she only know you as Maxwell Cooper?"

"She knew me as both, but James would have only known the name Cooper, if he wasn't too young to remember anything at all. That's why I continued using the name Cooper all these years and remained here in London. I hoped he would seek me out by going to the paper factories in the city where he'd last seen his father." He closed his eyes and swallowed heavily.

"James remembered nothing. Or if he did, he never mentioned it to me. But I doubt he could recall that far back. He would have tried to find you if he remembered Cooper or London, or even paper magic."

His eyes flew open. He thumped his fist on the table. "That bloody woman."

"Don't speak about my mother that way," I snapped. "She had her faults, but she had her reasons for doing what she did."

Two men entered the café. Although they showed no interest in us, Melville angled his hat lower to obscure his face. He hadn't taken it off when we sat. He was the only man in the café still wearing one.

"How strong is your magic?" he suddenly asked.

"Quite strong, so the Petersons told me. I'm still learning." I said it almost apologetically. I couldn't explain why, but Melville made me feel inept for being naive about my ability.

"I remember Rosina had a son. Is he a paper magician?"

"No, and nor is her daughter. You knew she had a daughter. Why didn't you ask about her?"

He ignored my question. "Did Myrtle and Naomi ever reproduce?"

"No."

He stood again. "Don't follow me."

I indicated the coffee and pastry that I was yet to try. "I'll finish this before I leave. Melville," I said, addressing him by his name for the first time. "Your sisters would like to see you again."

He sniffed. "I doubt that. They were ashamed of me once they learned that I was..."

"Not like other men?" I finished.

"They told you," he said flatly.

"They didn't seem to have an issue with that. It was your

actions years later that brought shame on the family, when the police came looking for you."

He quickly looked around, worried I'd been overheard. But there was no one in the immediate vicinity. "I have no interest in seeing any of them. I doubt they've changed much."

"Have *you* changed?"

His direct gaze drilled into me. Then, with brisk steps and hat pulled low, he strode out of the café.

With a sigh, I tucked into my pastry. I hardly tasted it.

* * *

DESPITE THE THOUGHTS whirling around in my head, I managed to keep alert to my surroundings. I intended to take Mr. Jakes's warning seriously. I arrived safely at Gabe's house where the elderly butler, Bristow, welcomed me with his usual stiff formality. The twinkle in his eye was new, however.

"You're in a good mood," I said. "Have I missed a funny joke?"

"Nothing like that, Miss Ashe," he intoned. "I'd just like to say that on behalf of all the staff, we're very happy to see you again."

While I didn't think anyone had seen Gabe and I kiss that day in the corridor, perhaps one of the staff had been nearby after all. Or perhaps Gabe had given them clues. Some of the staff had been with the family so long they'd known him since he was born, and they'd want to see him happy. The fact that I made Gabe happy warmed me. Some of the tension I'd felt ever since being accosted by my father in Crooked Lane eased.

I heard a male voice coming from the drawing room. It didn't belong to Gabe, Alex or Murray the footman.

"Mr. Glass is with friends," Bristow said.

"I don't want to intrude. Please tell Gabe that I called, and we'll talk later."

"I'm sure he'll want to see you, Miss Ashe." He shuffled off and opened the door to the drawing room. "Miss Ashe to see you, sir."

Gabe rose and invited me in.

"I don't want to intrude," I said.

"You're not. You know these fellows, anyway."

His three chums who'd helped us solve the codes in the Medici Manuscript all greeted me with varying degrees of enthusiasm. Juan Martinez was the most effusive, kissing both my cheeks and smiling from ear to ear. It wasn't flirtatious. It was simply his way. Francis Stray shook my hand. The quiet, reserved mathematician smiled as he did so, but it seemed unnatural, as if he only did it because he knew it was the correct thing to do. He'd always been awkward, not just with me but with everyone. He and Gabe had been friends since their school days, where Gabe had protected the shy, intelligent boy from bullies.

The third man was Stanley Greville, a friend of Gabe and Juan's from the army. The war had affected him more than Gabe, Alex and Juan. Although physically uninjured, he'd suffered from shell shock. After he demobilized, he'd been admitted to Rosebank Gardens hospital. He had checked out of the facility after a few months and seemed to be getting better, by all accounts. He'd even found himself work at a pharmacy, as he'd not wanted to return to his studies. But lately he'd seemed to relapse and retreat into himself. It was good to see him out and about with friends, although he was clearly not well. The bloodshot eyes and sallow skin were testament to that, even if he did try to hide his trembling hands.

He gave me a nod and a polite but curt "Miss Ashe" when I greeted him. He did up his jacket buttons. "I should go."

"Please don't leave on my account," I said.

"I can't stay. I have things to do."

"As do I," Juan said.

Francis checked the clock on the mantelpiece. "My lunch

hour is almost over, and I must return to work. Good day, Miss Ashe, gentlemen. Thank you for your hospitality, Gabe."

The three men filed out of the drawing room.

I was about to apologize to Gabe for interrupting his get-together, but he preempted me. "They probably really do all have things to do. They were contacted at the last minute by Willie and asked to keep me company because she and Alex had to go out. When I say asked, I mean she insisted." He took my hands and rubbed his thumbs over my knuckles. "I'm glad they left. This way we can spend some time alone."

His kiss started out light, a mere skim of his lips against mine. But it quickly deepened, heating me from the inside, making my heart do mad flips in my chest. For one thrilling moment, I thought we'd retreat upstairs. Without his cousin and friend in the house, we had some privacy.

But we weren't really alone. Gabe's servants might be few in number for a house of this size, but there would be no sneaking around or secrecy while they were here.

As if by mutual agreement, we drew apart. Gabe's eyes remained a little glazed, his lips plump from the fierce kiss. They curved into a smile. "I'm glad you're here. I missed you."

I laughed. "We saw one another yesterday."

"Too long ago." The smile vanished. "As glad as I am to see you, you don't usually visit on a workday unless something's wrong." He must have seen something in my eyes that worried him. He led me to the sofa and directed me to sit beside him. "What is it? What's happened?"

"Nothing's wrong. Not really. Gabe, I met my father. I met Melville Hendry."

"Bloody hell." He cupped my jaw. "Are you all right?"

"We had coffee together at that French-style café with the avant-garde artwork on the walls. Well, *he* didn't have coffee. I ordered a cup and a pastry but didn't touch either until after he left." I was talking rapidly, the words spilling out of me. Unable to sit still, I stood and began to pace the floor. I shook my hands, trying to release some of the energy coursing through me. "We talked. He had no idea I even existed, which means my mother left him while she was pregnant with me. He kept the name Cooper so James could find him, but I told him James couldn't remember anything about our father. He was sad that James was dead and seemed not particularly interested in learning he had a daughter, although he showed a little more interest when I told him I'm a paper magician. Oh, and he doesn't want to see his sisters. He probably wouldn't want me to tell you that we met, but I had to come here immediately. I can't keep things from you, Gabe."

When I turned again, he was right there in front of me. He took my arms by the elbows and dipped his head to peer into my eyes. "Take a deep breath, Sylvia."

I did, but it didn't help overmuch. "Gabe… I felt nothing for him. No familial instinct, nothing, and that makes me feel awful. He's my father. I ought to feel *something*." I sighed. "It's all rather…wrong."

"It's perfectly natural. You don't know him, and what you do know about him is negative. It's understandable you feel no love for him. Love for one's family isn't automatic. It has to be earned, just like any other kind of love." He drew me into a warm, gentle hug, resting his chin on the top of my head. "It'll be all right." The velvety hum of his voice vibrated through my body.

I wrapped my arms around him and drew in a deep breath, drawing in his familiar scent. I tilted my head to look up at him. "Thank you. I needed to hear that."

He kissed me lightly then drew away. "It must have been strange to talk to him after all this time."

"Very."

We sat again and I told him how Melville had found me by following his sisters to the library. I didn't mention that he'd captured me. That would upset Gabe, and I didn't want to do that. It must be enough of a shock knowing the man who'd tried to kill his mother many years ago was the father of his current flame.

It was a very good reason for me not to see Melville again. I didn't want to encourage him into my life, lest it drove Gabe away. Gabe was too important to me.

He must have been thinking along the same lines. "It's probably best not to tell Willie that you met," he said carefully. "At least for a while, until we know for sure if he has changed."

"It's unlikely we'll ever see one another again. We both now have the answers to questions that had concerned us for years, and neither of us have any affection for the other. I'm happy to leave our acquaintance at that one meeting."

"He's probably harmless now that Coyle is long gone, and his influence with him. Hendry has lived many years in London, quietly going about his life without being a threat to anyone. There's no reason to believe that won't continue."

I leaned into him, and he placed his arm around my shoulders. "Thanks, Gabe. I knew you'd make me feel better."

He kissed my forehead. "Glad to be of service."

I went to kiss him back, but someone made a sound of disgust from the doorway, and I retreated.

Willie strode into the drawing room looking like a storm cloud intent on ruining a picnic. "Do you two have to do that in here?"

Alex followed her, plucking off his driving gloves. "Leave them alone. At least Gabe's here and didn't leave the house without an escort."

"I wouldn't dream of it," Gabe said, standing. He held his hand out to assist me to my feet. "We're going to drive Sylvia back to the library. I want to stay awhile and do some more research."

Willie made another sound of disgust in the back of her throat. "More reading. Are you trying to kill me with boredom?"

"No more than you're trying to kill us with your whining," Alex shot back.

With a sigh, Willie strode out of the drawing room.

"How are your friends?" Alex asked Gabe.

"Fine. It was good to see them, especially Stanley. With all of us together, it gave us an opportunity to try to talk him into returning to hospital. He refused. He said the doctors haven't got any new treatments to cure shell shock, and the old ones do more harm than good. It's hard to argue with that."

"I'm sure he'll get better. Give him more time."

Gabe's mouth twisted into a sardonic smirk. "Time seems to be the answer to everything."

Willie continued to voice her opinion about library research as we left the townhouse. Fortunately, a distraction emerged from the back seat of a motor vehicle that pulled to the curb. Unfortunately, that distraction was the imperious Lady Stanhope.

She waved away her driver who'd stepped out to assist her and held out her hands to Gabe. "My dearest Gabriel. How handsome you look."

"Good afternoon," he said. "I'm afraid I have business elsewhere. I'll telephone you later."

"Pish posh. What's so urgent that you can't spare a few minutes for your dear friend?"

Gabe's polite smile was strained.

Sometimes Willie could be extraordinarily rude. Sometimes that rudeness was a blessing, as it saved others from being the one to cause offence. "You ain't his friend. You're an acquaintance at best. State your business so we can all get on with our day."

Lady Stanhope glanced pointedly at the front door where Bristow stood, waiting for orders.

"Madam?" Gabe prompted.

She clasped his forearm. "What I have to say can't be discussed over the telephone. I have a plan, you see."

"A plan?"

Her narrowed gaze fell on Alex, Willie then me. "May we have some privacy?"

"Whatever you have to say to me can be said in front of them."

Willie crossed her arms over her chest and gave Lady Stanhope a look of childish satisfaction.

Lady Stanhope tensed. She tried to steer Gabe away from us, but he was having none of it. He stayed put. She finally gave in. "I wanted privacy because they are not magicians. They won't understand."

"I'm not a magician either."

She leaned closer to him. "You say that because you don't fully understand your ability yet."

"What ability?"

"To heal yourself."

Gabe sighed. "That report was pure fiction. The newspaper printed a retraction."

"Newspapers only print retractions when they can't prove their statements and they don't want to be sued. Most of the time, there is an underlying truth to the claims."

"Not this time. If you don't mind…"

She showed no inclination to leave. Her attention was now entirely focused on Gabe. It was as if the rest of us didn't exist. "I understand you believe your fast healing is natural, but it isn't. It's special. *You* are special, Gabriel. You're a magician of a unique kind. Discovering one's magic is a confusing time. I can help you navigate through it and direct you down a path that enables you to take advantage of it."

Gabe trapped her hand, resting on his arm beneath his own, and steered her back to her motorcar. "I can't heal myself any faster than you, Lady Stanhope. I'm sorry you were taken in by that article, but none of it was true." He opened the door and guided her to the seat.

Lady Stanhope wasn't giving up that easily. "I can introduce you to important people while helping you reach your full potential as a magician of the rarest degree. You'll attend exclusive parties, be invited to the homes of famous people. You'll be celebrated wherever you go."

"I don't want any of that." He went to close the door, but she put out a hand to keep it open.

"People will try to exploit you, Gabriel, but I can protect you."

Willie stepped forward, grabbed the door and slammed it closed. "Drive off now before someone scratches the paintwork. It happens all the time around here. It's a bad area."

The driver gulped and quickly obeyed.

"That was strange," Alex said as we headed to Gabe's Vauxhall. "Does she genuinely believe what she's saying?"

Gabe opened the rear door for me. "I think she wants the newspaper report to be true, and for me to desire fame and fortune."

"Why? What does she gain from it?"

Gabe shrugged. "To be there for the ride?"

I suspected he was right, in a way. Lady Stanhope liked to discover young magicians who were previously unknown. She nurtured them and introduced them to people who would pay handsomely for their magician-made wares. A few months ago, she'd discovered an artist at the Royal Academy exhibition, and wanted to act as his agent. She'd offered to mentor him in exchange for a reward of sorts. Unaware of his own worth, or how to navigate the new world he was being thrust into, the artist had naively believed she was acting in his best interests.

Her reasons then were selfish, as they were now. Gabe was neither naive nor desperate for fame, but if his magic became public knowledge, Lady Stanhope would benefit socially by simply being in his inner circle.

Willie grabbed the crank handle from the floor of the front passenger seat. "And they say I'm mad."

"She's just bored," Gabe said.

"Then she should get a hobby. Or shoot something. That's what I usually do."

* * *

ON THE DRIVE to the library, I told Gabe and the others about Mr. Jakes' visit and his warning that Thurlow might kidnap someone close to Gabe to force him to react. It meant they all took the walk down Crooked Lane very seriously.

Alex was the first to spot the parcel wrapped in brown paper and tied with string. "Stand back. It could be an explosive device."

It had been propped up against the door with a small card tucked into the string. The card bore my name in neat handwriting. I couldn't be sure if the sensation of magical warmth that I felt came from the card or the contents of the parcel. The fact I felt it at all from a distance away meant it was strong.

"How will we know for sure?" Willie asked.

"One of us will have to unwrap it," Alex said. "Very, very carefully."

"Why are you looking at *me* like that? Why should I do it?"

"I wasn't looking at you. But now that you mention it—"

"I reckon *you* should unwrap it, Alex. You had explosives training in the war, didn't you?"

"My only experience with bombs was nearly getting hit by them."

Gabe pushed past them. "I'll do it."

Their protests reverberated off the surrounding buildings, but before Gabe could reach the parcel, the library door opened from the other side. Professor Nash stood on the threshold. The parcel toppled over and landed on his toes.

"I thought I heard voices." He picked up the parcel and slipped the card out. "It's addressed to you, Sylvia. It's a book, if I'm not mistaken."

Willie huffed as she thumped Alex on the arm. "Told you it was nothing."

Alex rolled his eyes.

I unwrapped the parcel at the front desk. It was indeed a book, filled with pages infused with strong magic. The book wasn't particularly large or thick, but the black leather cover was smooth from years of handling. Inside, the pages were in good condition thanks to the magic, but the book was old according to the date written on the first page.

A thousand years old.

CHAPTER 5

We took the book to the first-floor reading nook, the larger of the two reading areas in the library. Light drenched the desk near the arched window, allowing us to inspect the pages closely. Some of the ink had faded, but most of the text was still legible.

The powerful paper magic seemed to ooze from every page, but it wasn't my area of expertise that was required to understand the contents. Professor Nash's knowledge of the ornate script and ancient spelling meant he was the only one who could read the title page.

He bent over it, adjusting his spectacles to get a better look. "It's in Latin. *Liber Familiae.*"

"Book of the Family," Gabe translated. He pointed to the word beneath *Liber Familiae.* "This looks like *Hendreau.*"

The professor pushed his glasses up his nose as he squinted at the faint text. "Yes, it is." He straightened and gave me the same degree of scrutiny he'd given the book. "The French form of Hendry, I suppose."

I wasn't altogether surprised. The card attached to the parcel had my name on it, and I'd already heard about the family journal that Melville Hendry had taken. "The Hendry sisters mentioned this. They were looking for it at Melville's flat yesterday. Apparently, it's passed down to the strongest male magician in the family. Given there are no male Hendry magicians of my generation, it has come to me."

Willie had been inspecting the book, but she suddenly straightened. "If Hendry had it, how did he know to bring it here? How does he know about *you*?" Her nostrils flared. "You met him, didn't you?"

"We spoke this morning."

Professor Nash gasped, "That's wonderful, Sylvia."

Willie scowled. "Where is he staying? He should be arrested—"

"Willie!" Gabe snapped. "Sylvia doesn't know where to find him."

She looked like she would protest again, but a glare from Gabe silenced her. Well, almost. She did mutter something under her breath that I didn't quite hear.

Alex had been carefully turning the pages of the book, but suddenly stopped and flipped back and forth. "All of these early pages are in another language. Latin, I presume. They're also written with the same handwriting, using the same ink." He pointed to some of the letters that were indeed identical. "That suggests they were written by the same person. But these are dates, yes? And they're all different."

The Latin was beyond me, but Gabe and the professor had been educated in the language and confirmed Alex's suspicion. They were different dates, spanning hundreds of years.

Professor Nash pointed to a word at the top of a page, then turned to the next one and pointed at another written in the top corner. "And these are places, if I'm not mistaken, both in France and England."

Alex took over again. "Then after about halfway, the handwriting changes, and the ink, too. It changes every page or two. And from here," he turned to a page about three-quarters of the way through the book, "I can read it. The words are in English and the formation of the letters more modern."

Willie shrugged. "What does that mean?"

"It means the first part was transcribed by one person from another document."

"Or documents," the professor added. "According to these early dates, the first few were written around the year 900. They would have been written on scrolls back then, and for hundreds of years afterwards. Books came later. Someone at some point decided all the information across several scrolls needed to be kept in the one place." He indicated the book with a flourish of hands, as a fairground magician would conjure a trick.

Alex continued. "Then midway through the book, in the 1500s, the handwriting changes. A different author added to it. The change in handwriting continues to the end, each page or two written by someone new."

"A new generation," I murmured.

Alex turned to the last page with writing on it, before the several blank pages at the very end. "This was written by Melville Hendry."

I sat in the chair and read. Melville's small, neat handwriting gave an overview of his magical skill, including which spells he could perform and how long the effects of each spell lasted. Following that was a brief account of the changes in laws affecting magicians and guilds in the early 1890s. Neither his role nor that of Gabe's parents was mentioned. Then, finally, he'd written the birth date and name of my brother, James. Marianne Folgate was listed as James' mother, however 'Folgate' was written in different ink.

"He probably added it after he learned about her family in Ipswich," I said, pointing to the surname. "He wrote my name today." In the same neat scrawl, he'd written 'Sylvia' below James's name, noting the year of my birth, but not the exact date or place since he didn't know them.

Gabe rested a comforting hand on my shoulder. "He's leaving it for you to fill in."

"Does he want the book back when you've done that?" Alex asked.

Willie snapped her fingers then pointed at Alex. "We can get Hendry when she returns it to him. We'll lie in wait while you speak to him, Sylv. Is there an address on the back of that card?"

The professor picked up the card with my name on it. "It says, 'This is yours now. Take care of it and give it to the strongest male magician of the Hendry line. A woman will do if there are no male heirs.'"

Willie pulled a face. "Chauvinistic turd."

Earlier pages in the journal also listed the names and birth dates of children, so it acted as a sort of family tree, but only following along one line, that of the strongest male magician in each generation. I'd need to read it more thoroughly to find out if I was the first female to inherit the book.

Rosina, Myrtle and Naomi were listed, along with the date of Rosina's disappearance, which had been crossed out. Melville must have done that this morning, too. Until very recently, only her two sisters knew she was alive.

I stopped at an early page that had a little more wear and tear than the others, and a few dense lines of text. "This is the paper strengthening spell. It must have been created by this fellow."

"Or he was simply the first to record it in here," Gabe said.

I carefully turned the old pages until I found another spell. I recognized it as the origami spell Rosina taught me. A third spell was titled the Moving Spell. Melville was the only one who knew that spell. Other pages contained accounts about the times paper magic played an important role in a family member's life. The professor interpreted some of the Latin and found the pages referring to the years when magicians were forced into hiding by the artless who persecuted them.

We spent an hour poring over the book, at which point Willie declared she needed tea and cake. She left with the professor to prepare it.

I decided to telephone the Hendry sisters. It was time they knew I'd met their brother.

All three arrived thirty minutes later, just after we'd discovered the section in the book that referred to the merging of magics, and how other magicians of various disciplines had discovered they could combine their magics to enhance one or both. Paper magicians decided to experiment, and invisible writing was discovered, but due to the need for secrecy, experimentation was curtailed and nothing more useful was created.

"That's it!" Naomi cried upon seeing the book.

Rosina picked it up and cradled it against her chest with a satisfied sigh. "Do you sense it, Sylvia? So much history and magic." She sighed again. "I haven't felt as fulfilled as this since holding my children after they were born."

"I'm so glad Melville saw sense and gave it back," Naomi said.

I felt Myrtle's sharp glare needling into me. "How did he know to give it to you, Sylvia?"

I cleared my throat. "We met this morning. Apparently, he followed you here, hoping you'd lead him to the woman Evaline Peterson said was his relative and a paper magician. We talked and I informed him I was his daughter. He didn't dispute the fact."

I went on to tell them that Melville had actually been searching for my brother, James, and had hoped Evaline had made a mistake about the relative being a young woman.

"What else did he say?" Myrtle asked.

"Not much. He and my mother never married. Their union was forced by Lord Coyle, but he didn't say how. I assume Coyle blackmailed them."

Myrtle huffed in disappointment and frustration. "I assume Melville has been in hiding all these years?"

"Mostly at the Peterson factory. He wanted James to be able

to find him, so he remained in London and continued to use the name Cooper. He didn't know that James couldn't recall anything about our father. He was too young when our mother left. I wasn't even born yet."

Rosina hugged the book again before setting it down on the desk and opening it. She slowly turned the pages.

"Do you have a translation of the Latin at home?" Professor Nash asked. "I could translate it myself, but it would take time."

Rosina shook her head. "If there ever was a translation, I never saw it. I was never allowed near the book. It was always made clear to me that it belonged to Melville. Even though I was a magician, I was weaker than him."

"And female," Willie added wryly.

Rosina turned to the last page, written in Melville's hand, and flipped backwards through the pages. The sisters talked about the names that appeared there, of aunts and uncles, grandparents, and even great-grandparents. They told me family stories that had been passed down through the generations. Even though they weren't about magic, I enjoyed hearing them. But the further back through the book they went, the more they learned about their ancestors, too.

Gradually, over the course of the afternoon, the others drifted off to do their research, leaving only the three sisters and me to digest as much of the book as we could comprehend. It was Rosina who found a curious Latin word that had us all intrigued.

"*Vaticinium,*" she said, sounding out the syllables. "Is it something to do with the Vatican, do you think?"

The professor stood on the mezzanine level, reshelving books. I asked him to join us and translate the text.

"*Vaticinium* means prophecy," he said as he read.

Naomi lightly clapped her hands. "A prophecy. How exciting! What does the next part say?"

Professor Nash wrote the translation on a piece of paper then handed it to me. "Most intriguing."

I read the words out loud. "'A magician from the line of Hendreau will save time.'" I looked up and shrugged. "What do you think it means?"

"Goodness knows," Naomi said.

"Probably nothing," Myrtle added. "Saving time could mean catching a train instead of walking. Prophecies are all hokum anyway. They can be twisted to mean anything you want them to mean."

Rosina reread the English translation of the prophecy. "Melville would have taken it seriously. That's why he needed to find his son. He wanted this book to be passed to him, his heir, if he turned out to be a paper magician."

"He wanted his son to know his Hendry ancestry," Myrtle added, quietly. "He wanted Sylvia's brother to pass the book on to one of his heirs when the time came. It must have come as a surprise to learn he had a daughter who was a paper magician, not a son. Melville never did like surprises. Order, tidiness and predictability, that's what our brother liked."

We spent the remainder of the afternoon looking through the journal, having the more intriguing passages translated by the professor or Gabe. Rosina and I practiced the paper-moving spell. It took several attempts at getting the pronunciation just right, but eventually she could lift a piece of paper off the table. I was able to make it fly, albeit erratically. Fortunately, it was more like the delicate flutter of a butterfly than the streak of a thrown knife, and posed no threat.

When it came time for the sisters to leave, I offered the book to Rosina. "This belongs to you, not me. You have as much right as Melville to keep it."

Rosina shook her head. "Giving it to you is the one commendable thing our brother did in this entire sorry saga. You're a stronger magician than me, Sylvia, and younger. My children are artless, as are our cousins' children. You're the only Hendry paper magician of your generation." She smiled gently. "Hold on to it until the time is right to pass it on."

I clutched the book against my chest. My heart thudded in response to the close proximity of the dense concentration of paper magic. Rosina was right. Possessing the journal fulfilled me in a way nothing else did.

After the sisters left, Gabe sought me ought. The light caress of his fingers on the back of my neck was cool and very welcome. When he stroked my cheek, I leaned into his touch.

"Are you all right?" His silky-smooth voice rumbled deep in his chest.

I looked up at him and smiled. "Thank you for being here."

He pulled over another chair and sat, bringing us to the same level. He caught my hands in his. "It must be overwhelming."

"It is, yet I wouldn't have it any other way. Meeting my father still feels somewhat surreal, but reading this journal is… well, it's just so wonderful. I've gone from having no knowledge of my ancestry to having a thousand years' worth." My eyes filled with tears at the enormity of it.

Gabe stroked his thumb over my knuckles as he leaned forward. "If you're happy, then I'm happy."

He kissed me, and I kissed him back. It began as a light, tender caress of lips, but quickly deepened. We'd moved past the tentative, uncertain stage of our relationship, and progressed to passionate desire, the sort that made my skin hot and my mind sharply focused on just one thing—Gabe. His hand moved to the back of my head, burying his fingers in my hair. My breath shuddered.

Alex cleared his throat. "Willie's coming."

I sat back with a thud.

"So?" Gabe's voice sounded gravelly. "Let her see."

I wasn't ready to face the censure of his cousin, however. My emotions were taut, albeit finely balanced. A confrontation with Willie might make them spill over.

* * *

When it came time to close the library at the end of the day, I placed the journal in the bottom drawer of the front desk. Gabe offered to drive me home, but I asked to be taken to The Home Emporium on Bond Street instead. I wanted to meet Daisy after she finished work. She'd started the day before, and I'd been a terrible friend for not checking to see how her first day went.

Petra apparently had the same idea. I spotted her approaching the shop and waved. Gabe felt comfortable leaving me to walk home in the company of both my friends.

"Do you want to see Daisy?" he asked Alex.

"Not today." Alex slammed the gear lever into place.

"Gentle!" Willie cried from the back seat. "She doesn't respond to rough treatment."

Gabe and I exchanged worried glances. I mouthed, "Speak to him," before the motorcar sped off.

Petra frowned, watching them go. "Is everything all right between Alex and Daisy?"

"Her parents weren't kind to him, so she's chosen Alex over them. I think Alex feels conflicted about her choice. He doesn't want to be the reason for her distancing herself from her family."

Petra looped her arm with mine. "He's not the reason. *They* are."

"Wise words. Now we just have to convince him."

Daisy joined us on the pavement a few minutes later, an embroidered bag in hand. The navy blue and white stitching matched the compact sailor-style hat on her head. While most ladies still wore hats that required other pedestrians to give them a wide berth or risk being struck by the brim, Daisy followed the modern styles of her French fashion magazines and wore small ones. She looked very fresh and modish today in her navy dress with the white silk collar, hem and belt.

She beamed at us, only for it to slip when she peered past me. "Did I just see Gabe's motorcar? Was Alex with him?"

"They had to hurry off," I said quickly.

Her smile slipped even more. "Oh."

Petra took her hand and led her away from the shop door. "Well? How have your first two days been?"

Her face lightened again. "Marvelous! I've enjoyed it immensely. The owner is kind, the customers are a little snooty at first until I happen to mention I'm the daughter of Lord Carmichael, and the things we sell are the bee's knees. But that's not the best part."

"Oh?" I asked. "What is?"

"The wages I'll receive at the end of the month."

We all laughed.

"Let's celebrate," Petra said. "Shall we find a teashop then go on to a restaurant for dinner?"

"I prefer cocktails to tea," Daisy said. "We'll go to my place where no one will look at us like we have loose morals for enjoying predinner drinks."

It was a good idea, until Daisy's third martini, after which her conversation continually turned to Alex. Thinking of the way her parents had treated him, and his avoidance of her since, erased her good mood altogether. No one felt like going out to dinner after that, so we ate whatever we could find in Daisy's cupboard. The canned ham and canned peas followed by canned pears were hardly a celebratory feast, but they soaked up the martinis.

By the time Petra and I left, Daisy was feeling a little better. She promised to try to speak to Alex again as soon as possible. Just in case she decided to continue with the martinis after we left, and risk oversleeping and being late for her third day at her new job, I squirreled her bottle of gin out of the flat beneath my jacket. Petra had the same idea. She showed me the bottle of vermouth she'd tucked into her bag as we walked back to my place.

I waved her off from the front door and joined the other lodgers sitting in the front reception room where one of them played the piano. Some of the other girls danced to the merry tune, while Mrs. Parry looked up from her needlework and smiled. She invited me to sit, but before I could, one of the lodgers took my hands and whisked me toward the dancers. Her laughter triggered my own. I suddenly couldn't stop smiling.

Despite Daisy's troubles, and despite discovering my father was not a good man, I felt lighter than I had in a long time. Years. A weight that I didn't know I'd been supporting had lifted off my shoulders. I could now move forward with more ease. The future was looking brighter than ever.

* * *

I AWOKE with a start to the sound of someone knocking lightly on my door. I threw a shawl around my shoulders and padded across the floor in bare feet to answer it.

Mrs. Parry stood there dressed in nightcap and dressing gown. "There's a young lady downstairs asking for you. She seems upset."

It must be Daisy, the poor thing. I hastily dressed and headed to the sitting room where I'd danced the evening away earlier with the other lodgers. Perched on the edge of the sofa was a teary Ivy Hobson clutching a lace-edged handkerchief. She shot to her feet and rushed toward me. She clasped my forearm, hard.

"Sylvia, thank goodness! You have to come quickly. It's Gabe."

Perhaps I was still sleepy because her words didn't immediately sink in. It took her shaking my arm vigorously to trigger my response. "What happened?"

"He's been kidnapped!"

The words punched me in the gut. I covered my mouth, thinking I was going to be sick, but it was just the agonizing pain of panic gripping my insides. "Oh God, no."

"Come quickly. You can help."

Her words didn't make sense. "Me? How?"

"Alex said to fetch you so I came here directly."

"Alex? Ivy, I don't understand. Alex knows about the abduction?"

She nodded quickly. "Willie, too. They're out looking for Gabe now." She bit her lower lip. "This is all my fault, but I had to do it, you see. I had to, or Bertie…" She pressed her lips together and turned her face away.

I grasped her shoulders and shook her. "Tell me what happened. Who kidnapped Gabe? Why is it your fault?"

"There's a man… My mother and I became entangled in his business enterprises. But he wasn't what we thought. He turned out to be a brute, and I think his businesses are involved in criminal activity."

"Thurlow?" It wasn't a great leap to make, considering we'd seen Ivy and Mrs. Hobson speaking to the bookmaker at the racetrack.

She nodded. "He came to me tonight and said he was holding Bertie captive." She pressed the hand that grasped the handkerchief to her chest. She seemed to be having trouble catching her breath. It came in short, sharp gasps as she tried to hold back her tears. "Thurlow told me he wouldn't release Bertie until I gave him Gabe."

My own breathing turned ragged. "Ivy, what did you do?" When she began to cry, I shook her again, harder. *"What did you do?"*

"I went to Park Street and lured Gabe out of his house, alone. Then Thurlow's men bundled him into their motorcar."

My fingers sprang apart, releasing her. I could have slapped her. I wanted to slap her. But I wanted answers more. "Go on." My voice was ominously low.

Ivy swallowed heavily. "I regretted it instantly. I raced into the house and alerted Alex and Willie. I think they know some of Thurlow's haunts so they were going to look there first. Before he left, Alex told me to fetch you and take you to the house. He said you'd want to know, and you'd be a help in keeping the servants calm."

I pressed my fingers into my scalp. It felt like a blacksmith had set up a workshop in my head. "Why didn't Gabe use—" I cut myself short. Even now, I wouldn't divulge his secret.

"Why didn't he use what?" Ivy asked.

I shook my head, dismissing her question. Gabe's magic only engaged when his life was threatened anyway. It didn't react to kidnap. I tried to think of something I could do, something more productive than sitting with the servants. But it was no use. I was consumed with fear. Thurlow was cruel, and he'd seen what Gabe's magic was capable of at Epsom Downs Racecourse when Gabe had slowed time to save me from being hit by a bullet. Thurlow must think he could harness the magic for himself somehow.

"Sylvia, please. Come with me now. The elderly butler looked dreadfully pale when I left."

I stopped pacing. When had I started? "Did you drive here?"

"Our driver brought me. He's waiting outside with the motor running."

"There's just one thing I have to do first."

"What?"

"This." I slapped the side of her face. It could have been harder, but it was enough to sting, and get my point across.

She clutched her cheek with a shaking hand and stared at me, mouth open.

I strode out of the sitting room, passing Mrs. Parry listening in at the door.

"Should I telephone the police?" she asked.

"No," Ivy said from behind me. "Please, don't. If Thurlow finds out, he might do something awful to Gabe."

I tried to reassure Mrs. Parry, but I doubt I succeeded. My own fears were on full display as my eyes filled with tears.

I drew in a deep breath to steady my nerves. Crying wouldn't get Gabe back. Only action would. I'd go to Park Street and discuss what to do with the footman, Murray, the former police constable who'd been forced to change occupations after getting injured in the war. I rushed out of the house and raced toward the idling vehicle. I jerked the back door open and slid onto the back seat.

I should have looked first.

Strong hands grabbed me, pulling me against a thickset body that reeked of sweat. I opened my mouth to shout a warning to Ivy, but a hand clasped over it. I bit into the man's palm. He grunted in pain and his grip slackened. I managed to free myself and dove for the door handle.

The door wouldn't budge. It wasn't locked; it was blocked from the other side. Ivy stood there, pressing against the door. She glared down at me through the window aperture above it.

My stomach plunged, and my heart with it. She'd tricked me.

I opened my mouth to scream for Mrs. Parry, but the man beside me grabbed me again, and this time he shoved a cloth in my mouth. I choked on my cries for help.

I recognized the man as one of Thurlow's thugs.

"Get in," he ordered Ivy as he tied my hands together in front of me.

"I will," she said. "But first, there's something I need to do."

"What?"

She reached into the vehicle and slapped my face. Unlike me, she didn't hold back. My cheek and jaw stung; my head felt woolly. For a moment, I thought I'd pass out, but I managed to keep my eyes open.

I only had time to see that we were driving quickly along my street before the burly thug next to me covered my eyes with a blindfold. I tried to fight him, but with my hands tied, it was useless. There was no escape, and now no way of knowing where I was heading.

Ivy told me she'd lured Gabe out of his house so Thurlow could kidnap him. But he was probably still tucked up in bed. She hadn't tricked *Gabe*, she'd tricked *me*.

CHAPTER 6

The blindfold was removed at the top of a set of stone steps worn smooth from years of use. It took a moment for my eyes to adjust to a flickering, dim light coming from below. Once they did, I realized the steps led down to a cellar built of redbrick with arch supports. The light came from a single bulb hanging from the ceiling like a stalactite. There were no windows in the cellar, and the door through which I was pushed was the only exit. I wasn't surprised to see Thurlow waiting for me at the base of the steps. I *was* surprised to see Bertie Hobson with him.

Bertie chewed on his lower lip and didn't meet my gaze.

Thurlow smiled that slick smile of his. "Welcome, Miss Ashe. I am sorry for the subterfuge, but I thought it would be the only way to get you here. Did my man harm you?"

My cheek ached from where Ivy had struck me, but I wasn't going to let them know it.

"We'll remove that gag so you can talk." He nodded at the burly fellow who'd been seated beside me in the motorcar. "There's no point screaming. No one can hear you. If you do scream, I'll have to shut you up. I can't abide screeching women." His wince sharpened his weaselly features further.

It was a relief to have my mouth free again. I didn't scream, but I did spit a few strong curse words at him.

He merely smiled, revealing teeth crowded together, vying for space. "I've always admired your fire, Miss Ashe. It doesn't always reveal itself, but when it does, it's intoxicating." His tongue darted out and licked his lower lip. His gaze fell to my chest. "It's so much more attractive in a woman than ice."

Whether she suspected the comment was directed at her or not, Ivy employed that iciness she was famous for, and coolly asked Thurlow what would happen now.

He indicated I should sit on one of the three chairs. Aside from some barrels stored to one side, they were the only pieces of furniture in the cellar. "Now, we wait. A note will be slipped under the door at number sixteen Park Street, Mayfair, directing Glass to meet me if he ever wants to see Miss Ashe again. When the household awakes at dawn, they'll give him the note. Then we'll see how much he cares for her."

"I know what you're trying to do and it's pointless," I said. "Gabe is artless. He can't perform magic for you."

Thurlow ignored me and continued to speak to Ivy. "Fetch your mother, please, Miss Hobson. My driver will take you. She should be here, since she's the reason for this, after all."

Ivy jutted her pointed chin forward in defiance. "This is not her fault. She's merely trying to fix things. The fault lies with my idiot brother."

Bertie finally came to life like an automaton wound up and released. "I didn't engage his services! You and Mother did that."

"We wouldn't have to engage him if you hadn't drawn us into this predicament in the first place."

"It's not my fault I'm artless," he whined.

Ivy strode up to him, and I thought she'd strike him as she'd struck me. But she was composed, her piercing gaze the only sign of her fury. She'd never seemed more regal. "So now you want to play the artless card. It's too late, Bertie. The damage has been done, and you are responsible for *all* of it!"

She spun around so she didn't see her brother's eyes well with tears and his chin tremble. She hurried up the stairs and closed the door behind her with an ominous thud.

Thurlow grunted. "Families, eh? This is why it's better not to have one. Don't you agree, Miss Ashe?"

I ignored him and addressed Bertie. "You don't have to do as they say. Do the right thing and let me go."

Bertie blinked rapidly back at me. "I don't have a choice!" He indicated Thurlow and his thug, standing at the base of the steps, guarding the way out. "I'm sorry, Miss Ashe. Truly, I am." He indicated my tied hands. "Is that entirely necessary, Mr. Thurlow? She can't escape past your man."

Thurlow snickered. "It would be amusing to see her try." He untied me then stepped back, as if he expected me to leap at him like a wildcat.

I remained seated. Bertie was right; I couldn't get past the guard. The only thing I could do was to try convince Thurlow he would achieve nothing by luring Gabe here. "What do you think Gabe can do for you? I told you, he's artless."

Thurlow sat on one of the other chairs and crossed one leg over the other. He looked unruffled, as if this were simply a casual meeting between acquaintances. "Come now, you don't believe that and nor do I. Not after what I witnessed at the Epsom racetrack during the storm."

"I don't know what you mean."

"Someone fired a gun." He put up his hands in surrender. "Before you ask, I don't know who. I didn't organize a shooter. I was merely a witness. And what I witnessed was Glass saving you."

I crossed my arms. "That's absurd."

"You would have been shot if he hadn't pushed you out of the way. The thing is, he moved in the blink of an eye. Less than a blink." He clicked his fingers. "No one saw him actually move.

So I asked myself how that could be possible. How did a man save someone without being seen to move? It must have been the same way he survived four years of war unscathed, and saved that boy from drowning. He traveled through time."

I kept my features schooled, even though part of me wanted to laugh. He was right that Gabe's magic involved the manipulation of time, but he was quite wrong about the time-travel theory.

Bertie must have heard this explanation before because he didn't look surprised. Indeed, he clarified for me. "It explains a lot. Every time he was hit in the war, he used his magic as he lay injured, perhaps dying, to wind back time. Then he made sure he was prepared and out of the way when the attack came again."

"Just as he made sure you were out of the way at Epsom, Miss Ashe," Thurlow added. "It makes sense that he can travel through time. His mother is, after all, a watch magician. Her magic must have mutated within him somehow, or perhaps her husband isn't artless after all, and they've been fooling everyone all these years."

He might be wrong about how Gabe's magic worked, but he still believed Gabe was a time magician. And that was dangerous. So, I rolled my eyes and chuckled. "That is the most ridiculous thing I've ever heard."

Thurlow merely shrugged. "Deny it all you want, but I was there at Epsom that day."

It was best to steer the conversation in a different direction so that I wasn't in danger of accidentally telling him the truth. "How did you get the Hobsons to agree to kidnap me and lure Gabe to you?"

"After first meeting Glass, I did a little research and discovered Ivy was his fiancée for a time. I'd already read about the former soldiers whose Hobson boots had failed, and it made me wonder if there was something there that I could use to my benefit. I befriended Bertie and he admitted he was artless. From there, it was easy to put two and two together and realize he was responsible for the batch of boots failing."

"He tricked me," Bertie grumbled. "I thought he was my... particular friend. We became close and I thought I could trust him."

Had Thurlow and Bertie been lovers? It would explain why Bertie trusted Thurlow with an important secret.

"At first, I simply asked for money," Thurlow went on. "The time you saw Mrs. and Miss Hobson meet me at the racetrack, they were paying me for my silence."

I tried to meet Bertie's gaze, but he kept his head low. He sniffed.

Thurlow continued, unconcerned that Bertie was upset. "Then, once I witnessed Glass save you from the gunshot during that storm, I realized the Hobsons could be useful in another way." He gestured to me with a flourish of his hand.

"He's blackmailing us," Bertie muttered. "We wouldn't be doing this if we weren't being forced."

Thurlow made a show of being pained by the accusation. "Blackmail is such a dirty word. Let's call it payment for my services. In exchange for me not divulging their traitorous secret to the nation they are being useful by bringing you here, which will lure Glass. It's a neat scheme. I did consider having Ivy go directly to Glass and not involving you at all, but it was her mother who pointed out that he wouldn't be fooled. We had to be smarter. So we came up with this plan instead. I must say, Hobson, your mother is quite the shrewd woman."

Bertie sniffed again. "My mother is a she-devil."

Thurlow chuckled.

"You should be ashamed of yourself, blackmailing a widow," I said.

"She may be a widow, but she has always ruled the family and overseen the business. Her husband was little better than a puppet."

"It's true," Bertie muttered.

It was no use continuing to appeal to Thurlow's conscience. He didn't have one. I turned to Bertie instead. "It would be better to come clean about your artlessness yourself and face the consequences, rather than do this. Thurlow can't be controlled. If Gabe doesn't do as Thurlow expects, he'll kill Gabe, and me. Is that what you want? Our murders on your conscience and to never be free of him?"

Thurlow pressed a hand to his heart. "You wound me, Miss Ashe. I thought you and I could come to some sort of arrangement where I will let you go, and you will become my...particular friend." His smile turned as oily as his hair, slicked back with brilliantine.

Bertie sat heavily on the third chair, and finally lifted his head to look at me. He was a pathetic, forlorn figure. Although he and Ivy were similar in appearance, her bearing was imperial whereas the same features somehow made him look weak. No more so than now, with tears pooling in his eyes. "We've gone too far to come clean. It's not just the charges we would face for kidnap; we'd be charged with treason or criminal negligence. The newspapers would relish the story. Even if I was found not guilty, our business would be ruined. Now that Father is dead, I'm supposed to be the magician who infuses the leather in our boots with magic, but once everyone discovers I'm artless, no one will buy them. Customers will go to our competitors."

That's why the family refused to admit they'd made a mistake on a batch of boots in the war. They were protecting the future of Hobson and Son. A family business built on the promise of magic was in danger of becoming worthless if all living family members were artless.

"You could change your structure, and do as other artless businesses do," I said. "Sell lower quality goods than magicians, at a cheaper price."

"Our profits would fall dramatically."

"Not to mention no one would buy from a traitor," Thurlow added with a twist of his lips.

"Mother would hate existing on a more meager budget. Ivy, too. It would devastate them. It's hopeless."

"It's a matter of greed," Thurlow added.

"The Hobsons aren't the only greedy ones in this scenario," I snapped. "You're kidnapping Gabe to force him to use his so-called time-travel magic for your own ends. Do you hope he can wind back time so you can place illegal bets on horses that you know won? Or change the odds you offer at the tote?"

"Very good, Miss Ashe. You've guessed correctly." He got to his feet. "Come, Hobson. We'll let Miss Ashe rest until your mother and sister arrive."

Both Bertie and I looked around. There was a hard floor, hard chairs and hard barrels. I wouldn't be getting any rest. Bertie gave me an apologetic shrug then followed Thurlow up the stairs. Thurlow's man brought up the rear.

I saw a chance and took it.

When Thurlow opened the door, I raced up the stairs on my toes to be as quiet as possible. But my footsteps still echoed in the cavernous cellar. The thug heard my approach and blocked the exit with his barrel-sized body. I kept my distance. I didn't want to be pushed down the stairs. The last thing I needed was an injury.

He sneered as he left, closing the door behind him.

I returned to the chair, only to get up again. I checked the walls and floor for secret passages, scrabbling at the bricks until my fingers bled. Panic set in when I found none. My chest tightened, and my breathing became labored. Weak-kneed, I sat on the chair and bent over in an attempt to catch my breath.

At that angle, the chair legs came into view. If I could snap one off, I could use it as a weapon. If I were a wood magician, I might be able to wield it without touching it. But I wasn't.

I was a paper magician.

With a renewed sense of calm, I sat up straight and waited.

* * *

IT WASN'T TOO long before Ivy, Mrs. Hobson and Bertie returned. Thurlow wasn't with them, but his guard took up a position at the base of the stairs again. He'd dispensed with his jacket, revealing thick arms straining the seams of his shirt and a throat like a frog's, bulging above his neckerchief. The scars on his hands and cheek looked to have been inflicted by a knife. I was no match for him, physically.

I rose as the Hobsons approached, but I was still much shorter than all three. Mrs. Hobson made a point of looking down her nose at me. She and her daughter were alike, with their sleek dark hair and statuesque figures that suited the latest fashions so well, not to mention the sharpness with which they regarded me. Poor Bertie was an insipid imitation beside them.

"I believe you are responsible for my predicament," I said to Mrs. Hobson. "Your plan won't work. Gabe isn't a magician."

"We'll see." Her gaze swept my length, twice, before some of the tightness around her eyes and mouth relaxed. Had she been worried I was injured? "You'll be exchanged for Gabriel when he arrives. Mr. Thurlow gave me his word."

"His word is worthless."

Bertie nibbled his lower lip. "I think she's right. Mother—"

"Quiet!" Mrs. Hobson snapped.

Bertie seemed to shrink into himself. He once again gnawed his lower lip.

I indicated the thug. "You and I both know Thurlow won't simply let me walk out of here. You can't trust him."

Ivy glanced at her mother but didn't say a word. Mrs. Hobson looked in no mood to put up with another dissenting voice.

She folded her arms. "I suggest you leave London the moment you are released, Miss Ashe. For your own good, and Gabriel's."

I barked a harsh laugh. "Forgive me if I refuse to take the advice of someone responsible for my abduction."

"Think a little longer about it, then act based on common

sense not petulance. You can't marry Gabriel, even if he wanted to. You have no father, no family, no history. It's as if you don't exist. How could the Rycroft heir marry someone like that?"

She might be wide of the mark about my family, now that I'd discovered I was a Hendry, but in a way, that knowledge made it worse. Being Melville's daughter would remind Gabe's parents of a past they wished to forget.

I shook off the negative thoughts. Gabe had assured me he didn't care who my father was, and that his parents wouldn't either. I mustn't let Mrs. Hobson burrow her way into my mind and infect me with her poisonous words.

She slowly circled me, her arms still crossed over her chest. I felt like I was back at school with a strict headmistress checking I was following the uniform rules. "A marriage between you would have repercussions beyond the social. Lord and Lady Rycroft have significant influence over government policy surrounding magicians. Their son needs to marry a magician from a good family, not a mousy nobody. You would ruin him."

"Save your breath, Mrs. Hobson. You're going to need it when the police arrest you. It's *your* reputation that will be ruined."

Mrs. Hobson laughed, a brittle sound that echoed around the cellar. "You are so naive, it's almost charming. You will be the one wasting your breath if you go to the police upon your release. *We* didn't abduct you. Mr. Thurlow's men did. Who would take your word over ours when there's no evidence we were involved?"

"There is evidence. My landlady can identify Ivy."

None of the Hobsons showed a flicker of concern. They'd already thought of that. "Did she actually witness me kidnap you?" Ivy asked. "Or simply call on you? It's not my fault I got the wrong end of the stick and thought Gabe was being kidnapped, or that you then followed me out of the house. I thought I was taking you to my motorcar, but it seemed you got into a different one. The vehicle sped away before I had a chance to stop you. My driver tried to follow, but we lost sight of you, alas." She shrugged and batted her eyelashes oh-so-innocently. "Nobody witnessed us get into the same vehicle."

A jury would adore her. They would eat up her testimony, particularly if she added a few tears.

Mrs. Hobson laid a hand on her daughter's arm. "We'll wait upstairs. The air is unpleasant down here."

The thug moved aside to let them pass. The women lifted their skirts and marched up the steps. Bertie hung back, watching them go with stooped shoulders.

"May I have a book to read to pass the time?" I asked.

Mrs. Hobson paused on the top step and looked down. "No. Bertie, come."

Bertie cast me a look filled with hopelessness, then followed his mother and sister out. The thug exited, too, and locked the door behind him.

I sat on the chair and buried my face in my hands. I prayed they were right and Thurlow would follow through on his promise to release me. Unlike the Hobsons, I was confident I could get Scotland Yard to believe my account of the abduction. Alex's father, Cyclops, worked for Scotland Yard and would be on my side, and perhaps even Mr. Jakes. He would be very interested in hearing my account of Bertie's admission.

But I had very little confidence that Thurlow would keep his word to the Hobsons and let me go.

When the door opened again, I thought it might be him, but it was Bertie, along with the guard. The thug remained by the door at the top of the stairs this time, instead of at the base.

Bertie gave me a weak smile as he handed me two books. "I could only find texts about leather goods, I'm afraid. There are no novels here."

I accepted the books gratefully and held them against my chest. "Where are we?"

"I'm not supposed to tell you." He glanced up at the guard

then lowered his voice. "After his death, we discovered my father kept a small house in Bethnal Green."

Bethnal Green wasn't the sort of place where a respectable gentlemen had a house, particularly if he lived not far away in a much better area with his family. The fact he hadn't told his family about it meant Mr. Hobson hadn't been a respectable gentleman, after all.

Bertie smirked. "Mother was livid when she found out."

I'd never had much to do with Bertie in the past. He'd simply been there in the background, looking like he would rather be somewhere else. I regarded him with renewed interest. "You don't like your family, do you?"

"You've met them. What do you think?"

"I think you loathe the way they treat you."

"My mother calls me to heel, like a dog. If I don't come running, she has me whipped. Not physically," he conceded. "But her verbal lashings have left scars nevertheless."

I nodded in understanding but remained silent. I got the feeling he wanted to talk to someone who would just listen. He'd probably gone his whole life without being truly heard.

"When I came clean to my parents about my artlessness, they told me I was pathetic, useless. I was the son in Hobson and Son. I had a job to do; make the leather in our boots stronger by using magic. I'd pretended to be a magician when I was young to get them to like me, but they suspected I was artless for years before they finally admitted me to Rosebank Gardens in an attempt to draw it out of me." His mouth turned down as if he would cry, but he rallied and continued. "It was a horrid place. The treatments were painful. I wouldn't inflict them on my worst enemy. With Father alive, and Mother essentially running the show, it didn't matter that I was artless. We all simply continued on, fooling ourselves that I'd one day simply gain magic abilities. Then when Father unexpectedly became ill during the war, I told them I'd take care of everything, that I'd ensure the boots received their magic. I thought I could do it. I thought I *felt* magic inside me." He tapped his chest. "I must have been wrong."

"You probably convinced yourself because you wanted your parents' love and acceptance."

He shrugged. "Father was too sick to verify whether the boots held my magic, and Mother was busy ensuring his will and other financial details of the business were in place in case he died. Later, when we found out some of the boots failed and the batch could be traced back to the time when I was in charge, we all realized I was definitely artless. There was no longer any doubt, or hope. They blamed me for the boots failing, and rightly so. It *was* my fault." He closed his eyes and pressed his lips firmly together, as if that would stop him blurting out his emotions. When he reopened his eyes, the haunted look made him seem even more vulnerable. "Those poor soldiers who've lost their limbs… I tried to convince my parents that we needed to compensate them, but they refused. They said the future of the company depended on me being a magician. Admitting that a batch failed because I was artless would ruin us when it came time for me to take over."

"It's not too late to come clean."

"Mother won't let me. I don't even have an ally in my own sister. Ivy will do whatever Mother thinks is best."

"You are your own man, Bertie. Your future is what *you* make it, not what others want for you."

He lifted his gaze to mine, and for the first time, I saw a spark in them.

It gave me hope. "I know someone in Military Intelligence. Let me arrange for you to speak to him. If you explain that it was all a dreadful mistake, that you were under the influence of your parents, perhaps he'll be lenient."

The spark in Bertie's eyes flared brighter. "I *was* under their influence. And Father was still in charge, with Mother deputizing in his absence. Not me."

If he thought the only way to absolve himself was to blame

his parents, then I wasn't going to tell him otherwise. My plan had a better chance of working if he believed he could walk free.

Bertie glanced at the guard at the top of the stairs. "None of this can be blamed on me either," he said quietly. His face suddenly fell. "But I can't get you out of here, Miss Ashe. I can't fight him, let alone Thurlow and his other henchman."

I hugged the books tighter. "Leave that to me. When the opportunity arises, we'll make our escape."

He didn't look like he believed it would happen. I couldn't blame him for that. I wasn't sure my plan would work either.

He headed up the steps and left the cellar with the guard. This time, when the door locked, I didn't feel a sense of hopeless dread. I simply sat on the chair and opened one of the books.

I didn't read the title, but I silently apologized for the sacrilegious thing I was about to do. Then I tore out each page, one by one. When I'd finished with the first book, I went on to the second, piling each loose page up on one of the other chairs. Once both books were left with nothing between the covers, I quietly spoke the paper moving spell.

The top page lifted and flapped about before fluttering to the floor.

I tried again, digging through my memory for the way I'd emphasized the words not twenty-four hours ago in the library. More pages rose into the air and flew about, a little faster. I tried again and again, each time perfecting my pronunciation and altering the emphasis on the words I suspected affected speed and direction. The papers flew about, whipping through the air like blades, but I couldn't control where they went. I stopped, worried I'd cut myself.

It wasn't perfect, but it would have to do. I didn't have a watch on me, but I suspected it would be dawn soon. It was time to act.

With an armful of papers, I climbed the steps and thumped on the door. "I need to use the privy!"

The door opened and the guard regarded the papers. "Why do you need those?"

"Reading material."

He indicated I should follow him. The cellar opened into a kitchen, which led to a short hallway and the front door. Another of Thurlow's men stood there, guarding it. The voices coming from the only other room off the hallway belonged to Thurlow and Mrs. Hobson.

"Just one moment," I said to my escort.

I stepped into a compact parlor where the three Hobsons sat on stiff-backed chairs while Thurlow stood by a small fireplace that looked like it hadn't been cleaned since its last use. His casual stance stiffened upon seeing me. The Hobsons turned as one toward me.

"Why is she here?" Thurlow snapped at my escort.

The thug grabbed my arm.

I began the chant I'd learned from the Hendry family journal.

Ivy rose. "What is she doing?"

Her mother stood, too. "Is that a spell? But you're not a magician."

The papers in my arms flapped like birds wanting to be released. I let them go and watched them fly around the room as if a whirlwind had whipped them up.

Bertie laughed, until he had to duck under one of the pages that flew toward him.

The others ducked, too, including the thug. He released me to protect his head with his arms. Ivy screamed, drawing the second man into the parlor to see what the commotion was about. He realized too late what was happening and was cut by a paper's edge. Another one nicked his forehead before he fell to the floor and covered his head, too.

There were so many pages, over five hundred, and the noise of flapping papers all vying for space in the small parlor was louder than I expected. As with my experiments in the cellar, I failed to control them, and had to duck out of the way, too. I didn't stop speaking the spell, however.

"Get her!" Thurlow growled. "Shut her up before your bollocks are sliced off!"

The man closest to me covered his crotch with his hands, leaving his head exposed. He received a cut to his cheek and another to his shoulder. Blood tinged his shirt.

The second man was a little further away, but he blocked the doorway. His gaze narrowed as he readied himself to leap at me, low to the ground. I spoke the spell faster, changing the emphasis of a syllable here and there. Suddenly, the pages dove toward him, like a swarm of bees at their hive. He swore as he tried to bat them away.

There was no time to wonder at how I'd managed to direct the paper onslaught at him. With both men occupied, I ran past them, but hesitated in the doorway. "Bertie?" I managed to say between spell repetitions. I held out my hand.

He leapt up and took it. Thurlow tried to follow him, but the swarm of flying paper blocked his advance.

Bertie and I ran onto the road and spotted Thurlow's motorcar. Like Gabe's vehicle, it required a crank to start the engine, not a key like some newer ones. I took the driver's seat while Bertie cranked. Only once the motor rumbled to life did I stop speaking the spell.

Gabe had given me driving lessons, so I knew what to do. I pulled away from the curb, expecting to hear a gunshot. But the house was silent. I hoped no one was terribly injured. Individual cuts shouldn't be deep enough to bleed out or leave scars, but if they received too many…I shuddered to think.

It was fortunate that there was very little traffic on the road because the motorcar steered differently to the Vauxhall. I quickly got used to it, however, and headed in the direction of Mayfair.

"You've been cut." Bertie pointed at my neck.

I touched it. My fingers came away sticky and the cut stung. I glanced at him. In the soft light of dawn, I could make out two cuts on his face. "So have you. Sorry."

He dabbed at them with a handkerchief. "I didn't know you're a paper magician."

"I just found out myself."

After a few more turns, he added, "We're heading to Gabe's place, aren't we?"

"I have to retrieve that note Thurlow left for him." I flexed my fingers on the steering wheel and blew out a fortifying breath. "Can you look around for something to write with?"

He opened the glove compartment and found a notepad and pencil. When we stopped around the corner from number sixteen Park Street, I penned Gabe a note of my own.

It was the hardest thing I'd ever written.

My feet felt like they were bogged in clay as I made my way up the steps to Gabe's front door. Another deep breath did nothing to steady my jangling nerves. Despite every part of me screaming that what I was doing was wrong, my head knew it was right.

I had to stay away from Gabe. Not to protect his family from social disgrace, but to protect him from Thurlow. Even if Thurlow was caught, someone else would take his place. Indeed, someone else had tried to kidnap Gabe before Thurlow even came onto the scene, and they were still at large.

I made Gabe vulnerable. His affection for me was a weak spot to be exploited by those who wanted to use his magic for themselves. I must leave London, leave my friends, and leave Gabe and the Glass Library behind.

I raised my hand to knock.

CHAPTER 7

It was surprisingly easy to swap Thurlow's letter for mine. Bristow held it in his hand as he answered my knock. He must have spotted it on the floor when he came to open the door. He looked stunned to see me at such an early hour. He would barely be out of bed himself.

"Good morning, Bristow." I whipped the letter out of his hand before he realized what was happening and held out my piece of paper, folded in half. "I changed my mind. *This* is the one I want delivered to Gabe."

He took it and I crumpled Thurlow's note in my fist.

"Will you come in for breakfast, Miss Ashe?"

"Not today. That letter isn't urgent. Don't wake him." On a whim, I kissed Bristow's cheek.

His cheeks pinked. "Is everything all right, Miss Ashe?"

"Fine. I have to go." I hurried down the steps and along the pavement to the corner. I tried not to think about Gabe's reaction as he read my note, but my mind continued to wander there anyway. He would be furious and worried, and perhaps confused. He would go directly to my lodgings then on to my friends' homes to search for me. I must be quick if I didn't want him catching up to me, even though I had a head start.

It wasn't until I was driving home that I suddenly realized Bertie could have easily escaped while I was at Gabe's house. Indeed, I'd expected him to. Yet he had not. That changed things a little.

The house where I rented a room was quiet. It was too early for any of the lodgers or our landlady to be up. Mrs. Parry must have gone back to bed after I'd been abducted, none the wiser to my predicament. My room was paid in advance, so after I packed a few essentials, I quickly dashed off a note of farewell without explaining why I was leaving in a hurry. I hadn't yet thought of a suitable excuse for my sudden departure, so it was best to say nothing.

I drove to the home of Cyclops and Catherine Bailey next. I knocked several times until he finally answered. His eyepatch was in place, but he clutched the waist of his trousers to stop them falling down. He held a belt in his other hand. He seemed relieved that it was me on his doorstep.

"I thought you were a constable come to tell me something terrible had happened." He peered past me at Bertie Hobson. "Has something happened, Sylvia? It's very early. Are you all right?"

"I am now, but before I give you an account of my night, I need you to promise you won't tell Gabe."

He shook his head. "I can't do that."

"Then I can't tell you what happened, but I will tell you that you must warn Gabe not to trust any of the Hobsons."

"It's true," Bertie said from behind me. "My mother and sister are up to their necks."

Cyclops scratched his bald head with the hand that held the belt. Then he stepped onto the porch and closed the door behind him. "I don't want to wake Catherine or the girls." He threaded his belt through his trouser loops. "You have my word I won't tell Gabe...for now. Go on, Sylvia. I'm listening."

"The Hobsons and Thurlow abducted me in the middle of the night."

He stopped doing up his belt and stared at me. His one eye blinked back at me then narrowed as it shifted to Bertie. "I take it you were set free."

"I escaped."

"Bloody hell." He rubbed his jaw. "Are you sure you're all right?"

"I'm fine, just a paper cut here." I showed him my neck.

"Ah. So that's how you escaped. And you brought one of your abductors to me to turn him in?"

"Not quite. I want you to arrest Mrs. Hobson, Ivy and Thurlow, if you can find them. I'd also like you to contact Mr. Jakes at Military Intelligence. Bertie wants to talk to him about a batch of army-issue boots manufactured by his company, but it's too early for Mr. Jakes to be at his office."

"I'll make a telephone call. Wait inside where it's safe. I assume your abductors are cut, too, but not dead?"

"I think so. Make your telephone call, then we'll tell you about it."

A few minutes later, we got back into Thurlow's motorcar and drove to Scotland Yard where Cyclops had arranged to meet Mr. Jakes.

As I drove, I told Cyclops about the abduction, including the excuses Mrs. Hobson and Ivy planned to use to place the entire blame on Thurlow so they could walk free. He scribbled down my statement in his notebook.

When we arrived at Scotland Yard, I informed Bertie I'd drop him and Cyclops and go on my way, but he begged me to stay for the duration of the interview with Mr. Jakes. I reluctantly agreed. Time was marching on, and Gabe would wake soon.

As I parked the vehicle, I reminded Cyclops not to tell Gabe anything about my abduction. He must carry out the investigation in secret for as long as possible.

"I assume the reason you want me to keep it from him has something to do with that?" He pointed his pencil at the two small cases on the back seat beside Bertie.

I remained silent.

"Running away won't solve anything, Sylvia." When I didn't respond, he added, "So you plan to leave without talking to him?"

"She left him a note," Bertie piped up.

Cyclops shook his head. "Whatever excuse you wrote, he won't believe it. You two love each other. It's obvious to everyone, including him. Talk to him, Sylvia. Be honest."

"I'm leaving for his safety," I finally said. "That's also the reason why I don't want you to say anything about my abduction. You know he'll put himself in danger to exact justice. It's better if you do it. Just as it's better that I go. Last night proved that I make him vulnerable"

He sighed and shook his head again.

"Warn Gabe about Ivy and Mrs. Hobson," I urged him. "They may still try to lure him to Thurlow."

"How do I warn him without telling him about the abduction?"

"Bertie informed you of their plans for Gabe when he turned himself in. Didn't you, Bertie?"

"Er, all right," Bertie said.

"You've thought of everything," Cyclops said heavily. "Very well. I agree not to inform Gabe just yet."

I thought he'd eventually see it from my point of view. He knew as well as I did that I made Gabe vulnerable. It wasn't just Gabe. Where he went, Alex followed. Cyclops would do anything to protect both.

While we waited for Mr. Jakes, Cyclops sent a team to the Bethnal Green address where I'd been kept captive, and another to the Hobsons' home.

We didn't have to wait too long before Mr. Jakes arrived. It was still early, and traffic hadn't yet hit its morning peak, but I suspected he must have been nearby when he learned he was wanted at Scotland Yard. He looked as dapper as always, with his neatly combed brown hair and dark lashes framing light blue eyes that seemed to miss nothing.

He sat in a chair and removed a gold cigarette case from his inside jacket pocket. Cyclops asked him not to smoke in the confined space, so he returned it. "This must be important."

Cyclops clasped his hands on the desk. "This is Bertie Hobson. He wants to confess something to you."

Mr. Jakes must have known who sat with us, because he showed no surprise at the mention of Bertie's name. The only sign he gave that he'd not expected a confession was the sudden arch of his brows.

Bertie glanced at me. At my encouraging nod, he cleared his throat. "It wasn't my fault. It was my father's," he said in a rush of words. "He fell ill and told me to perform magic on the leather while he was confined to his bed. Naturally, I told him I was artless and couldn't, but he didn't believe me. He'd always suspected I was a magician, that my magic was simply buried within me. That's why he and Mother sent me to Rosebank Gardens years ago. You can check for yourself. I'm sure they still have the old admissions records somewhere. If only he believed me when I protested, those boots would never have been distributed to the army." He sat back, satisfied with his statement.

Mr. Jakes's cool gaze gave nothing away. "Come with me and we'll put it all in writing at my office. Scotland Yard isn't the place for you."

Bertie looked relieved. Perhaps he thought he'd be released. I wasn't so sure he would be, however. But whether Mr. Jakes believed the blame belonged solely to the deceased Mr. Hobson, or he believed Bertie should hold some accountability, it didn't matter to me. I shook Bertie's hand and wished him good luck.

He exited Cyclops's office, but Mr. Jakes hesitated in the doorway. His fingers drummed on the door jamb. "Why did he come to you with this, Miss Ashe?"

"That's not important."

"Let me be the judge of that."

I simply shrugged.

"Does it have something to do with the attempted abductions of Gabriel Glass and the speculation surrounding his magic?"

"Gabe is artless," I said, parroting the words I'd repeated several times overnight.

I went to push past him, but Cyclops asked me to wait. Mr. Jakes left the office and closed the door.

Cyclops rounded the desk. "Sylvia—"

"Nothing you say will convince me to change my mind."

"I can see you're determined." He took my hand in his huge one. "I'll just say good luck, but not goodbye. I believe we'll see one another again soon." He kissed my forehead then reached past me and opened the door.

"Take care," I said and left.

I didn't cry as I walked through the warren of halls to the main exit. My heart didn't thud, my stomach felt settled. Either I was too tired to feel anything, or too numb, because seeing Cyclops for the last time should have drowned me in misery.

* * *

I LEFT Thurlow's vehicle where I'd parked it and took a taxi to my next stop. Fortunately, I'd asked the driver to wait for me because I was there an even shorter duration than I'd expected. Daisy didn't answer my knock. She must be sound asleep still, or in the bathroom getting ready for work.

I scrawled a note and slipped it under her door. It felt woefully inadequate, but I couldn't stay to say goodbye in person. After my lodgings, this would be one of the first places Gabe looked for me after reading my note.

I didn't know where Petra lived, and her shop wouldn't be open yet, so I headed to the next person on my list, since he lived closer to Daisy than the Hendry sisters and I didn't want to double back. Nor could I go to the library to farewell Professor Nash. After my flat and Daisy's, Gabe would go there. I would post the professor my key when I found a new home.

To my surprise, Huon answered the door almost immediately after my knock. He must have been passing it and not bothered to wait for his butler or footman. His hair was messy, and he wore a blue-and-white striped dressing gown without shoes. Thankfully, the dressing gown was tied at his waist because he didn't appear to be wearing pajamas underneath.

"Good lord, Sylvia, you look like you could do with this more than me." He handed me the cup of coffee he'd been holding. "Come in. I have so much to tell you."

"I can't. I have to go." I sipped the coffee, closing my eyes as the warm, bitter liquid hit the back of my throat. I suddenly felt overwhelmingly tired. It was the only explanation I could think of for why I let Huon draw me inside.

"Where do you have to go at this hour? It's early." He checked the clock on the hall table. "The shops and the library don't open for at least another hour."

His butler passed, carrying a tray. He was about to go up the staircase when Huon stopped him.

"Change of plans," Huon said. "Serve breakfast in the dining room, after all." He bent his head to his butler's and whispered something in his ear.

"Very good, sir," the butler said, turning around.

Huon invited me into the dining room. I glanced toward the taxi waiting for me. My cases were in the back seat. I signaled to the driver that I would only be a few moments while I finished the cup of coffee. I was going to need its stimulating effects if I wanted to stay awake all day.

Once we were seated at the polished table, Huon gave me his news. "You are looking at the newest businessman to gain a government contract."

"What?" He wasn't making sense. Or perhaps my mind wasn't working properly. It was beginning to feel woolly from lack of sleep.

He beamed. "My invisible messaging business will provide services to the Ministry of Labour, but I can't tell you in which particular aspect of their vast portfolio. Let's just say, my service will become more important if the government's theory about the rise of trade unions is proved correct."

"I'm so pleased for you, Huon."

"Thank you. I'm pleased for me, too."

"Did you tell your father about the contract?" I knew Huon's relationship with his father had been a rocky one ever since Huon demobbed. Instead of returning to the family's ink-manufacturing business after the war, he'd settled into a hedonistic life that revolved around the next party.

"I telephoned him yesterday. He said he was proud of me. Then he said he'd reinstate my allowance to tide me over until the business returns a decent profit."

"Wonderful."

"I told him where to shove it. I don't need his help."

"Family is important, Huon. Don't cut yourself off from them." Tears suddenly welled as I thought about the aunts and cousins I'd found. I might never see them again.

"Are you all right, Sylv?"

I nodded and attempted a smile. "I should go. My taxi is waiting."

"Nonsense. Stay for breakfast." He asked the footman who'd been bringing in covered platters and placing them on the sideboard to pay the driver.

"Oh, no, don't," I said, rising. "I need that taxi."

"Nonsense," Huon said again. "You need to eat something. You look peaky. Besides, I want you to see that I've become a better person. More settled and mature."

I sighed as I watched the footman leave. I really ought to go after him, but I suddenly didn't have the energy. "Yes, of course," I murmured dully.

"Then I want you to tell Petra how much I've improved."

"I can't. I—"

"Please, Sylv. Do it for me. I really like her, and I am trying very hard to be the man she deserves."

My eyes welled with tears again as I realized I would never see how things played out between Huon and Petra. I would never be part of their lives, or Daisy's. Would she and Alex find a way to be together? I was going to miss so much. I was going to miss them all, my dear friends.

Huon saw my distress but got the wrong end of the stick. "Don't fret, dearest Sylvia. We will find a way to surmount the differences between our families, as long as Petra sees me as worthy enough to put up a fight when her parents inevitably tell her ink is inferior to graphite. So will you go to bat for me?"

"I can't. I won't see her—"

"Actually, you can see her now." He stood and held out a hand toward the door.

I spun around to see Petra standing quite still in the doorway. She stared at me with an expression somewhere between confusion and sheer panic.

"Sylvia! What are you doing here at this hour?"

I was about to ask the same question, until I realized the answer was rather obvious. Unlike Huon, she was at least dressed, but her hair hung loose past her shoulders. She must have come downstairs in a hurry after the butler sent someone up to fetch her when I arrived.

She frowned at Huon as she took a seat near him. "You didn't think to turn her away?"

"She's our friend and she looked like she needed coffee." He reached across the table to take Petra's hand. "You look beautiful, my love. I do like your hair like that."

"It's not done yet."

"Undone is my favorite style." He rose. "Help yourselves to breakfast, ladies. There's a good selection this morning since I knew I was having a special guest stay."

Petra patted her hair but didn't look at me. Her cheeks flamed as she continued to fuss with her hair.

I got up and hugged her from behind. "I'm happy for you," I whispered in her ear.

"You shouldn't be," she whispered back. "It's a mistake. This is...wrong. *He's* wrong for me. I shouldn't—" She cut herself off and glanced at his back as he stood at the sideboard, oblivious to our discussion.

I hugged her tighter. "Yes, you *should* love him. He's quite sweet and a good man, underneath it all. The war's effects on him are starting to wear off." I gave her shoulders a gentle shake. "Thanks to you. You saved him, Petra. Now, allow yourself to be happy. You both deserve it."

She sighed. "Our families won't accept it."

"You'll find a way to make them accept it. I know you will."

"Daisy was right. Our situation is a modern-day *Romeo and Juliet* story."

"That was Shakespeare's story, not yours. You have it in your power to write *your* version." I clasped her shoulders, turning her to look at me. "We are all the authors of our own stories, Petra. Certain twists and turns might be out of our control, but the overall tone and direction of the plot are ours to write."

Petra wasn't entirely convinced. "I agree about that, but there's still the matter of Huon's arrogance. I don't want to give in to him or he'll be impossible."

I glanced at his back. "Then don't give in easily."

One side of her mouth lifted with her crooked smile. "I'm glad you're here, Sylvia. You deserve happiness, too. Speaking of which, how is Gabe?" She seemed to notice my state for the first time. "You look pale and tired. And your hair is down, too. Is something wrong?"

Huon dropped the fork he was using to pile bacon on his plate. The clatter shattered my fragile nerves completely. "Help yourselves, ladies, or I'll eat it all myself." He turned around, a rasher of bacon pinched between thumb and forefinger, just in time to see me burst into tears.

Petra guided me to a chair. "Sylvia, what is it? What's the matter?"

Huon patted my shoulder. "It's Glass's fault, isn't it? Want me to challenge him?"

"This isn't the Middle Ages, Huon. You can't challenge people to duels."

Huon handed me a napkin. "I didn't mean a *physical* challenge. I'll have a stern word with him, that's all."

I gathered up my frayed nerves and dabbed at my damp cheeks. "It's not Gabe's fault, although it does concern him. It's a rather long story, but the upshot is, I've come to realize I'm a danger to him. Terrible people are after him for the time magic they believe he controls. Because he's proven so difficult to kidnap, they will come for me since he cares about me. So, I've decided to leave London. It's the best way to keep him safe."

Huon folded his arms. "That makes sense, I suppose."

"No, it doesn't," Petra said. "It's true that Gabe cares about you, Sylvia, but he cares about other people, too. Not in the same way, obviously, but there are other people in his life he'd want to protect. Willie and Alex, for example."

"They're more capable of looking after themselves than me."

"True," Huon said, nodding.

Petra shot him a glare before turning back to me. She took my hands in hers. "You can't leave now. Everyone you care about is here. Not just Gabe, but Daisy and me, Alex and Huon, and the professor, of course. Besides, you adore your work at the library." She squeezed my fingers. "Running away might throw Gabe's kidnappers off for a little while, but not forever. They'll find another way to get to him. The only way to protect him is to stop them. All running off will do is cause you both to be miserable."

Running away…

It was what my mother had done. She believed moving from city to city had kept us safe from Melville Hendry, and perhaps it had. But it also caused disruption for James and me. We'd had no stability, made no friends, known no other family. Every time we had started to set down roots, we'd been wrenched away again. I was a shy child who took time to get to know others, so moving frequently made me withdraw further. I was the outsider at every new school and neighborhood, and my lack of confidence meant I never developed the skill to make true friends.

If Daisy hadn't been so open and vivacious, I might never have made a single friend in London yet. I owed her a great deal for taking me under her wing. I shouldn't abandon her now when she needed me.

A knock on the front door startled me into action. I folded the napkin up and set it on the table. "Thank you both. You've been a great help."

"Well?" Huon prompted. "What have you decided to do?"

The butler appeared in the doorway. "A Detective Inspector Bailey to see you, sir."

Cyclops pushed past the butler. He breathed a sigh of relief upon seeing me. "I hoped I'd find you here, Sylvia. I've been looking for you everywhere. Your landlady said you'd gone, Daisy wasn't at home, and the library was locked."

Huon indicated the sideboard. "Would you like some breakfast?"

Cyclops didn't seem to hear him. He looked pained.

I rose, although my legs weakened at the sight of Cyclops. I'd never seen him look so worried. "What is it? What's happened?"

"It's Gabe. He's been abducted."

CHAPTER 8

I felt sick. I couldn't breathe. All my efforts to keep Gabe safe, and he'd been kidnapped anyway. My body started to tremble, and I suddenly felt cold to my bones.

Someone guided me to sit again. "Alex? Willie?" I managed to ask.

"Out searching for him," Cyclops said. "So are most of Scotland Yard."

I pressed a hand to my throat as bile rose.

Cyclops crouched before me. "The kidnapper won't harm him. They need him alive and well to learn more about his magic."

"Isn't he artless?" Petra asked.

Neither Cyclops nor I explained. He rested a hand on my arm. "I wanted to find you to tell you in person, and to ask for your help, too."

I sat forward. "How can I help?"

"Sally, the young maid who works for Gabe, saw one of the men just after she arrived this morning. But she's too scared to give an account, so Alex told me over the telephone. I thought perhaps you could coax something out of her."

I shot to my feet. "Let's go."

"What can we do, Detective?" Huon asked.

Cyclops placed his hat on his head. "Nothing at this point."

We left the house without saying goodbye, only pausing long enough to collect my two cases from the entrance hall. Cyclops placed them in the back seat of the waiting police vehicle. I sat beside them while Cyclops got in the front. He instructed the driver to take us to Gabe's house.

When we reached number sixteen Park Street, it was clear that an incident had occurred. Constables kept watch from the pavement and the front door stood open. Murray ushered us inside.

"Anything?" Cyclops prompted him.

The footman shook his head. "No, sir. Sally hasn't stopped crying. Mrs. Bristow is at her wits' end, which is making Sally more scared. She says she can't remember a thing, except that the man was big. The sketch artist has arrived, but he can't work until Sally remembers something."

A thud upstairs had us all looking up at the ceiling.

"The sergeant is leading the search for clues in Mr. Glass's bedroom," Murray went on.

"You seem to have it under control. Well done." Cyclops clapped the former policeman on the shoulder before taking the staircase to check on the searchers.

Murray led me through the door near the back of the entrance hall and down the service stairs to the basement. We found all the other servants in the room where they took their meals, along with a man I assumed was the police artist going by the sketchbook in front of him. He stood upon my entry.

"Miss Ashe!" Mrs. Ling, the cook, grasped both my hands. "We are glad you are here."

I suddenly felt the need for maternal comforting and drew her into a hug. "I'm glad I'm here, too."

Mrs. Bristow sat beside a weeping Sally. Her husband, the

butler, stood behind her, a hand on his wife's shoulder. She'd been crying, too, but at that moment she seemed more frustrated than upset. Sally was under her charge, and she must feel as though the girl's failure to remember was somehow a reflection on her.

I asked Mrs. Bristow to tell me what they already knew.

"Well," she began, "when Mr. Bristow and I came down this morning, we found Sally in the kitchen, crying." The Bristows were the only live-in servants. Sally and the others lived at their own homes, and Sally, being the youngest maid, always arrived first to light fires, and perform other chores before the rest of the household arrived or woke. "We asked her what was wrong, but she wouldn't answer. She just kept shaking her head, over and over."

"We thought it was problems at home and she'd tell Mrs. Bristow when she was ready," Bristow said. "But an hour went by, two, and she still didn't tell us. Then suddenly, Mr. Bailey and Miss Willie burst in, looking for Mr. Glass. They seemed worried and became more worried when they realized he wasn't in here. They said he wasn't in his bedroom and there were signs of a scuffle. The bedclothes were all over the floor as if dragged off. We all suspected the worst had happened. Mr. Glass wouldn't have left in the middle of the night. Then Sally burst into tears again."

"You didn't hear anything during the night?" I asked the Bristows.

Mrs. Bristow and her husband exchanged looks. "We're a little hard of hearing these days," she said.

It wasn't surprising. They must be well into their seventies, perhaps even over eighty in the butler's case.

"Sally became hysterical when she heard about Mr. Glass," she went on, her tone rather tart. "That's when we realized she'd seen something, but she wouldn't say what at first. Miss Willie finally got it out of her that she'd seen someone, but no amount of encouragement would get Sally to say more. Her memory of it has gone, so it seems."

Sally merely sat there, sniffling, her head bowed low. She didn't offer any further information. I understood Mrs. Bristow's frustration at her lack of cooperation, but unlike the housekeeper, I knew that if I was going to succeed in getting the maid to open up, I had to keep my irritation in check. We needed Sally to describe what she'd seen sooner rather than later. When his kidnappers realized he wasn't a magician, they would have no further need of Gabe. But they wouldn't be able to simply let him go. Gabe would be able to identify them.

They'd have to kill him.

I pulled a chair closer to the maid. "Hello, Sally."

She blinked damp lashes at me. "Hello, Miss Ashe. I know what you're going to ask me, but I can't..." She let out a sob. "I can't remember. I've told them...it's all a blur."

I peered past her to Mrs. Bristow. "Perhaps Sally and I can have a little chat alone."

Mrs. Bristow hesitated, but Bristow urged her to follow Mrs. Ling, Murray, Dodson the chauffeur, and the sketch artist into the kitchen. The butler gave me a grim nod of encouragement before closing the door.

I took Sally's hand. "It can be difficult to think when you're afraid."

She teased a wet handkerchief between her fingers and nodded.

"It's as if there's a lot of noise and you can't hear the person opposite you talking, even though you can see their lips move."

"Yes, that's it. I'm trying very hard, Miss Ashe, honest I am. But I can't recall anything." The higher her voice rose, the further her mouth curved downward.

Before she started to cry again, I patted her hand. "Take a deep breath and release it slowly." I kept my voice even, my tone soothing, so there was no evidence of my strained nerves. "Good. Now tell me what fear looks like to you."

She frowned. "What do you mean?"

"For me, my fear looks like a heavy fog. I hate fog. I hate not being able to see what it's covering. There could be a vehicle advancing toward me and I wouldn't know, or a hole in the ground that I might unwittingly step into. I hate the way fog deadens sounds, so that if I screamed, I wouldn't be heard."

"Oh, that's awful."

"But that's what *my* fear looks like. What about yours? Does it look like a snake? Fire? A sharp object?"

"Water. It looks like a gushing flooded river. I can't swim, see."

"No wonder you're afraid of water, then. Now, I'm going to teach you a technique my mother once taught me. It helped me to become less anxious. Close your eyes and picture a river. Can you see the water flowing fast? There's debris being tossed around in the churning current. The water is muddy. You can't see the river bottom."

She shuddered. "I can picture it."

"Now draw in a deep breath, and this time when you release it, picture all that water flowing out with the breath. Blow out all the air in your lungs until you have no more breath left in you. Only then will all the flooded water be gone."

She did as directed, releasing her breath at a measured pace until her chest deflated.

"The river is now just a harmless little brook. The flood has receded, and the water is merely ankle-deep as it trickles over smooth pebbles. Can you picture that?"

Sally nodded.

"Now open your eyes."

She sat back and opened her eyes. "I feel better now. Thank you, Miss Ashe."

"You did very well." I continued with my gentle tone to keep her calm. "Using the same breathing technique, cast your mind back to when you arrived at the house this morning."

She drew in a deep breath and released it slowly. "I arrived at five, as I usually do, letting myself in through the service door with my key. I collected my broom and went upstairs to sweep out the entry hall, but as I stood there, I saw a man. It was still dark, but he held a lantern, so I saw him clear enough. He was a big brute of a fellow. I heard his footsteps, but also heard a second set, up ahead on the stairs. I gasped. The brute stopped and looked my way. He must have seen me because he put a finger to his lips then drew it across his throat." She showed me the gesture using her own finger, then began crying again. "He means to cut me up if I don't keep quiet, Miss Ashe."

I put my arm around her shoulders. "Did you carry a lamp or candle?"

She shook her head. "No need. I know my way around every inch of this place."

"Then he can't have seen you. You said yourself it was still dark. He also held a lantern, which means the light was in his eyes. He heard your gasp and realized someone was there, and that's why he made the threatening motion, but he didn't see *you*. He won't come for you, because he doesn't know who saw him."

She sniffed. "But he knows I work here."

"But he doesn't know which member of this household you are."

"I suppose."

It was curious that the man didn't attack when he heard her gasp. He must have been confident his threat would work.

I tightened my grip around her shoulders. "Well done, Sally. You've been marvelous so far. Now, can you describe him?"

"Yes! Yes, I remember!" She gave me a tentative smile. Her confidence and her memory had returned now that she didn't feel as though she was in danger. "He was a large man with a thick neck and broad chest. There was nothing particular about his face, it was just ordinary, but his hair was something I remember. He was bald on the top of his head with stringy blond hair reaching past his collar. He could have plaited it, it was that long."

It was a distinctive feature, but I knew no one fitting the description. None of Thurlow's men had hair like that. "You said there was another fellow."

"He was already up the stairs when I arrived. I never saw him but I heard his footsteps. After the first man threatened me, I retreated downstairs to the kitchen and stayed there until the Bristows came."

"Did you hear any other sounds?"

"No. Not even their footsteps. The basement is a long way below Mr. Glass's bedchamber"

"Will you speak to the police artist now? He'll draw your description of the man, which the police will then use to help identify him."

"All right."

I stood, but Sally caught my arm.

"I thought they were burglars," she said. "I thought they'd take some valuables and leave. I didn't know they were kidnapping Mr. Glass." Her face crumpled. "I didn't find out until Mr. Bailey and Miss Willie came into the kitchen, looking for him. I'm real sorry, Miss Ashe. I hope the police find him."

"They will, Sally. They will." I repeated myself for my own benefit rather than hers.

I opened the door that led to the kitchen to see Willie and Alex standing with the servants. Alex embraced me, but Willie crossed her arms and glared. She didn't need to speak for me to know she blamed me. She spoke anyway. Indeed, it was more of a shout.

"This is your fault!" She lunged toward me, her finger pointed at my face.

Alex caught her before she got too close. "Calm down. This is not Sylvia's fault. It's Thurlow's."

"It's *hers* and her low-down cur of a father's. If she hadn't brought Hendry into Gabe's life, none of this would have happened."

"Why would Melville kidnap Gabe?" I asked.

"Because he's mad!"

Alex had clearly heard this argument before. He simply rolled his eyes. "Stop carrying on, Willie. Hysteria won't get Gabe back."

Willie's nostrils flared and the muscles in her jaw hardened. If I hadn't seen the tears in her eyes before she turned away, I would have thought she was too angry to snap back at him. But I suspected her sudden silence was due to her attempt at containing her rampant emotions. She wouldn't want to cry in front of others.

I swallowed the lump forming in my throat and addressed the artist. "Sally's memory has returned. She'll describe one of the men to you."

Willie whipped back around. She went to follow him.

I grabbed her arm, halting her. "Not you. Sally needs to feel safe."

"I ain't going to hurt her!"

Alex closed the door and blocked it, arms crossed over his chest. "You can scare the moustache off a grown man without even trying."

Willie sniffed then wiped her nose on her sleeve. With a *humph*, she leaned against the central bench.

Mrs. Ling and Mrs. Bristow worked around her. Dodson left while Murray returned upstairs to make himself available to the police.

Bristow laid a gentle hand on his wife's shoulder. "You don't have to work at a time like this. Nor you, Mrs. Ling. No one feels like eating."

"I have to work," Mrs. Bristow said without looking up from the kettle she was placing on the stove. "I need to keep busy."

Mrs. Ling removed a jar of flour from a shelf. "As do I. I will bake something for the policemen."

The idea of keeping busy appealed to me. I offered to help, and Mrs. Ling handed me a spare apron then set me the task of mixing.

When I caught Willie watching me, she *humphed* again and presented me with her back.

It felt like an interminably long time, but the artist finally emerged from the adjoining room.

Willie pounced on him. "Show me!"

He turned the sketchbook around. She studied the image of the man's face then shook her head. Alex peered over her shoulder. He tugged on his lower lip, frowning, but didn't say anything.

The artist took the sketch upstairs to give to Cyclops. Willie and Alex followed.

I removed the apron and handed it to Mrs. Ling, then I sought out Sally. She still sat at the table, dabbing the handkerchief to her swollen eyes. "Thank you, Sally. You've been a great help."

"You will find him, won't you, Miss Ashe?"

I managed a smile and a nod, but she didn't look convinced.

Bristow followed me up the stairs. Before we emerged into the entrance hall, he withdrew something from his pocket and pressed it into my hand. "You may want this back."

I hesitated, then took it. "Thank you, Bristow." I tucked my farewell note to Gabe into my skirt pocket.

We found Cyclops in the library, studying the artist's sketch. The proximity of so many books comforted me a little, as paper in all its forms did, but the effect didn't last long. The anxiety of those present was infectious.

Alex paced the floor, while Willie stared out of the window. Cyclops dismissed the artist and asked Bristow to leave us, too, and to close the door.

"Well?" Willie asked once we were alone. "Recognize him?"

Cyclops shook his head.

"Damn it. Nor do I."

Cyclops watched his son pacing back and forth. "You do, don't you, Alex?"

Alex stopped. "I think so."

Willie strode up to him and poked him in the chest. "Why didn't you say so in the kitchen?"

"Because I can't recall where I've seen him."

"At the racetrack? Is he one of Thurlow's men?"

"I'm not sure."

"Think!"

"I'm trying." Alex scrubbed a hand down his face. "I haven't seen him recently. A few years ago, perhaps."

"When you worked for the police? Or in the war?"

"Stop pestering me. It's not helping."

"A good slap might knock something back into place," she muttered.

"Try it," he dared her.

She merely crossed her arms.

I addressed Cyclops. "Did your men find anything upstairs?"

"A cloth that had been soaked in chloroform," he said. "That explains why Gabe didn't fight back. When they dragged him off the bed, the bedclothes fell on the floor. The two men must have then carried him between them downstairs. If Sally saw them arrive, then it happened a little after five."

Which meant Gabe was already gone by the time I left my note with Bristow.

I pressed a hand to my chest as my heart pinched.

Cyclops dipped his head to peer at me. "It must be Thurlow, given what he did to you."

"What did he do?" Alex asked.

"He kidnapped her."

"What?" Alex exploded. "Are you all right, Sylvia?"

Even Willie looked concerned, although it only lasted for as long as it took me to reassure them I was fine.

"I escaped using my paper magic."

She grunted. "So, you can wield deadly paper now, too."

"I learned the spell from the Hendry family journal."

"That's your man, Cyclops. You find Hendry, you find Gabe. I reckon the intruder Sally saw was a hired thug Hendry found in some register of henchmen that madmen share among themselves. Alex probably arrested him once, back when he worked for the Met."

"You're ridiculous, Willie." Alex turned to me. "Tell us about your abduction and escape."

I detailed my evening for them, including my visit to Cyclops after my escape and handing over Bertie to Mr. Jakes. "Speaking of Jakes, we can't discount him as a suspect in Gabe's kidnapping. His interest in bringing the Hobsons to justice over their failed boots doesn't negate his interest in learning more about mutated magic, and Gabe's magic in particular."

Alex wasn't so sure. "Thurlow has to be the top of our list now. He already committed one abduction."

"I doubt it's him. Not only is the man Sally described not one of the men guarding me last night, Thurlow slipped a note under the front door here for Gabe, informing him that I was his prisoner. He was using me to lure Gabe out of the house."

"Perhaps he didn't get around to leaving the note before you escaped and decided he had to strike immediately once you did. He could have collected a new henchman along the way." He indicated the sketch.

I withdrew two notes from my pocket. "I brought a message here as soon as I got away. I gave it to Bristow and exchanged it for the one that had been slipped under the door overnight." I showed him Thurlow's note. "When Gabe was abducted, I hadn't escaped yet, although I did shortly after. I don't think Thurlow had time to get back to the house where I was being held after abducting Gabe, but if he did...why go back at all? And what was the point of using me to lure Gabe if he planned on abducting Gabe anyway? Why bother to leave a note for him? It doesn't make sense."

Alex shrugged. "Thurlow may have simply changed his mind."

Willie wagged a finger at me. "I doubt he did. I think Sylvia's right. So that leaves Hendry."

"Jakes," I countered.

Cyclops rubbed the back of his neck but didn't offer an opinion. Alex watched his father through eyes narrowed to slits. Something passed between them. Something that made them both even more grim.

Willie hadn't noticed. "What did you say to Gabe in your message?" she asked me.

"It doesn't matter now."

"Course it matters. It might be relevant."

Alex saved me from answering. "I can't stand around here doing nothing. I'm going to hunt for Thurlow. Even if he's not responsible for Gabe's abduction, he is responsible for Sylvia's. I'd like to punch him."

"You won't find him," Cyclops said. "The house where they kept Sylvia was empty. He will have gone to ground by now. The Hobsons, too."

That was a surprise. Mrs. Hobson sounded like she was going to place the entire blame on Thurlow. Perhaps Ivy encouraged her mother to flee after Bertie left with me.

"I have to *do* something," Alex growled. "I can't sit around here waiting." He strode out of the library.

Willie followed him. "I'm coming."

"As am I," I said.

I didn't immediately follow, however. I wanted a quiet word with Cyclops first. "There's something you're not telling me. Something Alex has realized, too. What is it?"

He pressed his lips together and I assumed he wouldn't answer. But he must have decided to trust me. "The front door wasn't forced, nor was the service entrance or any of the windows."

"So how did the kidnappers get inside? Who has a key?"

"The Bristows, Sally, Gabe, Alex and Willie. Mrs. Ling, Dodson and Murray don't, but could have easily taken one and made a copy without anyone knowing."

My stomach dropped. "You mean…"

"The intruders were either let in or got their hands on a key. Since Willie and Alex are above suspicion, that means the kidnappers had help from someone who works here."

CHAPTER 9

I left Cyclops with the unenviable task of questioning the servants about keys and joined Alex and Willie in the Vauxhall Prince Henry. We drove to the house where I'd been held prisoner.

In the early hours of this morning when I'd escaped, the parlor had looked sinister. Brown cheerless curtains covered the windows, the cast-iron fireplace was cold, and there were no cushions or rugs to soften the hard surfaces.

In daylight, with policemen crawling through it looking for clues, it was no less cheerless, but it wasn't sinister. It was quite ordinary. The sergeant in charge recognized Alex and invited him inside. Willie followed. After taking a few fortifying breaths, I entered behind them.

Pages from the books blanketed much of the parlor. They covered the chairs and table and piled up in corners like drifts of snow. The only visible parts of the floor were where my kidnappers had cowered during the paper tempest, hands over their heads. Some of the pages' edges bore bloodstains.

I picked one up. How much blood signaled a fatal wound had been inflicted?

In an uncharacteristic show of sympathy, Willie put a hand to my lower back. "You didn't kill any of 'em."

"Are you sure?"

"That ain't enough blood."

I blew out a shuddery breath.

"Next time, don't give up until one of 'em bleeds out." She gave my back a hard pat.

The sergeant indicated the papers. "We're going to tidy this up now. Don't know what happened in here. Do you, Miss Ashe?"

I tried to look innocent as I shrugged.

Alex cleared his throat. "Have you found any clues as to Thurlow's or the Hobsons' whereabouts?"

The sergeant shook his head. "Nothing. The Hobson women haven't showed up at their home or the factory, and we only have an office address for Thurlow. He wasn't there. Men have been dispatched to the Epsom Downs racecourse, so that might yield something."

"Willie and I already went there this morning. It's the first place we looked. We'll head back now and see if there's any news. Sylvia, do you want to look around here a little more?"

"Absolutely not. I never want to see this place again." I strode out and did not look back.

* * *

THE SCOTLAND YARD team conducting inquiries at Epsom Downs were conspicuous because they were doing very little compared to everyone else. It was race day, but too early for the public. Most of the horses were still arriving with the trainers' teams, and officials strode across the course with purpose. More staff came and went from the main members' pavilion, the grand building with the expansive veranda and the best views over the finish line.

We spoke to the detective in charge who had very little to

report. No one knew where Thurlow could be hiding out. "I've just come from his office myself, and he wasn't there. It was locked up, good and tight."

"That ain't normal," Willie said.

Alex checked the time on his watch. "It's still early."

"It's race day. The office would be open by now, taking bets, both good and illegal. Then he'd close up around eleven and make his way down here to oversee the bookmakers operating under his license." She nodded at the empty betting circle.

Several of the bookmakers who would set up stands there later would owe Thurlow a portion of their takings. Those who tried to cheat him risked his wrath. We knew from personal experience what happened when Thurlow was crossed. We'd been run off the road as a result of trying to trick him. If it hadn't been for Gabe saving us when time slowed for him, we'd have died.

Gabe.

A pain gripped my chest, as if a hand were squeezing my heart, wringing out every last ounce of strength I had left.

Alex pressed his fingers into his forehead. "All right. We'll wait a little longer. When Thurlow's bookmakers show up, we'll question them."

"Thoroughly," Willie ground out through gritted teeth. "I ain't leaving here without an address for that cur."

After ten minutes of waiting, I fell into step alongside Alex. Together, we paced along the fence that separated the spectators from the track. The physical exercise alleviated our restlessness but did nothing to increase our levels of patience.

Willie had disappeared, heading in the direction of the stables. I wasn't sure how she could think about placing a bet at a moment like this, but we all coped in different ways and if checking out the runners in today's races kept her out of our hair, then I was in favor of it.

Finally, the bookmakers began to arrive. They marked their territory in the betting circle by positioning their chalkboards and the crates they'd stand on to be seen above the crowd. There was a lot of chatter between them today, more so than the other times I'd visited on race days.

"Something's amiss," Alex said as he walked off.

I trailed after him, trotting to keep up with his long strides. Willie joined us before we entered the betting circle. Her fists were closed at her sides, and I knew her gun was tucked into the waistband of her trousers, hidden by her jacket. I hoped she wouldn't need to use it, but for once I was glad she had it.

She thumped Alex's arm and nodded at a scruffy looking fellow with a droopy left eye. "He's one of Thurlow's. We'll start with him."

The scruffy bookmaker was talking in earnest to another two men. They stopped when they saw our approach and broke apart. They recognized us.

Always as blunt as a hammer, Willie took the direct approach to questioning. "Where's Thurlow?"

The bookmaker shrugged. "Don't know. I ain't seen him."

"Don't try that with me. I ain't got the patience for it today."

The bookmaker put up his hands. "I'm telling the truth. He wasn't at the office. I thought he might come here."

"Tell us where he'd be if not in his office."

The bookmaker shrugged again.

Alex addressed one of the others. "Have you seen him?"

"Not today," the man said. "None of us have. He might turn up here before racing starts."

"Where could he be? Home? A pub?"

The bookmaker snorted. "Don't know, and if I did, I wouldn't tell the pigs."

Most of the others in the betting circle either chuckled or nodded. One left the betting circle altogether.

I watched him out of the corner of my eye as he headed to the stable block and disappeared around the side.

The others hadn't noticed. Willie was getting frustrated with the wall of silence. "I'm going to blow your bollocks off if you don't give us an address for Thurlow."

That elicited a round of raucous laughter from the bookmakers. The scruffy one looked her up and down. "Not sure I want you blowing mine, but Wally over there's desperate enough to risk it."

"I said *off*! I'm going to blow 'em *off*!" She went to pull back her jacket to reveal her gun, but Alex grasped her arm and marched her away.

"Don't show that around here," he growled at her. "The officials will throw us out and I'm not finished yet."

She wrenched free. "Who're you going to question next?"

He sighed. "I don't know. Course officials, perhaps."

"I have an idea," I said, walking in the direction the bookmaker had gone. "Come with me."

We spotted him crossing the paved yard outside the stables. Instead of heading back to the betting circle, he was walking quickly to the members' pavilion. Beyond that was the exit gate. Willie wanted to accost him immediately, but Alex and I both told her to wait. We watched as he hurried off, his head low, his face covered by his hat.

When he reached the back of the members' pavilion, Alex said it was time. I picked up my skirts and ran, but my quicker companions reached the bookmaker first. Alex already had him in a headlock by the time I arrived.

"Where is he?" Alex growled. "Where can we find Thurlow?"

The man was aged about thirty, but had the yellowing teeth of someone who rarely cleaned them. He smelled like tobacco and unwashed man. Alex loosened his grip just enough so the bookmaker could tell us he didn't know where to find Thurlow.

"He wasn't in his office this morning," he gasped out.

"So where else might he be?"

"I don't know."

"You do, or you wouldn't be trying to leave now to warn him."

"I was going to use the privy!"

"It's back the way you came, unless you planned on using the private one in the members' pavilion."

The man tugged on Alex's arm, but that only made Alex tighten his hold. The man's face turned a violent shade of red.

Willie withdrew her gun and pointed it at the bookmaker's temple. "Where. Is. Thurlow?"

The man put up his hands and Alex released him. "I don't know! I just want to take a piss!"

"There ain't no privies back here."

"The tree. I was going to go behind the tree."

Willie flexed her fingers around the gun handle but kept her gaze on her quarry. Alex and I both glanced toward the tree. It was large enough to shield a man from the prying eyes of anyone wandering past.

Willie pointed the gun at the bookmaker's crotch. "Tell me where to find Thurlow or I'll shoot."

"You wouldn't," he sneered.

"Do I look like someone who cares about the bollocks of scum like you?"

The man gulped.

Willie cocked the gun.

"All right! I'll tell you. The only other place I know him to go is a pub near Borough Market, The Fisherman's Inn."

Willie stepped back. "See, that wasn't so hard."

The bookmaker glanced around. When he was sure no one was watching and we wouldn't recapture him, he hurried off, back the way he'd come.

"I thought you were going to take a piss behind the tree," Willie called out.

"Think I'll use the privy, after all."

Willie returned the gun to her waistband. "Do you think he told the truth?"

"Only one way to find out," Alex said.

I fell into step alongside him. "I truly don't think Thurlow took Gabe."

Alex sighed. "Where else do we look?"

"Jakes."

"If Jakes has Gabe, then his capture was sanctioned by the government, and they won't return him until they're ready. Besides, I don't see Jakes breaking into the house at five in the morning with a thug in tow."

"What if his activities aren't sanctioned by Military Intelligence? What if he's acting outside the scope of his orders?"

Alex eyed me sideways. "You may have a point, but I think we should go to Thurlow's pub first. If that yields nothing, we'll look into Jakes."

Willie must have thought my suggestion had merit, too, because she gave me another pat on the back, this one gentler than the last.

* * *

It was impossible to find parking close to Borough Market, so we parked the motorcar a few streets away and walked. Tucked behind Southwark Cathedral and a stone's throw from London Bridge, the market was dusty, busy and noisy. Stallholders shouted over the top of each other, vying for customers, but they were intermittently drowned out by the trains traveling on the viaducts above. The stalls, selling fresh farm produce, were crammed into any available space, including under the railway arches and on neighboring streets. The loud, thriving center of activity epitomized London in this postwar, post-influenza era of enterprise and energy. I wasn't sure whether I liked it or loathed it, but I appreciated it nonetheless.

The Fisherman's Inn was jammed up against one of the massive viaduct supports. A patchwork of posters and flyers were pasted to the support's brickwork. The old timber pub with its low doorway and mullioned windows looked out of place beside the more modern architecture, but I was pleased to see the railway hadn't consumed the historic building altogether.

Like most of the pubs in the market's vicinity, The Fisherman's Inn opened at six AM to serve beer to thirsty porters who assisted stallholders in the early hours of the morning. Some of them had lingered, chatting quietly at the bar, or napping in a corner booth. Thurlow wasn't among them.

I let Willie and Alex question the barman and the drinkers. The response from all was the same—no one knew a man named Thurlow, nor did they know of anyone matching his description. It wasn't obvious if they lied or not, but it was clear we weren't going to get a different answer. Willie didn't even attempt to threaten them. Perhaps, like me, she doubted that Thurlow was guilty of capturing Gabe, after all.

Outside, we trudged back the way we'd come. "We'll call on Jakes," Alex said.

I looked up at him, but something past his shoulder caught my eye. I stopped and pointed at one of the posters pasted to the viaduct support. "That's him! That's the man Sally saw!"

I tore the poster off the wall and studied the sketch. The brutish face with the scraggly hair past the shoulders matched the police artist's drawing. The figure on the poster was thickset and he stood in a boxer's stance, fists at the ready. He glared back at me as if daring me to take him on.

Willie took the poster and read. "'See Mad Dog Mitchell fight for the bare-knuckle championship this Thursday at The Rose and Thorn.'"

Alex slapped the poster with the back of his hand. "That's where I've seen him before: The Rose and Thorn. I went to that fight. It was last year. He lost, then disappeared from the fight scene altogether. He never entered another bout as far as I know."

"Isn't bare-knuckle boxing illegal?" I asked.

Alex looked sheepish. "I went from time to time after the war ended. I needed the distraction in those days."

The brutal sport had been outlawed for good reason. Without gloves and with few rules, fighters received terrible injuries. Clearly his loss hadn't affected Mad Dog Mitchell physically. He was still capable of abduction.

Willie folded the poster and tucked it into her pocket. "I reckon he's a hired thug for sure. Who better to carry out illegal activity than a big man who can take care of himself and doesn't care about laws."

"Change of plans," Alex said as we set off again. "We'll go to The Rose and Thorn. Jakes can wait."

It was a good plan, since none of us thought we could make Jakes confess anyway. We needed irrefutable evidence of his involvement. Hopefully Mad Dog Mitchell could give it to us. First, we had to find him.

* * *

THE ROSE and Thorn pub was located in a grimy East End slum that time seemed to have forgotten. There were no motorcars in the narrow backstreet, nor electricity wires feeding into the crumbling and rotting tenements. It was quiet considering it was mid-morning. Small children played in the gutter, their parents nowhere to be seen. There weren't even any housewives on their way to or from the shops. The only adult we saw was a drunkard, sleeping in a recessed doorway.

"The women around here are mostly whores," Willie told me. "The men are mostly involved in some sort of criminal activity."

Alex indicated the Rose and Thorn with its faded sign hanging above the door, and peeling paintwork. "The pub is the hub for that activity. The publican spent some time in prison before the war and has been holding underground fights here for years." He advanced toward the pub, only to stop. "Don't tell anyone I was once a constable, or that we're working with Scotland Yard."

Willie grunted. "'Course we won't. We ain't stupid. Mention

the pigs around here and they'll close up tighter than an old spinster's quim."

The pub was closed, but we could see someone behind the bar, pouring liquid from one bottle into another through a funnel. When Alex knocked on the window, the man returned the bottle to a shelf under the bar before opening the door to us.

He was entirely bald, with deep folds in his leathery skin and a crooked nose. He was a large man who may have once been capable of beating another man in a fight, but nowadays he looked like he'd be breathless after a few minutes. He shook a bent finger at Alex. "I remember you. Haven't seen you here for a while." His tone was friendly enough.

"The fights don't have the same appeal for me as they used to," Alex said. "Can we come in?"

"Pub's closed, but I ain't going to turn away paying customers." He stepped aside."

"These are my friends, Willie and Sylvia. We want to speak to Mad Dog Mitchell."

The publican had been eyeing Willie and me, getting our measure, but turned sharply to Alex at the mention of the boxer. He indicated the empty taproom. "Well, he ain't here. You're welcome to go through to the snug, but he ain't in there neither."

"When did you last see him?"

The publican became more guarded. "Couldn't say. Why do you want to talk to him?"

"Our friend is missing. An eyewitness saw Mad Dog Mitchell and someone else capture him. Mad Dog hires himself out from time to time, doesn't he? Does he conduct his business in here? Have you seen him with anyone lately?"

The publican sucked air through the space in his top row of teeth where one at the front had been knocked out. The one beside the gap was broken in half. His answer was a shrug of heavy shoulders.

Alex offered him some banknotes. "Will this jog your memory?"

The publican snorted. "Keep your money. I'm no squealer." He headed to the bar, his rolling gait making him slow.

"Stay here where I can see you," Alex growled.

"No one tells me what to do in my pub."

Willie withdrew her gun. "Don't move or I'll shoot."

The publican halted and whipped around, surprisingly fast for a large man. As he did, he picked up a tankard off the bar and threw it at Willie. It missed her but the gun went off.

The bullet hit the bottles lined up on the shelf behind the bar, shattering them. I wasn't sure if Willie had missed him on purpose or not.

Before I could register the damage, the publican withdrew his own gun from his inside jacket pocket. He aimed it at Willie. She aimed hers at him.

"Get out of my pub," the publican snarled.

"Nope." I always knew Willie was brave, or a little mad, but she didn't show an iota of fear that the publican would shoot her before she could pull the trigger. In fact, her lips curved with a smile. She seemed to be enjoying herself. Definitely mad.

I began to shake uncontrollably.

"We ain't leaving until you give us answers," she went on. "What do you reckon, Alex? You reckon Mad Dog Mitchell did meet someone in here and this moron knows who?"

Alex withdrew a gun too. I hadn't known he'd brought one. I didn't even know he owned one.

With both guns pointing at him, the publican gave in, swearing under his breath. He put his gun down and put his hands up. "Don't shoot any more of my supplies. That stuff's top shelf." He indicated the smashed bottles and the liquid dripping onto the floor. "Costs me an arm and a leg, it does." He perched himself on a stool by the bar. "Mad Dog comes in most nights. Folk know to find him here if they need him. He does hire himself out, mostly for jobs that need someone with muscle and experience with his fists. Someone who doesn't ask questions."

Alex returned his gun to the waistband at his back. "Did he meet anyone in here last night?"

"Last night, and the night before that, he met the same fellow."

"Describe him."

"Tall, about thirty. Red hair. He's not from around here. I'd never seen him before and he wore good clothes. Not like a toff, but not like the sort that usually come in here."

Red hair, good clothes… The description rang a bell. A rather large, loud one.

It did for Alex and Willie, too, going by the flicker of excitement to cross their faces. Alex wasn't ready to leave, however. "Do you have a telephone?"

The publican pointed to a booth near his office. "Who you calling?"

"Scotland Yard."

"I don't want the pigs crawling around here! They're bad for business, and for my health."

"I'll tell them to be discreet, and just send two men. One will be a sketch artist. You're going to give him a description of the redheaded man who spoke to Mad Dog and he's going to draw his likeness."

The publican grumbled his irritation over the disruption to his day.

Alex handed him the money he was going to give him earlier. This time the publican took it.

Alex made the phone call, then we waited. Willie ordered a drink, and brought it over to where I sat with Alex, waiting for the sketch artist and his escort to arrive.

Willie thumped Alex's shoulder. "We got her! After all these years, we finally got her!"

"Her?" I prompted. "Don't you mean him? Valentine?"

"Nope. His mother, Hope. Lady Bloody Coyle. I knew she was no good the first time I met her years ago. Now she's gone and done something real stupid and we're going to put her behind bars. Her and her idiot son, Valentine." She smirked before she downed her drink.

Alex drummed his fingers on the table. "She might not be involved. Valentine could have acted alone."

"He can't plan his way to the mailbox and back. She *must* be behind it."

"Why would either of them want to kidnap Gabe?" I asked.

"For his magic," Willie said. "Just like Thurlow and Jakes."

Alex glared at the window, as if willing the police to hurry. "We'll call on them and find out what they have to say for themselves."

"Are we meeting your father there?" I asked.

"No. He doesn't know we suspect Valentine. I want to question him myself without my father present."

Willie let out a *whoop*. "This could get interesting." She held up her empty glass. "Another, barkeep!"

CHAPTER 10

Gabe's father's cousin, the widow of the manipulative Lord Coyle, lived in a modest flat with her adult son. Despite owning a Rolls-Royce—driven by the chauffeur rumored to be Valentine's real father—she had found herself in reduced circumstances in the years following Lord Coyle's death. Her son's answer to their situation was to invest heavily in financial schemes I'd never heard of. From the look of their flat, his latest was yet to bear fruit. There was less furniture than on our last visit.

Willie picked up a shirt from the pile in the basket beside the table that was currently being used as an ironing board. The hot iron sat in its cradle out of harm's way. "Someone steal your furniture, Hope? Or did the debt collectors catch up with you?"

Lady Coyle's blue eyes flared with her fury. They'd once been her best feature, so I'd been told. Apparently, she'd been a beauty in her youth. But her blonde hair was now white, and her hourglass figure was shaped more like a barrel. Her lace dress only enhanced her age. It was at least a decade out of date.

She snatched the shirt from Willie. "I assume this isn't a social call?" Her gaze flitted between the three of us. "Where's Gabriel?" Her words slurred a little. It wasn't the only evidence she'd been drinking. A bottle of gin sat on the floor beside a chair.

A door opened, revealing a bedroom beyond. Valentine, the current Lord Coyle, emerged wearing trousers and an undervest that had gone gray after years of use. His feet were bare. "Is my shirt ironed yet? Oh. You lot. What are you doing here?"

Willie regarded him, hand on hip. "Nice to see you, too, Val. Now, where is he?"

"Where is who?"

"Gabe."

He shrugged. "I don't know. At home?"

"Don't be cocky with me." She pushed back her jacket to show her gun.

Valentine swore, making his mother wince. "Are you going to shoot me?"

"You, your mother… It depends on who I think is responsible for Gabe's abduction."

Valentine stared at her, his mouth ajar.

Hope bristled. "You think *we* abducted Gabriel? I always thought you were mad, but now I have proof."

Willie was in no mood for exchanging insults. She wanted answers.

It was Alex who made the next move, however. He shoved Valentine in the chest, sending him careening over the sofa's back, onto the cushion, and tumbling to the floor on the other side.

Hope gasped. "Get out!" she ordered Willie and me. "And take that savage with you."

Willie placed the end of her gun to Hope's temple. "I might be mad, and you might have been brought up a lady, but I got better manners than you."

Valentine picked himself up and dusted himself off. He jutted his chin at Alex in defiance, but the moment Alex moved, Valentine scurried backward. He appealed to me. "Miss Ashe, what is all this about? Why am I being treated like a criminal? I don't know anything about an abduction."

"If Gabriel is in some sort of trouble," his mother added, "we ought to be told. We're his family."

"A man matching your description was seen talking to a hired thug by the name of Mad Dog Mitchell," I said.

Valentine tucked his undervest into his trousers. "That's absurd. I'm an earl, for God's sake. I don't associate with men whose given name is Mad Dog."

"You were seen talking to him at the Rose and Thorn pub."

"I don't know it."

"Mad Dog and another man kidnapped Gabe from his bed last night," Alex said.

"From his own bed?" Valentine echoed. "You mean you two were there and you didn't stop them? Ha! Now that is amusing."

Alex grabbed Valentine by the front of his undervest and forced him to sit on a chair.

Valentine shrank back, expecting to be struck. Alex simply stood over him, his hands closed into tight fists at his sides. He was keeping his temper in check, but only just. "You were seen at the pub talking to Mad Dog last night and the night before. Now, you can answer our questions from the comfort of your sofa, or you can answer Scotland Yard's while sitting in a prison cell. The choice is yours."

Valentine gulped.

"Where is Gabe?"

A bead of sweat dampened Valentine's temple. "I don't know! I swear to you, I'm not involved in any of this. If someone says they saw me, then they've made a mistake. I wasn't anywhere near a pub called the Rose and Thorn on Thursday night. I can call on three people who can vouch for me."

"Who?"

Valentine began to rub his thumbs over the fingernails of both hands. "I can't tell you. They're important people, and I...

we..." He looked down at his hands and suddenly stopped fidgeting. "They're married."

Willie barked a laugh. "You want us to believe three women were desperate enough to be with you?"

Valentine blushed fiercely. "They weren't women," he muttered under his breath.

Hope covered her gasp with her hand. "Val! You told me you'd given them up."

"Shut up, Mother."

"What if you get caught? You'll be arrested!"

"I happen to think it's worth the risk."

She pulled a face. "You disgust me."

"The feeling is mutual, I assure you."

Alex stepped back and indicated we should leave. Unless we were willing to shoot one of them, we wouldn't get answers. I worried that Willie might be willing, but she followed us to the door, her gun tucked back into the waistband of her trousers. We would wait for Cyclops to interrogate Hope and Valentine officially, once the sketch artist's drawing proved it was Valentine who met Mad Dog Mitchell.

Hope followed us to the door. "This is harassment. You three are no longer welcome back here."

"I didn't think I ever was welcome," Willie said with mild indifference. "Alex, neither. You always made that real clear."

"Matt will hear of this."

"That's true. I'm going to make sure he and India know what you and Val did. They'll be back soon from America. Won't that be nice? You can have a good family chat with him. Pity it'll take place in prison."

"You will regret your tone, Willie, when Valentine becomes rich from Mr. Ponzi's scheme. We expect an enormous return on his investment any day now." With straight back and flashing eyes, she was every bit the regal lady. I could imagine the men admiring her beauty and strength of character when she was younger. She rather ruined the effect when she looked down her nose at Willie, however. "You and my sisters will come crawling to us, begging for help. I look forward to turning you all away."

"Val won't make you rich," Willie said with the most sympathetic tone I'd ever heard her use when speaking to Hope. "If he dragged you into his scheme to abduct Gabe, then you shouldn't protect him. I know he's your son, but he doesn't even like you." She touched the brim of her hat. "You know where to find us if you want to confess."

As we descended the stairs, I asked Willie if she truly believed Hope would come forward with information.

She shook her head sadly. "I don't think Val had anything to do with it, after all. If I did, the end of my gun would still be against his mother's head until he talked. But I reckon he was telling the truth when he said he was with three men on the night the publican saw someone matching his description speak to Mad Dog."

"So was the publican lying?" I asked. "Is he involved somehow?"

Willie shrugged.

It was Alex who responded. "I think we need to see the artist's sketch. It's possible we all jumped to the wrong conclusion because we wanted to believe it was Valentine. He would have been an easy nut to crack. The fact that he didn't crack is why I agree with Willie. I don't think he had anything to do with it."

* * *

We called at Scotland Yard, but the police artist hadn't returned, and Cyclops wasn't there. Instead of becoming frustrated with waiting, we decided to visit Mr. Jakes at Military Intelligence. It wasn't the best plan. Indeed, we had no plan unless directly asking him if he'd abducted Gabe could be considered one.

As we drove to the War Office building at Whitehall, I tried to think how we could trick or coerce Jakes. But by the time Alex pulled the motorcar to the curb to park, I had no ideas. My mind was incapable of plotting. Indeed, it was becoming consumed with the fog of my anxiety. Gabe had been abducted hours ago. He could have been subjected to all manner of awful things by now.

"Wait," Willie said, grasping Alex's arm as he was about to open his door. "That's him."

I followed her gaze to see Mr. Jakes exiting the building, cigarette in hand. Head bent into the breeze, he strode along the street. Although the area was busy with men wearing similar suits, I managed to keep track of him as he headed for the corner.

"Let's follow him," Alex said. "He could lead us to Gabe."

As we hurried after Jakes, I was very aware of how conspicuous we were. If Jakes turned around, we'd be seen.

But he did not turn around. He continued walking north toward Trafalgar Square. Nelson's Column was visible ahead, but Jakes didn't cross over to it. Instead, he went right, dodging the traffic, before taking The Strand. The entire area was chaotic with vehicles—both horse-drawn and motorized—jostling for position as they approached the square. Jakes threw his cigarette stub under the wheel of a lorry without breaking his stride.

Moments later, Alex slowed his pace. "Where did he go?" His superior height meant he was in a better position to spot Jakes in the crowd. If Alex couldn't see him then it meant we'd lost him.

Willie swore. "You were meant to keep an eye on him. Sylvia and I are too short. Now we'll never know where—"

Jakes stepped out of a recessed doorway and blocked our path. "Don't reach for your weapons," he said calmly. "There are too many witnesses."

"Where's Gabe?" Willie snarled.

"Why would I know where he is?"

"He was abducted."

Mr. Jakes's gaze slid to me. "I thought Miss Ashe was the one who was abducted."

"She was, then she escaped, then Gabe was."

"Sounds complicated."

Alex stepped closer. He towered over Jakes, but Jakes simply tilted his head to peer up at him. If he felt intimidated, he didn't show it. "Don't make light of this. Gabe has been abducted, and you are a suspect."

"I assure you, Military Intelligence are not in the habit of abducting Englishmen from their beds."

"We didn't tell you he was in bed. Only the kidnapper would know that detail."

"I merely assumed, since you said it happened last night."

"We also didn't say the War Office sanctioned it," Alex added.

Mr. Jakes arched his brows. "What are you suggesting?"

"That you did it with the help of a hired man for reasons of your own."

"What reasons?"

"You think Gabe's a magician, and you want to study him."

Mr. Jakes barked a laugh.

I'd had enough. My nerves were stretched to breaking point, my head felt woolly, and I was tired and on edge, not to mention frustrated at our lack of progress. Mr. Jakes's casual dismissal was the last straw. I moved up alongside Alex so that I was toe to toe with Jakes. Then I balled my hand into a fist and jabbed him in the gut.

He grunted, wincing.

I stepped back. "Next time, it will be your bollocks."

Willie clapped me on the shoulder. "You continue to surprise me, Sylv."

I didn't take my eyes off Jakes. "Some time ago, you came into the library and asked to see books about magic mutations because you assumed Gabe's luck could be explained that way. Nobody believes you've suddenly stopped being interested."

Mr. Jakes went to remove something from his inside jacket pocket, but Alex caught his wrist. "I'm just reaching for my cigarettes."

Alex released him and Jakes pulled the gold case out. He offered Alex a cigarette. Alex simply glared at him.

Mr. Jakes lit the cigarette and took his first puff. "It's true," he said, blowing out smoke as he spoke. "I do want to study Glass and his magic. Don't bother to deny it or pretend he's just lucky. No one is that fortunate. I know he can perform magic to save himself and others. What I don't know is how it works. His mother couldn't do it, nor her ancestors, as far as we know, which leads us to the theory of mutation. His mother received an unprecedented dose of magic while she carried him in her womb, so the theory isn't completely wild." He took another puff. "But even my department draws the line at abducting members of the British aristocracy to get answers."

He drew on his cigarette again, the action languid. He was so unruffled that I began to wonder if he was acting. No one would be that cool with a furious tower of muscle standing before them, alongside an armed madwoman and another woman stretched to her limit.

Mr. Jakes pointed his cigarette along The Strand. "You're welcome to continue following me. I have a dentist appointment." He touched his jaw. "A molar has been giving me trouble."

When none of us moved, Jakes took a step away from Alex, as if testing what he'd do. He addressed me, however. "Oh, Miss Ashe, I want to thank you again for bringing in Hobson. He has been most helpful. He claims he did nothing wrong, but further investigation will reveal the truth."

"Have you found Mrs. Hobson or Ivy?" I asked.

"Not yet."

"What will happen to Bertie?"

"That depends on what the factory's paperwork reveals, and also what his mother says."

"If you find her."

"We'll find her. Women like her don't hide forever. They get lawyers." He walked off, but stopped once again and turned back to us. "Odd how Glass has gone missing at the same time as his former fiancée and her mother, just one day after you were also abducted, Miss Ashe."

Willie charged after him. "What are you suggesting?"

Alex grabbed her and stopped her from making a scene in public. The last thing we wanted was for her to be arrested.

Mr. Jakes put up the hand that held the cigarette. "I'm suggesting you should look to the Hobson women if you want to find Glass. Not me or my department." He plugged the cigarette between his lips and sauntered away.

Willie blew out a long, ragged breath. "I can't stand that smarmy smile of his. Next time I see it, I'm going to wipe it off his face with my fist."

Alex headed back the way we'd come, a determined set to his jaw.

I hurried after him. "Where to now?"

"We should go home to see if Gabe returned. Our best chance of finding him is there, not running over the city chasing our tails."

"Why do you think that?"

"Because he's more than capable of escaping imprisonment."

Willie agreed. "If you can do it, Sylv, then it'll be easy for Gabe."

"I escaped because my captors didn't know I was a magician. In Gabe's case, they do, or they suspect. They'll be more prepared. He also can't use his magic at will."

It was a sobering thought, one that kept us silent all the way to Park Street.

* * *

Gabe had not escaped. He was not at home, waiting for us with a smile and warm embrace. The concern on Bristow's face when he opened the door was enough to tell us that.

I burst into tears.

It wasn't Alex, Willie or one of the servants who comforted me, however. It was Daisy. She drew me into a hug and stroked my hair until my sobs subsided. Then she led me into the drawing room.

I looked up to see Huon and Petra had joined her. Huon handed me a handkerchief. I'd never seen him look so grim.

Petra clasped my hands. "We couldn't settle all morning. We arrived a little while ago. Mrs. Bristow has been kind enough to serve tea."

Daisy directed me to sit on the sofa, then sat beside me. "Mrs. Ling made cake. Do you want a slice?"

"I can't eat," I muttered.

"Me either." Her gaze lifted to Alex. "Can I do anything to help?"

Alex sat on a chair and rested his elbows on his knees. He dragged a hand over his head but did not look up from the floor. "No."

Daisy pressed her lips together as her eyes welled with tears. I suspected she wanted to go to him, but the distance he'd maintained since meeting her parents made her hesitant. She obviously didn't know how she'd be received.

Willie cut into the cake. "I love lemon drizzle." She placed a slice on a plate and sat in another chair before taking a large bite.

"Shouldn't you be at work?" I asked Daisy.

"It's my half day on Saturdays. I worked this morning." She leaned closer and lowered her voice to a whisper. "After reading the note you'd slipped under my door, I couldn't concentrate anyway." She tucked my hair behind my ear. "I am glad you haven't disappeared, but I wish Gabe's kidnapping wasn't the reason why you changed your mind."

"I'm glad you're here, Daisy. I doubt I'm the only one happy to see you." I looked pointedly at Alex, who was trying so hard not to look at Daisy that it was obvious that he really wanted to. "And you?" I asked Petra, seated on my other side. "Shouldn't you be at work?"

"My mother sent me home when I kept making mistakes. I returned to Huon's place, then we met Daisy when she finished work. We updated her on Gabe's abduction and decided to come here. If we can't help search, then at least we can offer support." She took my hand again and gave me a wan smile.

Bristow had been hovering in the doorway and now cleared his throat. "Detective Inspector Bailey informed me he would return at intervals throughout the day. He asked me to inform you that if you returned before him, you are all to remain here."

"We have no reason to leave at this point," Alex said. "We've reached a dead end."

Willie flopped back into the chair with a sigh, like a restless boy told to play indoors.

Bristow narrowed his gaze at her.

"What?" she snapped at him.

"Shall I have Mrs. Bristow brew more tea?"

"I don't want tea. I want something stronger."

"There's brandy in the decanter." He indicated the drinks trolley with the crystal decanters and glasses. Then he left, closing the door behind him.

Alex sliced himself some cake. "Being stroppy with the servants isn't going to make you feel better, Willie."

"He was looking at me oddly."

"He wasn't. Let him do his job. It'll help take his mind off Gabe."

She shot to her feet. "And what'll help us?" She began to pace back and forth. "I've got to leave again. This house is stifling." She strode toward the door.

"My father asked us to stay, so we'll stay. He might have news."

Willie changed direction and strode to the drinks trolley

instead. She poured herself a glass of brandy without offering a drink to anyone else, then sank into the armchair with another heaving sigh.

"Perhaps Cyclops has *good* news," Daisy said hopefully.

None of us believed that. If he had good news, he would have informed Bristow.

The butler returned a few minutes later with Mrs. Bristow. She carried a tray with a teapot and extra cups and saucers. Usually, Murray carried the trays. Bristow rarely attempted it since his shaking hands made the contents rattle.

"Where's Murray?" I asked as she set the tray down.

"Helping the police. He misses the work and Detective Inspector Bailey said he could assist them, since he's trained." She paused and glanced at Willie, then back to me. "Shall I pour, Miss Ashe, or would you prefer to do it?"

How odd that she would ask me. As the lady of the house in the absence of Lady Rycroft, *Willie* ought to be giving the staff instructions.

Willie didn't like being supplanted. Or perhaps she didn't like being supplanted by *me*, Melville Hendry's daughter. She took a sip from her glass, glaring at me as she did so.

"You do it, Mrs. Bristow," I said.

Mrs. Bristow poured the tea then left, followed by her husband who once again closed the door behind him.

Willie pointed at it. "There! Did you see that? He gave me a look."

Alex reached for his cup of tea. "Probably because he finds you annoying."

"That can't be it. I've been annoying for years, and he's never given me strange looks before."

"We all reach the end of our tether at some point." Alex sipped his tea then placed the cup back on the saucer. He got up and went to the drinks trolley. "Anyone else need a brandy?"

We all declined.

Daisy watched him, her brow deeply furrowed. With his back to us, Alex didn't notice.

His hand suddenly shook, causing him to spill the brandy on the trolley. "Blast." He put the glass down with a heavy thud and lowered his head.

Willie started to rise, but Daisy was already on her feet. She placed a hand on Alex's back. He turned and drew her into a fierce embrace, tucking her head under his chin.

Willie eased back into the chair and concentrated on her brandy. Despite their bickering, she clearly adored Alex as much as she did Gabe. It must be painful for her to see him distressed.

I would have tried to comfort her, but I doubted I would be welcome. Besides, I wasn't sure I had the capacity to comfort others. I was sorely in need of it myself.

Petra took my hand again and squeezed. Standing behind us, Huon laid a hand on my shoulder. I gave them smiles, attempting to reassure them that I was all right. But I wouldn't be all right until Gabe held me the way Alex held Daisy.

* * *

THE KNOCK on the front door had us all leaping to our feet. We couldn't wait for Bristow to announce the visitor, so headed into the entrance hall to see for ourselves. It wasn't Cyclops, however. It was the sketch artist.

"I hoped to find you here," he said. "I returned to Scotland Yard, but D.I. Bailey didn't return, so I decided to come here instead. I don't think he'll mind if I speak to you without him present."

Alex invited him into the library. "We already have a suspicion about the redheaded man's identity. Hopefully your drawing will confirm it."

"In case you were wondering," Willie added, "he's an entitled idiot who won't confess unless we present proof he was seen talking to Mad Dog. Mother's orders."

The artist eyed her warily as he opened his sketchbook. "The publican took a little prompting before he opened up, but he has a good eye for detail. I've made notes about coloring as that doesn't come across in pencil."

I expected Huon to remark on the superiority of ink and that his family could supply any color of ink, but he surprised me. "Miss Conway is a graphite magician. Her family makes excellent colored pencils using a binding agent they invented themselves. It enhances the durability of the core, and ensures the colored pigments adhere better to paper, compared to artless pencils. Naturally, Miss Conway can also use a spell in her pencils that make your drawings more vibrant." He removed a business card from his jacket pocket. "Come to her shop and try them for yourself."

Petra smiled sweetly at him.

The artist accepted the card. "Well?" he asked Alex. "Is it your suspect?"

Alex shook his head. "But he does look familiar." He passed the sketchbook to Willie and me.

"That ain't Valentine," she said. "I don't recognize him, though. You do, Alex?"

"I'm not sure."

He looked familiar to me, too. The memory was so close, yet still out of reach. I wanted to scream in frustration. I pressed my thumb and forefinger into my eyelids until someone shook me by the shoulders.

A seething Willie filled my vision. "You know, don't you?"

"I can't quite remember," I said.

"Think!"

"I'm trying, but you're putting me off."

Her lips pursed and she snatched the sketchbook off Huon who was studying it. She held the sketchbook at arm's length and squinted. "It's written here that the man was tall and strongly built, but not heavy or fat."

"Those are the publican's words," the artist said.

"And he was pale with reddish-brown hair." She grunted. "He said *red* hair to us."

Reddish-brown hair. I'd heard someone described using those exact words. Someone who was also tall and strong. Someone who'd paid another man to throw balls of paper at Gabe at Epsom Downs racetrack. We'd concluded it had been a test to study Gabe's reaction if a harmless projectile came his way. Later, bullets had been fired in what we thought was an escalation of the same experiment.

Alex remembered, too, and told the others about the incident. "I never saw the man; he was simply described to me."

"But you said he looks familiar," Willie pointed out. "You must have seen him somewhere."

"It's just a fleeting memory."

If Alex and I had seen him, but Willie hadn't… I tried to think of the places we'd been without her. Since the stabbing, Gabe had been watched closely by both his friend *and* cousin. The only times they let him out of their sight was when they thought he was safe, or he'd managed to slip away.

The stabbing…

I asked to see the sketch again. "I know who it is."

CHAPTER 11

The Rosebank Gardens hospital patient who'd stabbed Gabe in the shoulder had come at him from behind. At the time, I thought Gabe's magic didn't activate because he hadn't seen him, but considering Gabe hadn't seen bullets flying at him from all directions in the war, that explanation didn't hold water. Gabe's magic activated when it knew he was in a life-threatening situation. A stab in the shoulder didn't qualify as life-threatening.

The former soldier was arrested, but his severely shell-shocked state meant he couldn't answer questions as to why he'd attacked Gabe. His only response had been to say that God made him do it. We'd theorized that someone put him up to it, either to frighten Gabe away from the investigation we'd been conducting at the time, or to test his magic. Occurring before the incident at the Epsom Downs racetrack, it was now clear both attacks were tests, and the same man was behind them—the man with the reddish-brown hair whose face stared back at me from the sketchbook.

The shell-shocked patient had been jailed in a secure facility since the incident and a quick telephone call confirmed he was still there. As for the face the artist had drawn—the man who'd hired Mad Dog Mitchell in the Rose and Thorn—I'd seen him at Rosebank. It was a face I'd hardly taken notice of at the time, which was why I couldn't immediately identify him.

We'd had several visits to Rosebank Gardens throughout our recent investigations. The hospital for returned soldiers suffering severe shell shock had once been a private facility that subjected the artless children of magician parents to cruel treatments in an attempt to draw out their magic. Since magic didn't lie dormant within them, the treatments failed.

Rosebank Gardens was where Bertie Hobson spent time many years ago. The Hobson family knew it well. They must have first met the orderly with the reddish-brown hair then, and hired him more recently to conduct the experiments on Gabe. Perhaps the Hobsons were coerced by Thurlow. By the time we'd first visited the hospital, Thurlow was already known to us, and shortly afterwards, he made himself known to Mrs. Hobson. The links were there, as solid as an iron chain. It was too much of a coincidence to ignore.

Alex, Willie and I drove to the hospital, located at the north-eastern edge of London. The guard at the front gate recognized us and let us through. Not that the gate was locked to keep visitors out. It was locked to keep the patients in.

The overcast day threatened rain, but even so, several patients sat on chairs or wheelchairs on the lawn near the rose beds. Nurses and orderlies mingled with them, playing cards with those former soldiers who weren't suffering too greatly, or simply reading to those who'd retreated so far into themselves they could no longer communicate. The sight of fully grown men plunged into the deepest, darkest dungeons of their minds because of their wartime experiences never failed to disturb me.

The staff and some of the patients looked up upon our arrival. One of the nurses approached, a matronly woman with a confident stride and direct gaze. "Willie? What are you doing here?" Sister Matilda Wallbank asked.

We'd first met Willie's current lover at the hospital during an investigation. They liked and respected one another, despite their obvious differences. Willie was loud yet emotional, whereas Tilda had a quiet, inner strength. I suspected it was a case of opposites attract. Apparently, Tilda was a lot like Willie's first husband, who had been a detective with Scotland Yard. People had tended to misjudge him at first, apparently, but he was cool under pressure with a quick mind. He had also been completely besotted with Willie's fiery nature, so I'd been told. Tilda was too, going by the way she gave Willie an admiring look.

Willie showed her the sketch the artist had given us. "We're looking for this man. He works here as an orderly."

"Not anymore. He resigned not long ago."

Willie swore, earning a scolding from Tilda. "Sorry," Willie muttered.

"What's his name?" Alex asked.

"Frank Alcott. Why are you looking for him?" When none of us answered, she prompted, "Willie?"

Willie folded the sketch up and tucked it into her jacket pocket. "He was seen talking to a man known as Mad Dog Mitchell in a pub. Mad Dog is a thug who hires himself out for jobs that require some muscle. Gabe's maid saw him in the house moments before Gabe was abducted from his bed in the early hours of this morning. There was another man with Mad Dog, but she didn't see him."

Tilda gasped. "Good lord. That's awful. You've mentioned there have been attempts before, but Gabe always escaped unharmed."

"They used chloroform this time," Alex said. "He couldn't fight back."

She pressed a hand to her chest. "To go to such extreme lengths because they want to harness the magic they *think* he has...it's madness."

Clearly Willie hadn't told her everything yet. Perhaps feeling guilty for not confiding in her lover, Willie shuffled her feet and cleared her throat. "Tell us about Frank Alcott."

"He was a good orderly. They don't have to mingle with the patients, but he often did. He would play cards with the more social men or share a smoke and conversation with them." Tilda indicated a group of patients chatting quietly in a group. One or two cast anxious glances our way, and another's hand shook so much he had difficulty placing the cigarette between his lips, but they otherwise seemed well.

"I thought he liked working here," Tilda went on. "Then he left, so I assumed I was wrong, or he found a better position elsewhere. I did think it odd that he left without saying goodbye to staff he'd worked alongside for years, as well as those patients he'd bonded with. His sudden departure hasn't helped those who think they're still in the war. They think the Germans got him and are coming for them next. No amount of reassurance allays their fears."

"When did he resign?" I asked.

"Nine or ten days ago."

Around the time Gabe was subjected to the paper ball projectiles and gunshots at Epsom Downs. The timing couldn't be a coincidence. Any final doubts I harbored about Frank Alcott's involvement vanished.

Tilda set off toward the hospital building that had been a grand country manor in its former incarnation. "Come with me."

We followed her inside. The director we'd dealt with in the past no longer worked there, and his replacement was behind the closed office door. Tilda asked his assistant if we could see Frank Alcott's file. Knowing we worked with the police, the assistant gave us his full cooperation. He retrieved the file from the cabinet and handed it to Alex.

Alex memorized the address given for the orderly and handed the file back. "Thank you for your help."

Tilda followed us outside to the Vauxhall. Willie cranked the engine and the motor rumbled to life. Before she climbed into the front passenger seat, she and Tilda had a quiet word at the front of the vehicle. I couldn't hear what they said, but the looks they gave one another were tender.

"Do you think it's love?" I asked Alex.

"Not the forever kind. Not for Willie. She's fickle by nature. She'll grow bored eventually."

"Did she grow bored of her husbands?"

"The first one died before she could tire of him, although they were married for several years. The second..." He smiled. "Lord Farnsworth was a unique character, like her. They got along well. Perhaps too well. They were like naughty children who got up to twice as much mischief when they were together. But they were more friends than husband and wife. I think Willie really likes Tilda. She acts like a normal human around her."

"Perhaps you should ask her to move in. It would make for a more peaceful household."

He turned to look at me, seated behind him. "Don't let Willie scare you away."

"She doesn't scare me. I know she has Gabe's best interests at heart." I didn't tell him I'd planned to leave Gabe. I may yet and I didn't want Alex trying to dissuade me. I'd decide what to do later, when my mind was clearer. For now, my focus was to find Gabe.

* * *

WE DROVE to the address listed in Frank Alcott's file, not far away in the township of Watford. The sun reappeared, bringing out the afternoon shadows. Their long shapes were a cruel reminder of the passage of time. Willie grew impatient as we got stuck behind a horse-drawn wagon on the busy High Street. Despite shouting at the driver, the wagon with the Benskins Ales and Stouts sign printed on the cover, didn't move over until he reached a pub. He waved cheerfully at Willie as we sped past, which only annoyed her more.

Frank Alcott lived in a handsome two-story brick house in

what appeared to be a respectable street. The question of how an orderly could afford such a nice place was answered by the notice in the window advertising a furnished room for rent. He must have occupied one room, not the entire building.

"What do we do now?" I asked. "Knock on the door and introduce ourselves? Sneak in and look for Gabe?"

"Gabe won't be inside," Alex said. "Not if Alcott only rented a single room. He has probably left anyway. That sign would suggest as much."

Willie thumped the door. "Just our luck. Our only lead has disappeared."

Alex got out of the vehicle. "If there's a room for rent, it probably means there's a nice landlady in reduced circumstances. She might know where her former tenant went."

As we approached the narrow iron gate across the path, Willie pushed me ahead. "You talk to her. Little old ladies like you."

The landlady was neither little nor old and had a clear interest in Alex over me, going by the way she batted her eyelashes at him. After introducing myself and my companions, she put out her hand to him, and only him. She drooped it in front of him, inviting him to kiss it. He took it and bowed, all smiles. Her lashes fluttered even more.

"Are you wanting to rent the room?" she purred. "It's fully furnished, very warm and cozy in winter."

"No, unfortunately," he said. "You have a lovely house, madam. I'm sure your next tenant will be very happy here. Speaking of tenants, we're looking for Mr. Frank Alcott. We believe he rented a room from you."

"He did. He left just over a week ago."

"Do you know where he went?"

A small dent appeared between her brows. She might like flirting with Alex, but she wasn't a fool. She wouldn't give away personal information to strangers without a good reason.

"He's my cousin," I said. "Frank wrote to me to say he was

tangled up in something, then I heard nothing again. I came to London to look for him. My friends offered to help."

"Frank never mentioned a cousin."

"We weren't close, which is why when he wrote and told me about his problem, I grew concerned. He must have been desperate to contact me, of all people."

"He did seem different these last two or three months," she said. "He used to be a friendly chap, but then he became introverted. I blame that place where he worked, the hospital for the insane."

"They're not insane," Alex said. "Just troubled from the war."

"So do you have a new address for Frank?" I asked.

She shook her head. "He didn't give me one. He said any mail I received could be thrown away."

"That is even more worrying." I pressed my fingers to my lips as if to compose myself. "Poor Frank. What if something terrible has happened to him?"

The landlady looked concerned. "I wish I could be more help, but I don't know where he could have gone."

"Did he have friends?" Alex asked.

"No one called on him here. He sometimes enjoyed a drink after work. I could smell it on his breath when he came home. But I don't know if he drank alone or with friends."

Willie mentioned the notice in the window. "Is that for his old room?"

The landlady nodded. "I haven't found a new lodger."

"Can we look through it? There might be clues as to where he went."

"I've already cleaned it and found nothing."

"Can we look anyway?"

"Please," Alex added with a warm smile.

The landlady gave in and led the way. She stood in the doorway while we gave the room a thorough inspection. The bed had been stripped, so it made it easier to check the mattress and pillow. Aside from a nightstand by the bed, and a small table with one hardback chair, the only other piece of furniture was an old armchair upholstered in dark green velvet. There wasn't even a portable stove to boil a kettle on.

Alex slowly paced the floor, using his weight to test each board to find any loose ones. Willie got down on her knees and checked the small cast-iron fireplace before peering under the dresser. I contemplated unpicking the seams of the mattress and pillow but decided to look for wall cavities first.

The landlady frowned as I knocked on the panels. "Do you think your cousin hid something in here?"

"He was a secretive man," I told her.

I hadn't got far when Willie declared she'd found something. She brandished a small envelope as she stood. "Found this at the back under the dresser. It's addressed to Alcott."

Alex peered over her shoulder. "Who is it from?"

She turned the envelope over. "There's no return address."

"What's inside?" I asked.

"Nothing. It's empty."

"Then it's useless." I heard the bleak tone in my voice but couldn't help it. The hopelessness that had been creeping ever closer as the day wore on now washed over me. We had a suspect, but without a forwarding address, we were no closer to getting Gabe back.

Our search yielded no results and we returned to the motor-car. The drive back to Park Street gave us time to discuss our next move. Unfortunately, we had no ideas. Aside from alerting Scotland Yard to Frank Alcott's involvement, there was nothing more we could do. There was nothing the police could do either, if the former orderly had gone underground. If a man didn't want to be found in London, he could disappear with ease. Thurlow would be hiding, too, after his failed attempt to kidnap me, as would Ivy and Mrs. Hobson.

It seemed Alex's mind had turned to them, too. "Jakes is right about the Hobson women. They'll reveal themselves soon. A life in hiding, out of the social spotlight, is not the life they want to live. The moment they're found, we're going to grill them about hiring Alcott. It must have been them. It's too much of a coincidence that Bertie was a patient at the same hospital where Alcott worked."

Willie turned in the front seat so she could see both Alex and me. "What if we underestimated Bertie?"

Alex shook his head. "He's not smart enough or brave enough to orchestrate something like this."

"He might be desperate enough, though."

Alex adjusted his hands on the steering wheel. His silence was telling. He thought her theory had merit.

The timing didn't match, however. "Bertie was with me when Gabe was abducted. He couldn't be in two places at once. The same as Ivy, Mrs. Hobson, and Thurlow."

Willie's jaw set hard, and her eyes flashed. "Was Bertie with you *all* that time, or just when you escaped?" Before I could answer, she added, "He didn't need to personally abduct Gabe anyway. He could have hired a second man to work with Alcott. Bertie's a weedy little runt, so it wouldn't be surprising if he got *two* thugs to do his dirty work."

"At least he's currently incarcerated. I handed him over to Jakes." Even as I said it, I worried that he could have been released.

A dark pit opened inside me. Had I helped the mastermind behind Gabe's abduction escape? I pressed my fingers to my lips as bile rose up my throat. Willie's glare left me in no doubt that she blamed me.

Alex came to my rescue. "It's more likely that Ivy and her mother are behind it, not Bertie. They're ruthless and smart, and Bertie's mother is more desperate than either of her children to save the family business. Now that her husband has gone, they need to find a leather magician willing to work for them without getting any acknowledgment as the magician. Even if they found one who didn't work for his own business, he won't want to sit in the shadows for long. He'll want a slice of the company, perhaps a large one. She wouldn't like to go down that route."

"How will studying Gabe's magic help solve that problem?" I asked. "When Bertie was admitted to Rosebank Gardens, they thought his magic could be extracted, but everyone now knows that's not possible. Abducting Gabe won't help Bertie or the company."

"Maybe this ain't about studying Gabe's magic," Willie said. "Maybe it's about punishing him for not publicly supporting the Hobson family when they needed it. And for ending his engagement to Ivy." Her glare turned even colder.

Part of me thought she was being unfair. But there was a part of me that agreed with her. Gabe was an honorable man. Even if he realized he didn't love Ivy, he might have gone through with the wedding if he'd never learned what it meant to truly fall in love. He may never have known what he was missing.

Just as I may never have known what I was missing if he hadn't entered my life. Now I knew what passionate, selfless, all-consuming love felt like. It was deeply fulfilling, uplifting and powerful.

At the moment, my fear for his safety made love feel like sheer torment.

Tears welled and my chin shuddered as I tried desperately not to cry. In the end, I couldn't control the tears and they slipped down my cheeks. I looked away.

To my amazement, Willie reached out and rubbed my knee. When I risked looking at her again, her anger had vanished. Her own eyes welled with tears, too.

Unaware of our moment of shared distress, Alex pointed out an obvious fact that Willie and I had forgotten. "Frank Alcott was involved in testing Gabe's magic at the racetrack, so we can be sure Gabe's kidnap—which Alcott was also involved in—was magic-related, *not* revenge."

Willie faced forward with a *humph*. "That doesn't mean the Hobsons aren't behind the kidnap."

"True. But let's be clear about the reason and not blame each other. We need to support one another, not criticize."

"We're supportive. Ain't we, Sylvia?"

I leaned forward so they could hear me over the roar of the engine and the wind whipping past the window apertures. "We're a team, and a formidable one at that."

Alex's surprise at our unification turned to satisfaction. "We'll find Gabe."

"And when we do," Willie added, "I'm going to shoot the bollocks off whoever is responsible."

"And if it turns out to be Mrs. Hobson or Ivy?"

"They've got the biggest bollocks of them all."

* * *

THE MOMENT of shared distress we'd experienced in the motorcar didn't last. Willie might not blame me for attracting the Hobsons' ire, but she still blamed me for attracting Melville Hendry's attention. In her mind, my father was still a suspect.

She reminded me of that as we climbed the steps to the front door of the Park Street house. "It's too much of a coincidence that he comes back into our lives right before this happens. I know it ain't something you could have foreseen, Sylvia, so I don't blame you altogether."

I rubbed my arms as a chill rippled through me.

Alex touched my elbow and shook his head. The roll of his eyes told me what he thought of Willie's theory. "Why would he kidnap Gabe?" he asked her.

"He's ruthless, mad and hates the Glass family."

"Those aren't motives."

"They are to me."

"You're the one who's mad, Willie. He has no link to Rosebank Gardens hospital or Frank Alcott."

"That we know of."

The door opened and Bristow stood there. He always seemed

more upper class than Gabe, but now he looked positively imperious as he looked down his nose at Willie. "Detective Inspector Bailey wishes to see you in the library, my lady."

She wrinkled her nose. "'My lady?' You ain't called me that in years. You lost your marbles, Bristow?" She patted his arm as she passed him, thinking nothing more of it.

I saw his scowl, however. He'd never looked at anyone like that, not even when Willie was at her most irritating.

It wasn't until she saw Cyclops standing in the library's doorway with a similar scowl on his face that she realized something was amiss. "What's wrong? What's happened? Is Gabe—"

"Still missing." Cyclops stepped aside. "I want a word with you."

Alex and I exchanged glances as we followed Willie.

Cyclops shut the door, then stood with his arms over his chest. It was a formidable stance, and not one I'd seen him employ with friends or family. What made it more worrying was the grave look he gave her.

Willie rarely showed fear, but she swallowed audibly.

"The kidnappers had a key to this house," Cyclops said. "There was no sign of forced entry."

"Aside from us, only the Bristows and Sally have keys," Alex pointed out. "Are you suggesting one of them gave theirs to the kidnapper inadvertently? I can assure you, none did it on purpose."

Cyclops shook his head without taking his gaze off Willie. "I questioned all the servants after you left this morning. No one gave their key away, or lost it or misplaced it, not even for a few hours during which time one of the other servants could have made a copy."

Alex glanced between his father and Willie. "And?"

"Do you have a confession to make, Willie?"

Alex suddenly turned to her. "Did you lose your key?"

Her face drained of color. She reached out, her fingers searching for the table for support. I pushed a chair under her and guided her to sit. She lowered her head into her hands, muttering something we couldn't hear.

"Pardon?" I asked.

"It ain't my fault. I was drunk."

"Being drunk *is* your fault!" Cyclops snapped.

Alex stepped between them, like a boxing referee keeping the opponents apart. Not that it would come to physical blows between the old friends, but there was every danger their exchange would be heated.

Or so I thought, until I saw Willie's forlorn face as she glanced up at Cyclops. She blamed herself, too. So much so that she even admitted it with a groan. She buried her face in her hands again.

I rested a comforting hand on her shoulder. For once, she did not shrug it off. "Tell us what happened."

"I went out drinking a few nights ago. I didn't realize I'd lost my key until I got home. It was real late and I knew the Bristows would be in bed, so I went into the mews and slept in the motorcar until the house woke up. Later, I borrowed Bristow's key and got a copy made." She removed it from her pocket. "I told him not to say anything to anyone."

"Why didn't you want us to know?" Alex asked.

"Because you and Gabe made fun of me last time I came home drunk. You told me I can't hold my liquor anymore, that I'm getting old." She sighed. "So that's why Bristow's been acting odd. He didn't say anything earlier when we were here with Daisy and the others."

"I asked him not to," Cyclops said. "I wanted to speak to you myself, but I had to go out to check on my men's progress."

I'd not thought it possible to feel even more hopeless about our situation, but the pit of despair became an abyss. Willie could have lost the key anywhere on her way home, and anyone could have picked it up. There was no way of narrowing our list of suspects.

Willie, however, wiped her nose on her sleeve and sat up a

little straighter. "I reckon I've got an idea who took it, but…" She gave her head an emphatic shake. "No. Can't be. I must be remembering that night all wrong."

Cyclops and Alex crowded close. "Talk it through with us," Cyclops said, his earlier anger having vanished. "Where were you? Who were you with?"

"I was supposed to meet a friend at The Flying Duck for a drink, but he never showed up. Some people I knew saw I was on my own and asked me to join them. We drank together for a while. Sometime later, I remember I tripped over something. I went sprawling, knocking over a chair. I reckon the key fell out of my pocket then."

Alex sighed. "Anyone in the pub could have picked it up."

Willie rubbed her temple as she shook her head. "It was just us in the snug and I didn't leave then. I stayed on, as did they. One of us would have seen the key on the floor before we left. The snug ain't spacious, and they weren't as drunk as me."

"So, one of them saw the key fall out of your pocket and picked it up then and there. Who were you drinking with?"

Willie wasn't a ditherer in any sense, yet she was reluctant to answer Alex. She bent forward and groaned.

He glared at her as if that could gouge the response out of her. "Tell us!"

She lifted her head. She displayed not a single trace of the bravado she was infamous for, none of the cockiness and spirited sass. There was just despair. "You ain't going to believe it."

CHAPTER 12

"Who?" Cyclops pressed. "Who could have picked up your key, Willie?"

"I was drinking with three others: Stanley Greville, Juan Martinez and Francis Stray."

I gasped. "Gabe's friends? Surely not." Yet even as I said it, doubt crept in.

Alex shook his head. "Why were the three of them drinking together without Gabe? He's the mutual connection between them." He was right—Juan and Stanley had fought alongside Gabe in the Grenadier Guards, but Francis was an old school chum.

"Gabe had been at The Flying Duck with them earlier," Willie said. "He left before I got there."

Alex was still shaking his head, over and over, as if trying to dislodge an insidious thought. "It can't be one of them. It must have been someone else, Willie. Think."

"If I lost the key when I tripped, it *was* one of them. I'm sure of it."

Alex began to pace the floor, striding back and forth between bookshelves.

I edged closer to one of the shelves, too, seeking a measure of comfort from the paper in the books. This time, it offered none. The direction of my thoughts was awful. Almost too awful to say out loud, but someone had to. I suspected we were all thinking the same thing anyway. "Stanley Greville spent time in Rosebank Gardens after the war. He knew Frank Alcott. I remember seeing them talking in the hospital grounds."

Alex continued to pace. Willie's head didn't rise from where she'd lowered it, her fingers buried in her tangled hair. Only Cyclops was capable of acting. It was he who rallied Alex and Willie by taking the decision-making out of their hands.

"We'll visit him now. If we present him with our evidence, hopefully he'll give in and release Gabe."

"And if he doesn't?" I asked.

Cyclops didn't answer. He placed his hat on his head and strode out of the library.

* * *

NONE of us were particularly surprised to find that Stanley Greville no longer lived in the small flat where we'd visited him before. According to the new tenant, he'd moved out only two days prior and not left a forwarding address. Stanley's disappearance all but confirmed his guilt.

Willie slumped against the wall beside the flat's door and leaned forward, her hands on her knees. Her breaths came in shallow gasps.

"It's not your fault," Cyclops told her. "You had no reason to distrust Greville."

Alex leaned against the wall beside her. "None of us did." He tipped his head back and stared at the ceiling. "Now what do we do?"

"We call on Francis Stray and Juan Martinez," I said. "They might have a new address for Stanley."

Alex pushed off from the wall. He and his father strode

ahead and quickly descended the stairs. Willie hadn't moved. Her breathing was more even, but she was still bent over.

"Alex is right," I told her. "Don't blame yourself. The only one at fault is Stanley."

She slowly straightened. I thought my words had got through to her, but the haunted look in her eyes told another story. It reminded me of the look I'd seen in so many men's eyes since the war ended. I'd seen it in Gabe's, too, when we first met. It was guilt. In their case, it was the guilt of having survived when so many perished. In Willie's, it was the guilt of playing a role in Gabe's abduction.

Her mouth twitched and twisted with the effort not to succumb to her emotions. "Gabe's my family. He's like a son to me. Not only did I fail to protect him, I gave his abductor the means to enter the house. If it weren't for me… If I hadn't gone out that night… If I hadn't got drunk, I wouldn't have tripped…" She buried her face in her hands.

I put my arm around her shoulders. "Don't think like that, Willie." I gave her shoulders a little shake in an attempt to rally her. "Anyway, it's quite possible Stanley deliberately tripped you up and picked the key out of your pocket when he went to your aid."

She lowered her hands and fixed me with a wide-eyed stare. At least it was no longer haunted. "He *did* help me up. I reckon I didn't drop the key. He *stole* it from my pocket." She threw her arms around me. It was the most affection she'd ever shown me.

I patted her back, but she suddenly drew away.

She raced to the staircase, her movements quicker than a woman half her age. "Come on, Sylv, we got to interrogate Francis and Juan."

* * *

Gabe's mathematician friend, Francis Stray, was a literal man who found social interactions both confusing and taxing, so he tended to avoid people, particularly if he didn't know them well. Added to that, he wasn't very adept at reading a person's emotions, so when he immediately invited us inside upon seeing us on his doorstep, it was a testament to how worried and desperate we appeared. We were all finding it difficult to mask our anxiety.

"Gabe's been abducted by Stanley Greville," Willie said before I could think of a less confronting way to inform Francis of the reason for our visit. "Do you know where Stanley is?"

Francis blinked at her. "At his flat, I assume."

"He no longer lives there."

Willie looked around, as if she wanted to destroy something in frustration. Fortunately, she refrained. Francis's flat wasn't large, but it was neat and tidy, like the man himself. Nothing was out of place, not a single book or hair on his head. The only evidence he'd just arrived home from work was the steam rising from the spout of the kettle on the portable stove.

Francis's gaze shifted between each of us, but it settled on me. Perhaps he thought of me as the least intimidating. "I don't understand. Gabe is strong and capable. How could someone simply take him? Why would Stanley?"

I directed him to sit down, then sat opposite. Francis didn't like to be touched, so I kept my distance when usually I'd offer a comforting hand. "We're sorry to barge in like this, Francis, but it's important to act quickly. As Willie said, Gabe was abducted. It appears chloroform was used to subdue him."

He nodded. "That makes sense."

"We've uncovered a number of clues that point to Stanley's involvement."

"None of which we have time to go through now," Willie added.

Alex nudged her with his elbow.

I continued. "Stanley has vacated his flat and left no forwarding address. Do you know where he may have gone?"

"No." Francis's voice was small, thin.

He seemed to be trying to make sense of the situation but failing. Gabe had been a rock for Francis over many years. It had started when Gabe protected the weaker boy from school bullies. Recently, Gabe sheltered Francis from Thurlow when the bookmaker sought to employ him.

Gabe was a rock for many of us. It was only now that he was gone that I realized how easily I'd settled into London life thanks to him. I'd met new friends through him. I'd found my father and aunts because of his help. I'd emerged from my shell because his attentions made me feel beautiful, interesting, and worthy. He made me feel brave.

The tears that were never far away welled again. I looked down at the floor, not wanting to worry Francis.

Cyclops thanked Francis for his time. "If you think of anything, telephone or visit Gabe's house. It's acting as our hub for the time being."

Francis stood and crossed the floor to the tightly packed bookshelves. He removed a folio-sized book from the bottom shelf and placed it on the table. It was a street atlas, I realized when he opened it. "If Stanley moved out of his flat specifically because he knew he was about to kidnap Gabe and he didn't want to be discovered, he would have moved into a new place that met his specific purposes."

Willie leaned both hands on the table beside the atlas. "I don't understand. What purposes? To keep Gabe hidden while he performed his tests?"

Alex, Cyclops and I crowded around, too. Like Willie, I didn't quite follow.

Francis scanned the double-page key map at the front of the book. "Yes, but also the nature of those tests is important."

"We don't know what tests he'll perform," Alex said.

"While I would never advocate guessing, we can make some valid assumptions based on what we know of Stanley."

I tried to think of what we knew about our main suspect, but aside from picturing the nervous shell-shocked former soldier, I came up with nothing. Where my panic after learning Gabe's fate had scattered my thoughts and made it difficult to concentrate, Francis had set aside his worry after the initial shock wore off. It was as if he'd made a conscious decision to place it in a box and deal with it another time when he wasn't so busy. His practical brain got to work in a methodical manner, whereas mine was all over the place.

"What do you know about him?" Cyclops asked. "I don't know him well myself."

"He was a medical student before the war," Francis said.

Willie looked up from the atlas. "I'd forgotten about that."

"He never returned to his studies. His nerves were too wrecked, so he said, although he did plan to return one day when he was better."

Something occurred to me. "Do you recall the Medici Manuscript? We all worked together to decipher its codes."

Willie's features set hard. "Stanley *helped* us. Gabe trusted him enough to ask him to work alongside us to decipher the manuscript's secrets. But that dog had already tried abducting Gabe at that point, and he continued trying after, too. Traitor."

"He identified the medical symbols in the book," I reminded them.

Alex rested a hand on my arm and looked at me as though I may have lost my mind entirely. "You can't blame us for not anticipating that he was going to perform tests on Gabe. Not all the way back then."

"That's true," I said, "but there was other evidence that he was interested in Gabe's magic from a medical point of view. He was reading up on testing blood for diseases. I remember seeing a medical journal in his flat, opened to a page about blood carrying disease."

"It's an exciting field of study," Francis said. "The war spurred major advancements in research into diseases transferred between men who received blood transfusions." He seemed to cut himself short, perhaps realizing it was inappropriate to be so enthusiastic about scientific breakthroughs that only came about because of war.

"You reckon Stanley believes Gabe's magic is blood-borne?" Willie asked.

"Given Sylvia saw him researching hematology, there's a high probability he does."

"But why would he want Gabe's magic anyway? I don't reckon he cares much about money, so he probably won't sell his research if he could prove he's right."

"To cure his shell shock," I said.

From the lack of surprise on Alex, Cyclops, and Francis's faces, they'd already reached the same conclusion as me. It was the only conclusion that explained why a man would turn against his friend. Stanley probably didn't want to harm Gabe, but he wanted so desperately to cure himself of his shell shock that he'd stooped to an unfathomable low.

Stanley, and other former soldiers whose nerves had been shredded by their wartime experiences, had found the world unsympathetic when they returned. They were stigmatized, labeled pathetic, cowardly, and told to "just get on with it." Following demobilization and a stint at Rosebank Gardens hospital, Stanley was deemed well enough to be discharged. Although the government funded hospitals to treat some patients, there was no financial assistance once they left. Few could find work, let alone keep a job for any length of time. Stanley had taken a position at a pharmacy, but we'd recently learned he'd resigned. He'd retreated from the world again. It was a warning sign that all was not well with him. We shouldn't have ignored it.

But none of us could have guessed how unwell he was. None of us could have guessed that one of Gabe's closest friends would betray him in the most dreadful way.

Francis pointed to various locations on the key map. "Stanley will need access to laboratories to test Gabe's blood once he extracts it. The main hospitals have modern facilities, so I think his new digs will be near one of those."

Cyclops circled his finger on the eastern section of the city's key map. "He'd get a place somewhere where folk don't ask questions when they see an unconscious man being carried by two others. Somewhere Gabe would be just another drunk helped home by friends. The East End."

Willie whipped out the envelope she'd found under the dresser in Frank Alcott's room. She slapped it down on the table beside the atlas. "The postmark shows it was posted from the E1 district. That's the East End. It's dated last Tuesday. It could have been sent by Stanley from his new digs."

Alex flipped the pages until he reached the maps focusing on the East End. "There are a few hospitals in the area, the Royal London being the largest." He pointed to it, as well as another four. "There are a lot of buildings in the vicinity, each with many rooms. The search will take time."

"It's a start," Cyclops said. "I'll contact my men."

They sounded grimly determined. I held out much less hope of success, however. Scotland Yard could put as many resources into the search as they wanted, but I doubted it would yield results. The residents of the East End would be unwilling to tattle on their neighbors. The East End also covered a sizeable area. It had a lot of densely packed buildings crammed into its maze of streets, alleys and courts. The task of going through each room in each house and tenement was enormous.

We still thought it worth visiting Juan. He'd been closer to Stanley than Francis, having served alongside him in the same company, with Gabe as their captain. Perhaps he even had a new address for Stanley.

We thanked Francis and headed off. Cyclops took a taxi to Scotland Yard to redirect all available resources to searching the East End. Alex, Willie and I drove to Juan's flat.

Fortunately, we caught Gabe's Catalonian-born friend as he

was locking up. A few minutes later and we would have missed him.

"We need to speak to you," Alex told him.

Juan checked his wristwatch. "Can we talk while I walk? I have to go to work."

Willie blocked his path. "At this hour?" It wasn't yet evening, but most men were returning home from working in an office, not leaving.

"I am part-owner of a new nightclub. There is much to do before we open at ten. You should come one night, all of you. It is fun. The music is jazzy, and I will give you a free drink." He looked past us to the lift cage. "Where is Gabe?"

"That's what we need to speak to you about," Alex said. The neighboring door opened, and a couple emerged, arm in arm and laughing. "May we go inside? It's important."

Juan seemed to notice our grim faces for the first time. He unlocked the door and invited us in. His flat resembled Francis's, but without the books. He wasn't quite as neat as Francis either, but few people were.

He removed a newspaper from the table and put away a dirty cup before inviting us to sit. No one did. "Something is the matter, no? Where is Gabe?"

"Kidnapped by Stanley Greville," Willie said in her usual direct manner.

Juan sat, muttering something in his native language. "Are you sure it is Stanley? No, it cannot be him," he said before any of us could answer. "He and Gabe are friends. Gabe saved him in the war. He would not harm the captain."

Alex outlined our reasons for suspecting Stanley and what we believed to be his motive. "We need to find his new address. If he's not keeping Gabe there, we can still watch it in the hope Stanley will lead us to him. Did he inform you where he was moving to?"

Juan shrugged. "I did not know he moved at all."

Then we were no closer to finding Gabe. As much as we told

ourselves that Scotland Yard had a search of the East End in hand, the reality was quite different. It would take time. Time that Gabe may not have.

Juan clicked his fingers. "He owns a house. I remember, in the war, he told me this when we were up to our knees in a muddy trench, but he did not mention it since. If he still owns it, he could be there."

"He owns a house!" Willie cried. "Then why was he renting a flat?"

"Because it is in a bad area, and he did not want to live there himself. He rented it to the poor. When he told me this, in the trench, he was feeling guilty. He said when the war ended, he would fix up the house, and make it better for the tenants. He wanted to be a better landlord."

"What's the address?" Willie asked.

Juan shrugged. "I do not know."

Willie grabbed the front of his jacket. "Think!"

Juan put up his hands in surrender. "I am sorry, but I do not know."

"My father can find out," Alex said. "It shouldn't be difficult." He was already striding toward the door before he finished speaking. "I saw a telephone booth downstairs in the foyer."

Willie raced after him. I took the seat she'd vacated and released a pent-up breath. "Thank you, Juan. This could be the breakthrough we need."

He patted my hand. "You look very sad, Sylvia, but Gabe will be all right. Stanley will not hurt him." He didn't sound convinced, however. Like me, he knew Stanley was desperate enough to throw caution to the wind and take too much blood from Gabe.

Would Gabe's magic save him if that happened? What if he lost consciousness? Would his magic still work then?

What if Stanley wanted answers to those questions, too? If Gabe's magic failed because he was weakened through blood loss or unconsciousness, Stanley would have his answers—but perhaps at the expense of Gabe's life.

Juan and I joined Willie and Alex at the telephone booth that was available for the use of the building's occupants. Alex informed us that he was waiting for his father to telephone back with an address. The minutes ticked by interminably slowly. None of us spoke. Residents passed us, coming and going from the building as the late afternoon turned to dusk. Juan waited for a while then left to meet the co-owner of the nightclub before it opened. Time dragged.

The irony of the perception of how time seemed to slow wasn't lost on me.

We all jumped when the telephone rang. Alex snatched up the receiver and gave an uncharacteristically brusque response to the operator on the other end. Finally, Cyclops must have been put through. Alex listened then repeated the address out loud. "Milsom Court, Whitechapel."

"That's not far," Willie shouted into the mouthpiece. "We can be there in a few minutes if we drive real fast."

I could hear Cyclops's voice down the line, but not his words.

"We'll do whatever is necessary," Alex said into the receiver.

Before he hung it up, his father's final word came down the line, as clear as a bell. "Alex!"

"He ordered us to let the police handle it." Even as Alex said it, he was striding to the door. He had no intention of waiting.

Thanks to Alex's driving skill, we reached the Royal London Hospital mere minutes later. We turned down one of the streets to the east of it, then another and another, each narrower than the last, until the motorcar wouldn't fit if another vehicle passed in the opposite direction. We stopped at the entrance between two houses that had probably once been grand residences but had long ago been turned into lodgings that could be rented by the room. No wider than a doorway, we would have missed the entrance to Milsom Court if it wasn't for the sign attached to the bricks above the arch. There was just enough light for us to read it. Soon, these streets would be as black as night, while the more open avenues in the better parts of London would still be bathed in twilight's glow. I glanced at the nearest streetlamp, wondering if it worked.

Alex led the way through the passage into the court beyond. Buildings rose out of the gloom on all sides, suffocatingly close. The owner of the two houses must have built these dwellings in his backyard many decades ago, leaving just the oddly shaped courtyard in front of them. Hidden from the main street, the court appeared to serve as a laundry room, tavern, sleeping quarters, and meeting place for residents. Going by the scantily clad women lounging in doorways, it wasn't much of a stretch of the imagination to assume the sort of meetings that were conducted were mostly of the prostitution kind.

There seemed to be far more people about than could possibly be housed in the tenements, all of them watching us with the interest of a fighter sizing up his opponent before a bout. The buildings themselves didn't seem old, yet their roofs were missing tiles, some of the windows were missing glass panes and, in the case of one rotting wall, missing nails altogether. It seemed to be held up by nothing more than dirt and cobwebs. The landlords who built or owned cheap dwellings in their yards were called slumlords for a reason.

To think, Stanley was one of them.

It was in a court like this, not far from here, that the infamous Ripper had committed some of his murders decades ago. I could imagine a shadowy figure prowling the night, hunting for his next victim. The whores were easy prey, exhausted, drunk, and desperate as they were.

Whores beckoned Alex with a crook of a finger, not shy in their promises as they competed for the custom of the well-dressed newcomer who'd arrived in a flash motorcar. Some tried to lure Willie, too, but none bothered with me. The men, however, couldn't take their gazes off me. Fortunately, most seemed too drunk to be of any harm, but I kept a wary eye on them, nevertheless.

There was no sign of the police. Scotland Yard was some distance away, but Cyclops would have telephoned the closest station to Milsom Court and ordered men to be dispatched immediately. Neither Willie nor Alex suggested we wait for them. Nor did I. Every moment mattered and I wasn't going to waste a single second.

Alex bypassed a glassy-eyed man drinking from a tin cup and approached the most sober-looking woman. I stayed back with Willie and gazed up at the windows, searching for the face of Stanley Greville. Several residents stared down at us, but he wasn't one of them.

Moments later, Alex returned. Behind him, the woman's skirt pocket now bulged. He must have paid her a considerable sum. "Stanley owns this entire court and every building in it. Apparently he inherited it from his father before the war, but rarely came here. She recognized him, though. He's in there, first floor, at the back." He nodded at the building to our right.

"It could be a trap," Willie said, eyeing the door.

"He couldn't have known we'd find him."

"It's too easy."

Alex indicated a man slumped forward over a broken crate, an empty bottle lying on the cobblestones beside him. "We knew Stanley would take Gabe to a place where an unconscious figure is a common enough sight. But he hadn't factored in his tenants' dislike and distrust of their landlord. Add a healthy bribe into the mix and she gave him up without hesitation."

We could take Stanley by surprise if we acted quickly. He could look out of a window at any moment, or one of the other residents could alert him. "There's no reason to wait," I urged.

Alex grabbed my elbow and directed me deeper into the shadows. "We still need a plan."

Behind him, Willie withdrew her gun and marched toward the tenement. When he realized, Alex swore and ran after her.

She was already heading up the staircase, gun at the ready, when I entered the dingy house. Dampness and the stench of urine seemed to ooze from the very floor and walls. Fortunately, it was too dark to identify the stains. Carnal sounds coming from a nearby room covered the creak of floorboards beneath our feet as we crept up the staircase.

Then Willie tripped on a broken step. She fell to her knees but managed to quickly pick herself up and continue. She'd not let go of her gun.

Only one of the doors on the landing was closed. She checked the other rooms, but all were empty. Alex stood to the side of the closed door, clutching his own gun. He signaled for me to stand back, then indicated that Willie should enter behind him.

She didn't refuse, but she didn't obey, either. She tested the doorknob. Finding it unlocked, she gently pushed open the door and peered through the gap.

"Gabe!" She shoved the door open and barged into the room.

Her loud cuss was like a punch to my heart.

Alex went to follow her, but got no further than the doorway. He put his hands in the air and swore, just as loudly as Willie. I turned to flee, but the click of a cocking gun stopped me dead in my tracks.

"You too, miss," came a voice I'd never heard before. "Hands in the air where I can see them."

I turned around to see Frank Alcott holding Willie and Alex at gunpoint. Behind him, a barely conscious Gabe sat on a rickety bed, strapped to the bedhead to keep him upright. His eyes were closed, and his face was as pale as his shirt, thrown over the back of a chair. A dented tin bowl was placed under his arm at the elbow. Blood dripped from a deep incision in his inner elbow into the bowl.

I ached to see him so vulnerable. But what truly scared me was his rapid breathing, and the fact the bowl was almost full. He didn't have long.

CHAPTER 13

"Let him go!" I cried. "He'll die if you don't stop draining his blood."

When Frank Alcott didn't move, I tried to push past Alex and Willie to reach Gabe. Alex caught me, pinning my arms to my sides.

"Don't," he whispered in my ear. "We can't lose you, too."

Too.

I closed my eyes. I wouldn't concede defeat. Gabe's life was too precious. I loved him. I'd loved him from the moment I'd met him at the Royal Academy of Arts exhibition. I would do anything to save him.

But Alex was right. Rushing in would achieve nothing but a bullet in my head.

I opened my eyes, only to find myself staring into the barrel of Alcott's gun. If there was a way to free Gabe and not sacrifice any of our lives to do so, I could not yet see it. I willed my mind to focus and not give in to the fog of fear and despair lurking at the edges.

Willie swore at Alcott. "Are you mad? You're going to kill him!"

Alcott adjusted his grip on the gun. The former orderly

didn't look mad. Nor did he seem cruel. He looked like an ordinary man who was utterly convinced he was doing the right thing. "Stanley told me a man can lose a lot of blood without dying. He knows what he's doing. He was a doctor before the war took everything from him."

"He was a medical *student*!" Willie snarled. "He wasn't qualified."

That appeared to be news to Alcott, but he didn't lower the gun. "I am sorry, but I can't let him go."

"Why not?" Alex asked as he released me. "I just want to understand." Compared to Willie, he sounded calm, and genuinely interested in Alcott. It was his way to lull a suspect to get them to lower their guard.

Alcott seemed relieved to have a chance to explain. "Mr. Glass is too important. His blood could be the key to unlocking the secret of his time magic."

"That ain't how magic works, you ignorant moron!" Willie cried.

Alex hissed at her to be quiet. She bit down on her lower lip in an attempt to stop it trembling. When her teeth released it, they left behind indentations.

"She's right," Alex told Alcott. "You can't extract magic from a magician and transfer it into someone else along with the blood."

"Stanley says it might be possible, but only testing the blood will give answers."

"He's not basing that on fact. Don't believe him."

"It *is* based on fact."

"Gabe isn't a magician, anyway."

"Stanley says he is. He observed Mr. Glass in the trenches and realized he was saving himself somehow. Bullets and bombs didn't hit him, or his friends. That was strange, but not the strangest thing. You see, Mr. Glass would be in one spot then a blink of an eye later, after the bomb had gone off or the spray of bullets ended, he'd be somewhere else. Sometimes he'd even be in the enemy trench, having captured the Jerry shooting at them. No one knew how he got there. No one saw him move."

"It's difficult to notice details under fire."

"Stanley was—is—a scientist. It's in his nature to notice things, and to experiment. So that's what he did after he was discharged from Rosebank. He ran tests, and saw that Mr. Glass reacted instinctively when his life or that of someone he cared about was threatened." His gaze slid to me then back to Alex. "He didn't save himself consciously. He had no control. It just happened. Just like some diseases that are carried and transferred by blood. The mind can't will them away. The body can't always fight them off. Usually a cure requires medical intervention, or death is inevitable. Stanley noticed the parallels between some diseases and Mr. Glass's magic and thinks doctors can learn how to transfer the magic from Mr. Glass into others along with a blood transfusion, the way some diseases are transferred."

"Stanley's theory is flawed. It's widely known that magicians are born. Magic isn't in their blood. It's their essence. Like a soul," he added, grasping at the analogy.

Alcott jerked his thumb at Gabe. "He's not a normal magician. No one knows why *his* magic is different, but the why doesn't matter. What matters is that it *is* different, and so it needs to be studied to understand it. If the blood does carry his magic, and it can be extracted and recreated by scientists in a laboratory, imagine the benefits! Every British soldier could be given a transfusion before going into battle. Their chances of survival would increase enormously if time slowed for them when they were in danger."

That was a specific, and somewhat unexpected example, given what we knew about Stanley Greville. He suffered shell shock from the war. Why did he want to help the military justify sending more troops into battle? Was it about money, after all? The government would pay extremely well for medicine that could give men life-saving magic. Either we'd been wrong about Stanley's motives, or Alcott's reasons were different.

Willie swore again. "You'd kill Gabe to make a cure for something that's not even a disease? For something that won't even work?"

Mr. Alcott shook his head. "He'll be fine. Stanley doesn't want him to die."

"Look at him! He can't afford to lose any more blood."

Alex put a hand out to calm her, and addressed Alcott. "I've seen men who've lost too much blood. Gabe—" His voice cracked with emotion. He cleared his throat. "Gabe looks like them."

Mr. Alcott hesitated, then shook his head. "Trust Stanley. He's a good man. He only wants what's best for as many people as possible."

Willie scoffed. "At the expense of Gabe's life!"

"If he does die, then it's for the greater good. Why don't you want to save hundreds, if not thousands, of lives?" He shook his head at her, chastising her for her selfishness.

Willie stared at him, speechless.

I took the opportunity to try and reason with Alcott. "Did you enlist?"

He blinked, taken aback by my question. "I was a stretcher-bearer. My two younger brothers fought." The sudden shudder of his chin encouraged me to continue. I was on the right path.

"Does one of them suffer shell shock, like Stanley?"

"One does. The other..." He swallowed. "He didn't make it."

"I'm very sorry for your loss. I lost my brother, too. I miss him."

A wave of emotion washed over me, as it often did when I thought about James. We had been so close, because of our family's constant moves, our cold mother, and our absent father. He'd been my friend, protector, confidant and guide. There would always be a sense of something missing in my life without him in it.

"I understand that you wish you could do something to help your shell-shocked brother," I went on. "But this is not the way." I indicated Gabe, although I didn't look at him. I couldn't. My nerves were shredded and I knew they'd break completely if I saw his vulnerable form again.

"It's not just the shell shock," he said. "It's the deaths…the senseless loss of life. It's too late to help the ones who fought in this war, but there will be other wars, and there are many still employed by the military. We can save them. It might take years, but it begins with him, with studying his blood. Stanley has assured me he will recover."

"He won't if too much blood is taken. You say Stanley believes he won't take a life-endangering amount, but if that's so, why didn't he just ask Gabe to donate it? He could have given just a little over a safe period of time rather than all at once in this filthy hovel. The field tests at the races, the kidnap, the secrecy, all point to Stanley believing Gabe will die from this process and he doesn't want to be arrested for murder."

Alcott's head turned ever so slightly in Gabe's direction without breaking the connection with us altogether. My words had made an impact. Doubts were setting in.

Alex and Willie were utterly silent. I couldn't even hear them breathing. Perhaps they didn't dare for fear of startling Alcott, forcing him to double down on his denials.

"Please," I begged. "You can't murder one man to save others. It's not right. Gabe's life is no less valuable than anyone else's."

"It's mathematical," he told me. "That's what Stanley said. One man to save thousands." Alcott readjusted his grip on the gun handle and squared his shoulders. It was an argument I'd already lost.

I abandoned it. I had one more card to play. It was my last hope. If I didn't crack the shell and get through to him after that, then I had no more. The only recourse left was for one of us to charge at Alcott and draw his fire away from the other two who would rescue Gabe. It was a dreadful choice to make. My next words *had* to work.

I swallowed past the lump in my throat. "Are your parents still alive, Mr. Alcott?"

He shifted his weight from foot to foot. "My mother is."

"Do you remember her reaction to your brother's death?"

"I wasn't there. I was still in France."

"But you did see her, later. I'm sure the pain of losing her son didn't dull in that time. I'm sure it still feels very raw for her, and very painful." He lowered the gun a few inches, as if it were suddenly heavy. "Would you inflict that pain on Gabe's parents? He's their only child."

The gun lowered further. It was now aimed at my legs in a loose grip. Alcott's gaze turned distant, and immeasurably sad.

I tilted my head in the direction of Alex and Willie. "Would you inflict that pain on his friends? On his…his fiancée?"

He gave no sign that he knew it was a lie, and that Gabe had ended his engagement. He simply lowered the gun all the way to his side.

Alex rushed forward and grabbed Alcott's wrist. He disarmed Alcott before I'd even moved.

Willie raced to the bed and pressed a hand on the gash at Gabe's inner elbow, then raised his arm to direct the blood to flow back the other way. As an ambulance driver in the war, she'd picked up a thing or two from the medical staff.

"Find something to use as a tourniquet," she said as she set aside the blood-filled bowl. "Sylvia!"

Her bark snapped me to attention. The knot securing the rope tying Gabe to the bedhead was complicated, but I managed to undo it. I wrapped it around his arm, making sure it was tight, then tied it. Now that I was close, I could see the web of blue veins on his pale eyelids and feel his clammy skin. He was cold.

I fetched his jacket from where it had slipped off the chair to the floor and placed it over him, then I sat beside him on the bed and drew him against me, tucking his head under my chin. I wrapped my arms around him, holding him there, warming him, willing him to wake up and reassure me that he was fine. But his eyes remained closed, and his heart fluttered like a trapped butterfly's wings, weak yet dangerously rapid.

Willie removed her jacket, too, and settled it around him. Then she marched up to Frank Alcott, held at gunpoint by Alex, and punched him in the stomach.

He grunted and doubled over.

Outside, a woman shouted, "Oi! This is private property!"

A male voice responded, but I couldn't hear what he said. Moments later, footsteps thundered up the staircase.

Alex moved so he could keep Alcott in his line of sight while pointing the gun at the door. He lowered it when a constable barged into the room, followed by two more and a sergeant.

Willie thrust her hands on her hips. "It's about time!"

The sergeant nodded at Alcott. "Is this the perpetrator?"

"One of them," Alex said. "He was just about to tell us where his colleague is."

Alcott shook his head. "I can't tell you."

Willie balled her hand into a fist, ready to strike again. "You damn well can!"

"I mean I don't know where he is. He didn't tell me where he was going."

"Is he at the Royal London Hospital? In their research laboratories, testing the first batch of Gabe's blood?"

Alcott shrugged.

I glanced at the bowl. My stomach rolled violently, but I managed not to throw up. I tightened my arms around Gabe. "Speaking of hospitals, Gabe needs a doctor."

The vibration of my voice must have stirred him. He murmured something I couldn't quite hear and lifted his head, but the effort seemed too much for him and he rested it against my chest again. That small movement made my heart explode with relief.

I cupped his face and titled it so I could look at him better.

Seeing his clear green eyes peer back at me shattered the remaining vestiges of my self-control. Tears rolled down my cheeks. "Hello."

"Hello." His voice was barely audible, but it was the most wonderful sound. "Where…?"

"You're sitting on a filthy bed in a Whitechapel tenement owned by Stanley Greville. Frank Alcott, a former orderly who worked at Rosebank, is being arrested as we speak, and we're about to take you to hospital. You've lost a lot of blood.

"Stanley…" he murmured. "Why?"

"It's a long story, but you can ask him yourself when you're better."

He tried to sit up, but couldn't, and slumped against me again. A shiver wracked him. "Cold in here."

"Someone fetch an ambulance from the Royal London Hospital," I said.

Willie shook her head. "That's a bad idea."

The sergeant agreed. "It'll be faster if you take him in your vehicle."

"I meant taking him to the Royal London is a bad idea. Stanley could be there. We have to take Gabe somewhere else."

"It's the closest hospital," Alex said.

Willie had a stubborn look about her. I'd witnessed it before. She wouldn't be moved from her stance. I never thought I'd be so happy to see her return to her demanding, fiery, somewhat irritating self. I wanted to hug her.

She would have voiced further opposition if Gabe hadn't tried standing, only to find he was too weak. He collapsed back onto the bed.

Alex and one of the constables helped him up, propping him between them. "He needs immediate medical attention, Willie," Alex said. "The Royal London is closest."

Willie bit her lip, no longer so sure of herself.

I put an arm around her waist. "We'll take him to the Royal

London and have him assessed. If he requires a transfusion, we'll all stay and keep guard. If not, we'll take him home to rest and have his usual doctor check him there."

She wiped her nose on her sleeve. "His usual doctor went to America with Matt and India, but his colleague will come. All right, we'll go to the Royal London first. But I ain't letting Gabe out of my sight."

Alex and the constable half-carried, half-assisted Gabe out of the room, meeting Cyclops on the landing. Cyclops embraced him. "Are you all right?"

"Fine," Gabe said, his voice sounding stronger.

"We're taking him to the hospital." Alex then told the constable they needed to carry him down the stairs.

Gabe scowled at him. "I can manage."

Alex exchanged a smile of relief with his father.

Cyclops pressed a hand to Gabe's shoulder but didn't speak. He watched Alex and the constable take Gabe downstairs, then cleared his throat and entered the room. He strode up to Alcott, his fists closed. I thought he'd punch Alcott, but he didn't. He drew in a deep breath, uncurled his fists and stretched his fingers.

"You're lucky," he told Alcott.

Alcott kept a wary gaze on Cyclops's hands. "Why?"

"Because Gabe's father isn't here. I swore to abide by a code of conduct; he didn't."

Alcott swallowed again.

"Where's Stanley Greville?" Cyclops asked.

"I don't know."

"We reckon he might be in the research laboratories at the hospital," Willie said. "Send some men to search it. We'll protect Gabe."

She left, but I waited while Cyclops instructed the sergeant to send men to the hospital and take Alcott to Scotland Yard for questioning. Once they were gone, I asked him about Thurlow.

Cyclops removed his hat and rubbed a hand over his head. "He's still at large, as are the Hobson women. Be careful, Sylvia. He might still target you."

"Since I'm going to stay with Gabe for now, I'll have the two best guards with me in Willie and Alex."

He gave me a flat smile. "Get some rest. It's been a long day for you."

I joined Gabe in the back seat of the motorcar and directed him to lean against me. I placed my arms around him and kissed the top of his head. I shouldn't have. I should have resisted my deep-seated urge to hold him if I was going to leave.

But I could not. The time for resisting my urges would come later. For now, I needed to feel his blood pulsing steadily in his veins as much as I needed to breathe.

Cyclops rested a hand on the door and peered inside, checking on Gabe again. "I'll do my best to find out what Alcott knows about Stanley's whereabouts." From the tone of his voice, he did not sound hopeful.

* * *

THE DOCTOR at the Royal London Hospital confirmed that Gabe wouldn't die from blood loss and dismissed the idea of a transfusion when Willie suggested it. "The science behind it is too new. I don't trust it yet. Besides, he's not in dire need." He nodded at Gabe, sleeping on a hospital bed in a busy ward. The pulse in his throat throbbed a little too quickly for my liking, but his breathing was steadier. According to the doctor, that was a good sign at this stage.

Willie began rolling up her sleeve. "If you're worried about finding a match, test my blood. We're cousins."

"It's not simply a matter of giving Mr. Glass blood from the same group as his own. There are other factors that haven't yet been studied sufficiently."

"I saw soldiers get transfusions in field hospitals all the time."

"Did you see them months later? A year or two? Some died, and the scientists don't know why. Is that a risk you want me to take with your cousin?"

Willie rolled down her sleeve. "I suppose if he ain't in immediate danger..."

The doctor hung the clipboard on the end of Gabe's bed. "He just needs rest."

The patient in the bed beside Gabe moaned in pain. Nurses in crisp white uniforms and orderlies in blue ones moved around the ward. A policeman appeared in the doorway, shook his head at us, then left again.

The patient in the bed beside Gabe's threw up.

"We'll take him home," Alex told the doctor.

* * *

WITH GABE SLEEPING in his own bed, Willie shooed Alex and me out of the room, or tried to. Neither Alex nor I wanted to leave Gabe. I suspected for Alex, it was to protect him. He peered out of the window at the street below, as if gauging how easy it would be to scale the wall. When he checked the window's lock was secure, I knew my suspicion was correct.

My focus wasn't on the bedroom's entry points, however. It was on the figure in the bed. The strong, capable man I loved, who looked so uncharacteristically vulnerable, yet I didn't love him any less. It brought out a side of me that I didn't know I possessed, the role of his protector. Willie and Alex could only do so much to keep him safe. I had a part to play, too, and I wanted to play it to the full extent of my abilities. It was all I could think about.

A doctor came and went. Nurse Tilda arrived, too, and promised to stay for as long as necessary. I suspected that was more for Willie's benefit than Gabe's. Willie was as tense as a wound-up toy, but Tilda's presence seemed to calm her.

Mrs. Bristow brought in food, but none of us felt like eating. She, Bristow and the other servants came in from time to time, using one excuse or another. They didn't fool anyone. They all needed to see Gabe for themselves.

The only visitor who managed to draw us out of the bedroom was Cyclops, and that was only because we didn't want to wake Gabe with our voices. We left Tilda to watch over him and retreated to the dining room where Mrs. Ling's delicious Chinese cooking enticed us all to finally eat something.

While he transferred food from the various dishes to his plate, Cyclops told us about the interrogation of Frank Alcott. "I'm positive he doesn't know where Stanley Greville is at this point in time. Stanley went to test the first batch of Gabe's blood, but he didn't tell Alcott where he was going."

"The Royal London Hospital," Willie said, as if it were obvious.

"My men questioned the staff, and no one had seen him. I've kept some constables there to watch for him, as well as at Milsom Court."

Willie snorted. "Reckon the whores ain't happy about that."

"Alcott told me that Stanley enlisted his help on a recent visit to Rosebank. His first task was to stab Gabe in the shoulder, but he didn't want to do it. He knew he'd be arrested immediately. So, Stanley concocted a plan to have one of the patients with little hope of a full recovery do it instead."

"That's despicable," I murmured. Stanley had been an excellent actor to keep this side of himself from his friends.

Willie picked up a spring roll from her plate and pointed it at Cyclops. "The attacker said God made him do it. Stanley must have told him he was God. Frank Alcott went along with it, maybe even encouraged the patient, too."

Cyclops nodded. "He admitted he did. He also admitted his role in this kidnap."

"It's too late to deny it! We caught him red-handed."

"What about the kidnapping attempts prior to the stabbing?" Alex asked.

"Alcott claims he wasn't involved then," Cyclops said. "Apparently Stanley hired help when he needed it. When they continued to fail, only then did Stanley resort to someone he knew from his time at Rosebank, someone capable who would be as invested as Stanley once he explained his motive for studying Gabe."

Willie stabbed a dumpling with the end of her chopstick. "Good job getting him to confess. You must have been real hard on him."

He looked up from his plate where he was expertly using his chopsticks to scoop up food. "I did nothing unethical."

She rolled her eyes. "You and your rules. I miss Duke."

I knew that Duke was a friend of Cyclops, Willie and Gabe's parents who'd moved back to America. He departed England years ago, but they often spoke about him as if he'd just stepped out to run an errand and would return soon.

Willie popped the dumpling in her mouth, but that didn't stop her talking. "Duke and I got up to a lot of mischief." She must have been directing her comment to me because Cyclops and Alex would already have heard her stories. It was so rare for her to include me that I stayed silent and waited for more.

Cyclops got in first, however. "I'm sure Tilda would like to know just how much mischief." He leaned back in the chair and rubbed his stomach with satisfaction. "I've been meaning to spend more time with her."

Willie glared at him as she stabbed another dumpling with her chopstick.

Alex looked between them, shaking his head. "Can you two stop reminiscing about your delinquent pasts and talk about finding Stanley?"

Cyclops sat forward. "You're right. This is serious. Willie, I didn't use underhanded methods to get Alcott to talk. I merely reminded him that he's in a lot of trouble. He then claimed that Stanley brainwashed him into believing that studying Gabe would have enormous benefits for thousands of men. He's not taking responsibility for his own actions."

"Coward," Willie muttered.

Cyclops turned to me. "I asked him about Thurlow, but he'd not heard of him. I don't think there's any connection between them. It just happened that Thurlow wanted to use Gabe's magic for himself, as Stanley did."

"What about the Hobsons?" I asked. "He knew Bertie."

"Alcott says he doesn't remember him. I believe him."

I pushed the rice around my plate with my chopsticks. I no longer felt like eating. Indeed, I felt sick to my stomach.

"Are you trying to make a pattern?" Cyclops asked gently.

I set my chopsticks down, my decision made. "Remember when you promised not to tell Gabe that Thurlow and the Hobson women abducted me? I'd like you to keep that promise."

Cyclops shook his head. "I don't like secrets."

"It doesn't have to be forever. Just while he's weak. He'll be worried and that worry won't help his recovery. He'll want to get out of bed before he's ready and look for Thurlow himself."

Willie and Alex understood my point and encouraged Cyclops to agree. Finally, he did.

"Speaking of not telling people about kidnappings," Alex said to his father, "have you told Mum about Gabe?"

"Not yet."

"Best not to."

"I definitely don't keep secrets from your mother. Trust me, Son, it's never a good idea to keep something from your wife. For one thing, she'll always find out. For another, women are stronger than they look. Sometimes I think they're stronger than us."

Willie scoffed. "Only sometimes?"

I hardly heard their banter. I was drowning in my own

misery, and everything else was simply background noise to the one thought screaming inside my head—Gabe wasn't safe from Thurlow and anyone else who decided I was the way to lure him. I had to protect him using every means at my disposal.

I had to leave, just as I'd originally planned.

CHAPTER 14

Mrs. Bristow made up the spare bedroom for me, while Sally found a nightgown and clean clothing that I could use. My initial thought was to refuse, since I'd packed my own things that morning, but my cases weren't in the room. With all the confusion and chaos of the day, I'd misplaced them. The last time I recalled seeing them was outside Huon's house early that morning when Cyclops transferred them from the taxi to his vehicle. They might still be on the back seat, forgotten. Or he might have deliberately not given them back to me in the hope I wouldn't leave London without my luggage.

I hadn't told him that I still planned to leave, and he gave no indication that he assumed I would. Perhaps he thought I'd changed my mind. After all, I'd been so relieved to see Gabe safe that I'd not hidden my love for him from anyone.

It was a setback not to have my personal things with me, particularly the sentimental items that had belonged to my mother and brother, and the Hendry family journal. Gabe would see that the Hendry sisters were given the journal, and he'd keep my other belongings safe. It's unlikely I'd see them again, unless Stanley, Thurlow and the Hobson women were all caught. Even then, there would be others who tried to use me to get to Gabe.

I twisted my mother's silver ring on my finger. It was all I had left of her.

The moment I climbed into the soft bed, exhaustion overtook me. The lack of sleep from the night before, as well as the emotional toll of the day, had finally caught up. I managed to set the alarm clock beside the bed before nodding off. It would wake me at a quarter to five, giving me time to leave before the servants started. I didn't want to face Bristow's censorious glare. I wanted to slip quietly away hours before my absence was discovered.

* * *

I HAD no idea what time I awoke. The room was dark, but that didn't mean it was still nighttime. The curtains were so thick, and covered the window so fully, that no light would have crept in even if it was sunny outside. The house was quiet, so that was no help either. I rolled over and glanced at the bedside clock. Ten past nine! Why didn't the alarm go off?

I flung off the covers and picked up the clock. Perhaps the time was inaccurate because Sally hadn't wound it recently since this was a rarely used room. But surely the clocks belonging to the world's strongest horology magician kept perfect time regardless of when they'd been wound. I looked closer and groaned. In my exhaustion, I'd mixed up the minute and hour hands and instead of setting the alarm for a quarter to five, I'd set it for twenty-five past nine. It was due to go off in fifteen minutes.

My plan to leave while the household slept was scuttled.

As I dressed, I considered whether to leave during the day while no one was looking or wait until nighttime, when everyone was in bed. Leaving later would give me the opportunity to find my cases.

I decided to see how the day progressed. If an opportunity arose to slip away unnoticed, I'd take it.

The one good thing about a delay meant I could see how Gabe fared. Hopefully after a solid rest, he was feeling stronger. The spare bedchamber was on the same floor as Gabe's room, but I passed it without knocking on the door. I didn't want to wake him. Indeed, I didn't want to speak to him. The fewer opportunities there were to surrender to my heart's desire, the better. This was a time for my head to rule.

I met Murray on the landing. He directed me to the dining room where breakfast had been laid out. He also informed me that Gabe was sleeping peacefully.

I found quite a crowd in the dining room. Joining Alex and Willie at the table were Nurse Tilda, Daisy, Petra, Huon, and Professor Nash. The sideboard was full, some of the serving dishes still covered to keep their contents warm. The smell of coffee beckoned me.

Daisy intercepted me on my way to the sideboard and embraced me in a fierce hug. "Thank goodness you're still here. I was so worried you'd sneak off in the night now that you know Gabe will be all right." She didn't whisper. Indeed, her voice was rather loud.

I glanced past her to see everyone looking at me, yet not a single brow arched in question at her words. Only Petra, Huon and Daisy knew I had planned to leave. I'd not informed Alex, Willie or the professor.

"We told them," Petra said, answering my unspoken question.

"And we're not sorry about it," Huon added. "Not even a little bit."

Daisy squeezed my hand. "We won't let you leave, Sylvia. While it's a good idea in theory—"

"No, it ain't," Willie said. "It's a bad idea. A real bad one."

Tilda, seated beside Willie, cleared her throat. "I'm glad to see you heeded my advice."

Willie sniffed. "I'm used to Sylvia now, and I can't be bothered getting to know another girl."

"What about my father?" Perhaps it was foolish of me to bring him up, but I wanted to test if she truly had accepted me. "Are you no longer worried I'll attract Melville Hendry into Gabe's life?"

Willie fished what appeared to be a bullet out of her pocket. "I'm ready for Hendry. If he comes here and creates a paper storm, I'll use this." She unscrewed the top of the casing to reveal a small wheel. "An injured soldier I drove to a field hospital at the Somme gave me this pocket cigarette lighter. He made it from a used shrapnel shell when he was waiting around in the trenches." She spun the small wheel with her thumb creating a spark that ignited the fuel inside the shell. "Fire beats paper. I win."

Daisy squeezed my hand again, but before she could ask me if I still planned to leave, I asked Tilda how Gabe was. I wanted a professional opinion.

"He awoke briefly in the night, disoriented but well enough to tell me he was thirsty. Hopefully he'll eat something this morning. Mrs. Ling is preparing him a steak. Red meat is what he needs now, and a lot of water."

I released a breath. "That is good news."

Daisy gave me a little push in the direction of the sideboard. "You need to eat, too. There aren't any steaks, but there seems to be everything else. I haven't eaten such a hearty breakfast since visiting my mother's cousin before the war. His estate was enormous, and he had triple the servants we had." She laughed, only to suddenly stop when she caught sight of Alex. "I never liked him much," she added quickly. "His children are as dull as a muddy puddle and his wife likes to remind my mother how much better off they are than my parents. I wouldn't care if I never saw any of them again."

Without looking at her, Alex got up and joined me at the sideboard. He took a long time searching for the perfect rasher of bacon. I'd poured myself a cup of coffee, and spread butter and marmalade on my toast before he placed a single rasher on his plate.

I took the serving fork off him. "You can't ignore her forever."

His jaw firmed.

"You love her and she loves you. Being together is what matters. Whether you decide to cut her family out of your lives or educate them, it's a decision you should make together. You can't decide what's best for her without consulting her."

"Is that so," he said with a heavy dose of sarcasm.

"My situation is different. Gabe's life is at stake."

He put out his hand, asking for the serving fork back. "You're going to go through with it, aren't you?"

I pressed my lips together.

He sighed. "I know I should encourage you to stay, but I know that real love makes you want to put their well-being above your own, even when they don't agree that it's for their own good." His gaze slid to Daisy seated at the table. She suddenly looked away, pretending she hadn't been watching us. "It bloody well hurts when you can't be together," he went on in a murmur, "but sometimes one of us has to be strong enough for both and make the difficult decisions. Gabe would do the same for you, Sylvia, if your positions were reversed."

He seemed to be waiting for me to tell him that Daisy would end their relationship if *she* was the reason for an estrangement from *his* family. But I couldn't give him that assurance. Alex's family made that scenario an impossible one to fathom. There was no comparison, as there would never be a situation in which his parents would deny him the woman he loved because they didn't like the way she looked or what level of society she came from.

I handed him the serving fork and joined the others at the dining table. I sat beside Professor Nash, knowing he would have something to say to me. I got in first, however.

"I wanted to say goodbye in person, but the timing… I had to hurry."

He pushed his glasses up his nose, but they immediately slipped down again because he didn't look up from his plate.

"I would have written as soon as possible and enclosed my library key."

"The key is unimportant. I don't want to lose you, Sylvia."

"You don't need my help, Professor. There isn't a great deal of work to do at the library, but if you feel as though you need an assistant, there will be many who would enjoy the job. There's a shortage of employment opportunities now that all the men have come home, and it truly is a wonderfully peaceful place."

"That isn't the point, Sylvia." The genial, even-tempered professor had never sounded so angry. Although his anger was mild when compared to Willie's ferocious temper, it startled me more.

"I'm sorry," I murmured, dropping my hands to my lap. I was no longer hungry.

The professor used a knife and fork to cut his buttered toast into small squares, but he didn't eat any of them. He didn't apologize for his outburst. I'd hurt his feelings deeply, and that hurt mine.

The only way to fix things between us was to admit the real reason I didn't make the effort to go to the library after packing my belongings. "I couldn't face you," I said.

He hesitated. "What do you mean?"

"I couldn't be in the library, surrounded by all those wonderful books with a close connection to Gabe's family, and have to say goodbye to someone who's been like a father to me these last few months. It was too hard, and I'm a coward."

He set the knife and fork down and placed his hand over mine. "You're not a coward, Sylvia. I think the word you're looking for is afraid. You're very brave, but you're not fearless. Few people are. Not even Willie, for all her swagger. In fact, I'd say the only people who are not afraid are those without feelings for others, because to care for someone is to fear for them, and to love them, sometimes without having that love reciprocated. Love and fear are inextricably bound together, and we mere humans can't accept one without the other." He shook my hand to draw my attention. I sat so still that he must have wondered if he'd got through to me.

My throat was tight, making my voice reedy. "You know that I'm still planning to leave to protect Gabe, don't you?"

He gave me a grim smile. "Before you came downstairs, they told me you were kidnapped to lure him. Your kidnappers haven't been caught, which means he's still in danger. But there is no guarantee running away will stop them altogether. The only thing it guarantees is the unhappiness of two people."

"He'll move on."

"Will he? To the outside world, he might appear as though he has, but he won't. Not truly. Not in here." He tapped his chest. "One day, perhaps years later, after thinking he has locked all thoughts of you away in a corner of his heart, a crack will develop. The memories will be released, a mere trickle at first, then they'll come flooding out." He gave my hand a firm pat and shifted closer to me in his urgency to get his point across. "You're fortunate that you have not only found a grand love, but you have the opportunity to hold on to it. Take it, Sylvia. It's not going away."

He spoke from the heart, with an earnestness that I felt through our linked hands. I couldn't dismiss such a passionate plea lightly, so I chose my next words with great care. "Gabe and I will both be deeply hurt, and perhaps that hurt will always be with us. But at least he'll be safe."

He sat back with a heavy sigh.

"Don't tell him I still plan to go," I said. "Or anyone else. Not yet."

"You mean not until after you've left?"

"He'll be all right. He'll have his friends with him, and his parents will return from America soon. Hopefully they'll help him find Thurlow and the Hobson women, and Stanley Greville, too."

"Will you return once they're arrested?"

I stared into my coffee cup. "There'll always be people who want to study him and find a way to replicate his magic. And yes, I know there are others in his life that he cares about who could be used to lure him, but I will be seen as the easier target, the one he cares about most." I shook my head emphatically. "I can't be the weak link that makes him vulnerable. I couldn't live with myself if something happened to him because of me."

The professor picked up his fork and stabbed a square of toast. "I see you've made up your mind," he said stiffly.

This was going to be harder than I expected.

"Prof, you strike me as a romantic." Huon's voice held a hint of humor, something we all badly needed at that moment. "We need your opinion."

The professor blinked back at him through his spectacles. "A romantic? Oh no, no, no. I've not been… I don't have…" He tugged on his cuff. "That is to say, women are a mystery to me."

"And to me, although I've been with—" Huon cleared his throat, taking great pains not to look at Petra, seated beside him. "That is to say, women are a mystery worth solving."

"Fun, too," Willie said, winking at Tilda.

With a light blush to her cheeks, Tilda rose. "I'd better check on my patient." She kissed Willie on the forehead and left.

"What's your romantic dilemma that requires opinions?" I asked Huon.

"I want to know what grand gestures a fellow can do for the woman he admires above all others." He still didn't look at Petra, and I realized I was the only one who knew they'd spent the night together. Although Daisy was aware of their previous encounters and probably suspected Huon was speaking about Petra, she didn't look her way either.

Petra tore off a corner of her toast and popped it in her

mouth. She tore off another piece, and another, giving the toast her full attention.

"I am unable to advise you," Professor Nash said. "Alex?"

Alex's looked somewhat startled. "Ummm…"

"I was thinking of a public declaration," Huon added.

"Of your admiration for her?" Willie shook her head. "The thing is, grand public gestures are for the one making them, they ain't for the one receiving them."

"What do you mean?" Daisy asked.

"The one making the gesture only does it publicly if they want *everyone*, not just the intended recipient, to think they're wonderful. It doesn't make her feel special because she knows it's not about her, it's about the one making the gesture. That's why some men propose in a public place. Steer clear of those men, ladies. They're seeking attention for themselves, which means they're too selfish to love completely."

Daisy nodded thoughtfully. "I always suspected you were wise, Willie."

Willie looked a little surprised. "I've always suspected it, too."

"After all, one doesn't get to be as old as you and not learn a few things along the way."

Alex snickered, which made Daisy smile.

Willie threw a sugar cube at him, but he caught it deftly and popped it into his coffee cup.

"Right, so no public declarations of love," Huon said. "Understood. What about public gestures of another kind, that are not romantic in themselves, but she will appreciate nonetheless?" When he realized none of us followed his meaning, he elaborated. "What if I place an advertisement in a newspaper stating that pencils are better for sketching than ink, and that as an ink magician, I fully endorse Petra's pencils which are available exclusively from her shop."

Petra choked on a crumb of toast.

Huon turned to her. "Will that prove to you that I'm serious?" There was no humor in his voice anymore, just the cadence of a man trying to make a good impression on a woman he admired, perhaps even loved.

We all leaned forward in anticipation of her response.

"He's awake." Tilda's words, spoken from the doorway, caused a flurry of activity.

Willie was the first one out of the dining room. I thought Alex might be next, but he hung back. I had no intention of seeing Gabe, so I remained in the dining room, too. As Huon passed him, Alex caught his arm.

"Your families don't get on, do they?" He nodded at Petra, already out of the dining room and heading for the staircase. Daisy walked by her side. "Putting an advertisement in the newspaper supporting her family's magic will disappoint your own. I know you haven't had a close relationship with your father in the past, but do you really want to be cut off now when you've recently got back into his good books?"

Huon's lips curved with a knowing smile. "She's worth it."

"It's a lot to give up. Are you sure?"

"If my family can't accept her, and accept that I love her, then losing them is a sacrifice I'm willing to make. That's what love means, Alex. It means making a sacrifice when necessary and making it willingly. If someone is prepared to do that for you, then it's pointless trying to oppose them because it means they are very much in love with you." Huon's gaze followed Petra and Daisy, climbing the stairs. "You may as well embrace her sacrifice, my friend. She's not going to change her mind." He rather ruined the lovely sentiment by adding, "Once a woman's mind is made up, it's almost impossible to get her to change it."

Huon left, and Alex went to follow him, but seemed to notice me for the first time. "Coming, Sylvia?"

"You go on. I need to speak to Bristow."

I found Bristow in the basement service rooms, instructing Murray on how to present Gabe's breakfast on the tray.

"I know how to do it," Murray growled.

Bristow slapped his hands together behind his back, the only sign that Murray's retort annoyed him.

He spotted me and welcomed me into the kitchen. He used to dislike it when I called on the servants during my visits. He'd been raised in a time when social hierarchy was the loom on which the fabric of society was woven, and he was struggling to adapt to the more fluid landscape of the postwar era. Although Gabe had told me his household had never been formal, Bristow had been in service for years before Gabe's father moved into the Park Street house, and his English relatives had been aristocratic to their core.

Mrs. Bristow gave me a soft smile that had all of her wrinkles crinkling. "Perhaps Miss Ashe would like to take Mr. Glass his breakfast."

I stepped back when Murray tried to pass the tray to me. "No, I'm not going there directly."

Mrs. Bristow's face fell. She and Mrs. Ling shared a frown.

"Bristow, did Cyclops leave some things here for me?" I asked.

"He did, Miss Ashe." He glanced at his wife.

Her smile of encouragement was fleeting, but I noticed it.

I was about to ask if there was a problem when Bristow offered to take me to my cases.

"Couldn't Murray just bring them to my room after he delivers Gabe's breakfast?" I indicated the footman as he left carrying the tray.

Either Bristow didn't hear me or he pretended not to. He simply asked me to follow him.

I cast a frown back at Mrs. Bristow and Mrs. Ling then followed the butler out of the kitchen. His gait was slow, particularly up the staircase, but we eventually reached the floor with the main bedrooms.

"If the cases are already in my room, there's no need for you to accompany me," I told him.

Again, he either didn't hear me or pretended not to.

As we approached Gabe's room, chatter spilled out through the open door to the passageway. A number of voices spoke over each other, all of them telling Gabe about the events of yesterday. He must be feeling much better, otherwise Nurse Tilda would have sent everyone out so he could continue to rest.

Hopefully with everyone crowding around and his breakfast now delivered, Gabe would be too distracted to see me sneak past his door to get to the guest bedroom.

Bristow stopped, however, ensuring we were visible from Gabe's room. The butler announced me before I could move around him.

All conversations ceased. Everyone turned to me, parting so that I had a clear line of sight to Gabe, sitting up in bed. If he was pleased to see me, he didn't show it. He scowled and crooked his finger, beckoning me.

"I want to talk to you, Sylvia."

CHAPTER 15

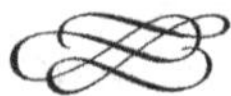

I swallowed the lump forming in my throat. Gabe looked so much better than the last time I'd seen him. Although he was still pale, some of his color had returned. The shadows under his eyes were dark, but the eyes themselves were bright and focused.

They were focused on me. "Can we talk, Sylvia," he said again.

"Perhaps later. Bristow was just about to give me something."

"Do you mean those?" Gabe pointed to the corner of his bedroom where my cases sat on the floor. "Mrs. Bristow thought they needed very particular attention so left them in my care while I was sleeping this morning."

"How can you care for them while you're asleep?" Willie asked.

Tilda jabbed her in the ribs with her elbow and shushed her.

Gabe put out his hand, inviting me in. "Sylvia. Please."

His earnest plea and imploring gaze almost shattered me. I folded my arms across my body, hoping that would hold me together, and shook my head. "No, Gabe."

"Very well. If you won't come to me, I'll come to you." He

pushed the covers back and swung his legs over the edge of the bed. He stood, but the effort made him dizzy and he sat heavily on the mattress again.

He received a round of scolds from everyone. Then they turned accusatory glares onto me.

I'd not been aware of having rushed forward when he collapsed, but I found myself standing several steps inside the room, so I must have.

Gabe patted the bed beside him. "If you don't come here then I'll have to try and stand again."

"This is emotional blackmail."

He smiled smugly.

Petra made a shooing motion. "Everyone out."

I turned to go, but Daisy, the nearest to me, caught me by the shoulders.

"Not you." She stood in front of me, blocking my line of sight to Gabe. "As your best friend, it is up to me to tell you that you are being an idiot, Sylvia." She put a finger to my lips as I began to protest. "I've already heard your excuses, and I think they're bollocks. We all do." She took my hand and dragged me over to the bed. She released it, only for Gabe to capture it instead.

I was trapped.

But I still had some fight left in me, and I still had right on my side. The only way to stay on course, however, was to not be in the orbit of Gabe's magnetic presence. I indicated the tray Murray had set on the bedside table. "Eat your breakfast, Gabe. Tilda, tell him he needs to eat."

There was no answer.

I turned around to see they'd all left, and the door was closed. I tugged my trapped hand, but Gabe's grip only tightened. "This conversation needs to happen when you're better," I said. "You're too weak now."

He pulled me down onto the bed beside him. His beautiful sea-green eyes raked over my face, as if he'd not seen me in a very long time. I was so distracted by his eyes that I didn't see his mouth until it was too late. "I'm not too weak that I can't do this." The smile teasing his lips vanished.

He kissed me.

There was no hesitation in it, no question that I might reject him. It was an utterly confident kiss, certain that I'd already given in and was going to stay.

It was wonderful.

Every reason I'd had for leaving fled. There was a part of me that still tried to listen to my head and not my heart, but it was drowned out by the tide of yearning. Gabe's kiss branded his point of view on me as thoroughly as his lips seared mine.

It took his dizzy spell to separate us. He sank into the pillows, his face dreadfully pale again.

"Gabe!" I searched his eyes and was relieved to see them refocus.

"I'm all right," he murmured. "I probably should eat."

I settled the tray across his lap and watched as he tucked into his steak. Only when he'd eaten half did I ask him what he knew. "Did they tell you what Thurlow did?"

"That he abducted you? And that my former fiancée and her mother helped?" He lowered the knife and fork to the tray with a shake of his head. "I can't believe how badly I misjudged Ivy. I knew well before I ended the relationship that I didn't love her and never had, but I thought she was a decent person. Then again, apparently I'm not a good judge of character, as evidenced by Stanley's actions." He heaved a sigh as he went back to cutting the steak.

"Both Ivy and Stanley have been driven to the brink, making them do things they wouldn't normally do. In Stanley's case, the war changed him. Returning home to a society that dismissed his shell shock as his own fault for not coping when other men did…it left him feeling isolated and alone."

"He wasn't alone. He had friends. Juan and I wouldn't abandon him."

"I know you wouldn't, but Stanley's mind is in a very dark place."

"Do you think he can be brought back from it? He was taking medication before. Perhaps he could have a stronger dose."

I curled into his side and hugged his arm. "I don't know, Gabe. I don't think anyone knows, including the doctors."

"I'll try to talk to him."

I sat up straight. "Don't deliberately place yourself in danger or I *will* leave."

He gave me a grim-faced nod. "I won't."

"Gabe, you have to be prepared for the worst. If he tries to kidnap you again, Alex, Willie and Cyclops will stop at nothing to release you. Nor will I."

He nodded again, even more grim-faced. He understood that Stanley probably wouldn't survive if he jeopardized Gabe's life a second time. "The thing is," he said, "that may be the whole point. He could be counting on retaliation. Hoping for it, even."

He finished his steak then set aside the tray. I poured him a glass of water from the jug and made him drink all of it then made him drink another. I refilled the glass and reached across him to place it on the bedside table nearest him. Once the glass was safely put down, he circled his arm around my waist and drew me on top of him.

He stroked my hair back and kissed me again. This time it was soft and tender, although no less confident. He harbored no doubts about his own feelings toward me, just as he harbored none about my feelings for him. In anyone else, it would be arrogant. On him, the self-confidence was natural.

After a moment, I could tell something was on his mind and drew back. "Go on, Gabe. Say it."

"With Thurlow and the Hobsons free, I don't want you returning to your place. You should stay here. Alex said there are constables at the front and back doors." He searched my face. "Please stay, Sylvia. I'm too weakened to worry about you, and I will worry if you're not here with me." It was the occasional vulnerable moments like this that stopped him from being arrogant. If I harbored any more doubts about staying, these moments would have banished them completely.

"I suppose I'd better, since I don't want Willie blaming me for making you unwell."

He cupped my face and kissed me.

A knock on the door separated us. I scooted off the bed and self-consciously adjusted my skirt and blouse. Gabe bade his visitor to enter.

The door crashed back on its hinges and Alex's three younger sisters barreled inside, followed by their mother, Catherine, at a more modest pace. I could tell from her face that she was no less relieved to see him well. Indeed, I suspected she'd been crying.

Lulu, the youngest at seventeen, was still crying as she threw her arms around Gabe. Mae, the middle sister, allowed her only a few seconds before she told Lulu to move aside. Ella, the toughest of the trio and policewoman in training, stood with hands on hips as she waited for her turn. When she finally hugged Gabe then pulled away, she wiped her nose on her sleeve.

Mae pulled a face. "That's disgusting. It's no wonder you don't have any suitors."

Lulu gasped. "Are you crying, Ella? Look everyone, Ella is *crying*. She *is* a real person and not an automaton."

Ella gave her sister a withering glare. "Shut up."

"All right, that's enough," Catherine chided. "You've all seen that he's well, now let him rest.

They filed out, joining Alex where he stood in the corridor.

Catherine stayed. She hugged Gabe fiercely. "I am very glad you're all right, but I'm not looking forward to telling Matt and India what happened."

"They don't have to know."

"If you think Nate and I are going to keep something so important from them, you don't know us at all." She handed him the glass from the bedside table. "Tilda says you need to drink lots of water."

"Sylvia just made me drink two glasses."

She continued to hold it out, so he gave in and drank. When he finished, she put the empty glass back on the table and tucked in the sheet under the mattress where it had come loose.

"Is Cyclops here?" Gabe asked.

Catherine continued tucking the sheet, shoving it again and again under the mattress, even though it was perfect the first time. "He's looking for your respective kidnappers." She smoothed the bedcovers beside him, flattening the wrinkles I'd created. "Speaking of which, Nate and I think you should stay here, Sylvia. I know India and Matt would approve, so you don't have to worry about how it looks."

"She has already agreed," Gabe said, watching Catherine vigorously whip her hand across the perfectly flat bedcovers.

"Good. Now, did Alex tell you there are constables at the front and back doors?"

"He did."

"I see you've eaten all of your breakfast." With the bedcovers smoother at Gabe's side than even Mrs. Bristow managed to get them, Catherine returned to tucking in the sheet under the mattress.

"Nurse Tilda threatened me with a lecture from Willie if I didn't," Gabe said.

"Good for her. I like her a lot."

Gabe caught her hand. "Catherine, I'm all right."

She stopped fussing and pressed her lips together as tears welled in her eyes. Once she was composed again, she gave him a wobbly smile. "I know. But it gave us all a scare." She folded her other hand over his. "Now, promise me you'll stay in this bed until the doctor says you're well enough to leave the house. Don't go gallivanting around the city looking for the kidnappers."

"I promise to listen to doctor's orders."

Satisfied, she pecked his forehead before leaving and closing the door again.

I stood beside the bed, arms crossed, my gaze narrowed.

He blinked back at me, all long dark lashes and innocent eyes.

"You may have hoodwinked Catherine, but it won't work on me, Gabe. We don't want your promise to *listen* to the doctor; we want your promise to *heed* his advice. There will be no leaving this house until he approves. Understood?"

His grin turned devilish. He suddenly circled me in his arms, drawing me onto the bed again. I rose above him, on my knees, and peered down at him. "I like this stern side of you," he said.

I unfolded my arms and rested them on his shoulders, stroking my fingers through his hair. "I want you to know that I am aware that you still haven't promised."

"Noted. But?"

"What makes you think there's a but?"

"Hope."

I smiled. "But we're alone and all I can think about is kissing you again." So I did.

* * *

THE FOLLOWING DAY, I felt like our troubles had melted away. Number sixteen Park Street became its own bubble of safety with friends dropping by and the constables guarding the doors. I ensconced myself in Gabe's library after the professor deposited a box of books at the house. He'd retrieved them from the Glass Library's attic and assigned them to me for cataloging. He knew being surrounded by paper and books was precisely what I needed. Not only did it keep my mind occupied, but the magic within me responded to all that paper. It soothed my nerves just as much as the presence of the constables did.

I suspected my magic also responded to the magic in the Hendry family journal. I'd started reading it before the box of books arrived, but set it aside to work. The paper magic infused into every page of the journal was a strong magnet, however, and I found my attention often wandering to it.

As if the book had summoned him, a most unexpected visitor in the form of Melville Hendry arrived. I was so surprised to see him—not least because he was wearing a false beard—that I forgot my manners and left him standing there in the library doorway looking rather uncertain. It wasn't until I shook off my surprise that I remembered he must have problematic memories of this house and its owners, just as they had of him. Bristow's severe scowl was testament to that. He and Willie had both been here all those years ago. I must never forget that my father had done terrible things to Gabe's parents. If I was to have a happy future as a part of Gabe's family, I mustn't let Melville ruin it.

It struck me like a hammer blow that this had to be our final encounter.

Bristow cleared his throat. "May I take your disguise, Mr. Hendry?"

Melville removed the false beard and placed it inside his hat, but refused to hand them to Bristow.

I invited him in, then asked him to sit. It wasn't lost on me that we were surrounded by weapons both of us could wield if necessary. Except I hadn't yet learned to control the paper I directed using the moving spell, whereas Melville had years of practice.

"I'll inform Mr. Glass of your visitor, Miss Ashe," Bristow intoned.

"He was asleep last time I checked, and I'd like him to keep resting. Please inform Willie and Alex instead. On second thought, just Alex."

"Isn't he the police detective's son?" Melville asked after Bristow left. "I don't want him to know I'm here."

"Then you shouldn't have come. Don't worry, he won't arrest you.

Having Alex as my guard was rather pointless, given all the

paper contained in the library. I simply didn't want Bristow waking Gabe, so having Alex nearby might appease the butler's concerns.

Melville looked around the library with wonder. "He's fortunate to have all this at his fingertips."

"He appreciates his good fortune."

"There's paper magic in that green leather-bound one on the second-top shelf."

"I know."

While he didn't smile, I could tell my answer pleased him. He studied me, his gaze lingering on the features that I'd inherited from the Hendry side. My fair coloring, freckled nose and the shape of my mouth, so I'd been told. "You *are* my daughter," he finally said.

"Yes."

This time he did smile, but it was fleeting, almost as if he was embarrassed. "You received the journal." He nodded at the family book on the table. "Keep it safe until it's time to pass it on to the next generation."

"I will. Speaking of time, the book mentions a prophecy whereby a member of the Hendreau family will save time. Do you know what that means?"

"No. It's not important anyway. What's important is that you learn the spells in the journal. Have you tried them?"

"I've been busy, but I learned the moving spell. I have trouble controlling the power, though. I suppose I just need practice."

He indicated the crate of books I still had to catalog. "Then why aren't you?"

"Because I have work to do," I snapped.

Alex entered the library. He nodded at Hendry but remained by the door, arms crossed over his chest. His gaze flitted around the room, taking in all the books packed onto the shelves. If he was worried about them being weaponized, he didn't show it.

Hendry smoothed his hand over the journal's cover. "The key to controlling your magic is to focus it."

"How do I do that?"

"Concentrate."

"On what?"

"The words, your target…" He sounded annoyed, so I didn't press him. "I've been thinking about you ever since we met in the café." He paused, perhaps waiting for me to say that I'd been thinking about him, too. Perhaps I would have, if I hadn't been so preoccupied. "I didn't want to tell you some things then. They were painful memories that I thought never to bring up again. But I stand by what I said in the café: every child has a right to know their origins. So, I've decided to tell you some things."

I was taken aback. I'd given up hope of learning answers to questions that had eaten away at me for years. "Thank you. That would be appreciated."

He shifted his weight in the chair, taking a long time to begin. I bit down on my tongue to ensure my frustration at the delay didn't boil over. "I already told you that Lord Coyle set Marianne and me up together. He blackmailed us both."

"I know he got you out of prison. You felt you owed him."

"He helped Marianne, too. We were both at our lowest points, desperate, afraid, alone. We both owed him favors in return for his help, and having children together was how he wanted us to pay him back. That was his only condition for his assistance, and we couldn't refuse."

"Even so, what he asked you to do is extreme."

"It wasn't easy to get me out of prison. I owed him an enormous debt, which I paid."

"Even though being with a woman was abhorrent to you."

"I don't dislike women, no matter what my sisters tell you." Despite the denial, he didn't meet my gaze.

"And my mother?" I asked. "How did Coyle save her?"

"Marianne's father was cruel. She ran away and came here to London, where she became known to Coyle. I suspect it was because she was selling off items containing her father's silversmith magic that she'd stolen before leaving Ipswich, and someone noticed and informed Coyle. Such a rare magic would have immediately grabbed his attention."

"So he helped her when she moved to London?" I shrugged. "That's hardly a favor worthy of her pound of flesh."

"His way of helping her was to kill her parents."

My head began to buzz, as if he'd struck me. In a way, he had. The news was so shocking that I could barely comprehend it. I remembered my mother's old neighbor in Ipswich telling us about the fire that had killed my grandparents, but it hadn't occurred to me that Marianne was the reason for the fire, even if she hadn't lit it herself. According to the neighbor, she'd left some time before that dreadful night.

Coyle had started the fire, or sent someone to do it, killing Marianne's parents for her sake, to keep her safe. At moments like this, when we used the name Marianne Folgate, it was a little easier to disassociate that person from my mother, the woman I knew as Alice Ashe.

But no amount of pretending ignorance could deny the fact that Alice was Marianne, and she'd either asked Coyle to free her from her cruel father, or known he was going to take matters into his own hands. Otherwise, she wouldn't have felt obligated to return the favor.

"Her father doesn't deserve sympathy," Melville said, following my train of thought. "He *was* violent toward her."

"And her mother? Did she deserve to die so horribly?"

"She was complicit, by not protecting Marianne. It's a mother's duty to take care of her children." He gave a humorless grunt. "It's rather an ironic admission for me to make, don't you think?"

I frowned. "Yes, I do. She fled from you for the very same reason."

"I was never violent."

I waited. There had to be more. My mother had run from him for years, well after Lord Coyle died.

Finally, he gave in. He cleared his throat. "I admit I was...

cruel to her in other, non-physical, ways. I took advantage of her anger and fear at the situation she'd found herself in, and her youth and loneliness. I let my feelings about women in general color my interactions with her. I was angry, too, at finding myself in that predicament. Coupled with the fact that I had to hide my natural instincts when it came to loving men rather than women, *and* hide my magic, as we all had to in those days…I lashed out at someone weaker than myself. I realized later that I should have protected her, should have talked to her. If I'd been willing to be her friend, perhaps we could have found a way to be content. We had James, after all. But I won't take the entire blame. She wasn't willing to try either."

"She'd been raised with a violent father and a mother who turned the other cheek. She didn't know how to love."

I'd meant it as an accusation against his lack of understanding for her situation, but he seemed to think I was absolving him from blame entirely. "She *was* rather difficult. I suppose you're wondering why Coyle chose us to be parents when we were clearly not suited."

"Is it not merely because you two owed him considerable favors?"

"That, and your mother's silver magic. It's incredibly rare. Some thought it had disappeared altogether. Did you say James inherited it?"

"We never discussed magic, but he alluded to it in his diary."

"Pity," he muttered.

I didn't know if he meant it was a pity James had died before he could learn more about his own ability, or that he'd inherited silver magic and not paper. "Did Coyle demand my mother use her magic to create silver pieces for him?"

"Most likely, but not for financial gain. He simply liked to possess magician-made objects. He was a collector. He appreciated them."

"Are there other couples like you and my mother? Magician couples blackmailed by Coyle into having children?"

"I'm quite sure we were the first, although I suspect we wouldn't have been the last."

"His death put an end to his plans," I murmured.

"If it hadn't, bringing magic out of the shadows would have. Giving magicians freedom from persecution would have diminished the power Coyle had over them."

"You mean the freedom that Gabe's parents were instrumental in bringing about? As a magician, you would have been free, too, if you hadn't attacked Gabe's mother and needed to go into hiding."

His lips flattened. "Ironic, isn't it?"

As ironic as the fact my very existence was thanks to Lord Coyle, a man who'd caused Gabe's parents so much trouble.

Melville pulled the journal toward him and opened it. "You should study this closely. We can practice the spells together, if you like. You seem intelligent, so I'm sure you'll pick up the nuances in the language quickly." He flipped through the pages until he stopped at the moving spell. "You should learn to control flying paper first. It's perhaps the most important spell."

"It's dangerous."

"Not if you learn to control it. It's a weapon, and like any weapon, it can be used to protect yourself. I want you to be safe out on the streets, Sylvia. There are some evil men out there."

I watched him carefully, but he showed no sign of recognizing the irony this time. "My mother taught me some self-defense moves."

"So I noticed. Now it's my turn to teach you other ways to protect yourself. No one expects paper to be turned into a weapon, so the element of surprise will work in your favor."

"I have already used it, as it happens. It was effective, but chaotic. I'll practice focusing until I've learned to control it."

I thought he'd be pleased to hear my promise, but he looked concerned. "You had to use it? What happened?"

I'd not wanted to go into it, but I'd come this far and I didn't want to brush him off entirely. "A corrupt bookmaker named

Thurlow abducted me in an attempt to lure Gabe, for reasons I don't really want to go into."

"Abducted you!" He reached across the table, but I withdrew my hands before he could touch them.

I crossed my arms. "I escaped by using loose paper to cut him and his assistants." I touched the cut on my neck. It no longer stung, and I'd quite forgotten about it in the turmoil of the previous two days.

"Well done, Sylvia. I like that you're a capable woman, not a silly flibbertigibbet."

"It's how my mother raised me."

He lowered his gaze to the journal. "This Thurlow fellow… have the police caught him?"

"Not yet."

He frowned at Alex, as if it were his fault Thurlow was still at large. "That's a concern. You must be very careful, Sylvia."

"I'm well protected."

"I want to help you catch him."

"How?"

"I don't know, but he *must* be caught before he strikes again. You're the only family I have. I don't want to lose you, too."

"I am not your only family. You have three sisters, a niece and a nephew."

He huffed out a breath. "My sisters don't care about me. They made that clear years ago when they learned that my inclinations lean toward men. Anyway, I don't care about them."

"They may have changed, as have you. If you tried—"

"No." He reached across the table again, but I kept my arms crossed. "You are my daughter, Sylvia. My flesh and blood. You won't fully understand until you become a parent, but having children will change everything you thought you knew about yourself. I never wanted children when I was your age. I was content never to marry, never be with a woman to…" He waved his hand in the air in dismissal. "Having James brought a different perspective and brought out a side of me that I wasn't aware existed. When your mother took him from me, I was devastated. When you told me he'd died in the war, it was a double blow." He offered me a tentative, hopeful smile. "But you are here, Sylvia, and I want to get to know you."

This was going to be harder than I thought, but I had to say it now before emotions deepened. "Melville, considering what Gabe means to me, and your past entanglement with his parents, I'm sorry but this has to be our last meeting."

I heard rather than saw Alex shift his weight.

Melville's shoulders slumped, before he seemed to rally a little. "I thought you'd say that, but now I have a chance to prove to you—and them—that I only have your best interests at heart."

"I don't follow."

"Your kidnapper, Thurlow…do you know where he lives?"

"We only know his workplace, but…" I shook my head. It was all becoming too much. "Melville—"

"Call me Father."

"No." I stood, hoping he realized I wanted him to leave. He stood, too, but made no move toward the door. "Thurlow has gone into hiding. Leave it to the police to find him."

He rounded the table and strode toward me, his intense bearing somewhat unnerving. "I know how to stay hidden, Sylvia. There are people and places—" He cut himself off and glanced at Alex. "I might succeed where the police failed."

I blew out an exasperated breath. He didn't seem to want to accept that we couldn't have a relationship. "Even if you find Thurlow, it won't change anything between us."

"Very well. I'll write and apologize to Mr. and Mrs. Glass, but you have to understand that I can't hand myself over to the police. I won't survive in prison." He attached the false beard that wouldn't fool anyone if they looked closely, and picked up his hat.

Seeing him in disguise was a reminder of how much he was risking by coming here. While Alex wouldn't turn him over to the police, Cyclops probably would, as would the constables guarding the exits if they recognized him. I should be more appreciative. I *tried* to be.

"You're right, you must be careful. You'd better not return here. You can write, if you like."

He placed the hat on his head. "I know this will take time, but hopefully you'll see how much I want to play some part in your life. The time for raising you has passed, but I like to think I can play another, equally important role in your life."

I couldn't be any blunter, but I decided not to repeat myself. I'd tell Bristow and Murray to turn Melville away if he came back.

He came back the following morning, and what he had to say changed my mind.

CHAPTER 16

Although I'd told Bristow to turn Melville away if he returned to the house, the butler nevertheless informed me of his visit the following morning while I was once again working in Gabe's library.

"He claims to have found him," Bristow told me.

"Found who?" I asked without looking up from the book I was cataloging.

"He didn't say, but he asked me to tell you that. If I report back that you have no interest in speaking to him, he claims he will leave and never return. But he begged me to say that much to you. Miss Ashe," Bristow prompted when I still didn't look up, "could he mean he has found Thurlow?"

I dropped the book. *Oh, God.* "Bring him in here, then inform Alex, but not Willie or Gabe. Thank you, Bristow."

When Melville entered, he peeled off the false beard and stuffed it inside his upturned hat. He placed the hat on the table. "Did the butler tell you I found him?" His eyes were bright, and his voice edged with excitement. "I found your kidnapper, Sylvia. I've set up a meeting so we can trap him."

"What?" I exploded.

Footsteps came running and Alex appeared in the doorway.

Seeing me safe, he released a breath. "Everything all right, Sylvia?"

"I'm not going to harm my own daughter," Melville said snippily. "In fact, I've found a way to protect her. I'm glad you're here, young man. You're part of my plan."

Another set of footsteps pounded on the staircase.

"I'm sorry," Alex said to me.

"About what?"

Willie charged into the library and aimed her gun at Melville's head. "Get down on your knees, put your hands in the air, and don't move. You're under arrest."

Melville put his hands up but didn't kneel. "You don't have the power to arrest me. Anyway, I have a plan that involves you, and your gun."

Willie screwed up her face. "Huh?"

Alex placed his hand over her wrist. "Don't shoot him in here. It'll make a mess." Once she'd lowered the gun, although not put it away, he asked Melville to explain.

Melville addressed me. "I found Thurlow for you."

Willie swore.

Alex shushed her and closed the library door. "Gabe is resting."

Even if Gabe wasn't resting, I didn't want him hearing what Melville had planned. If it involved flushing out my kidnapper to arrest him, Gabe would want to be a part of it. In his current state, he was too weak. If his magic activated, it could weaken him further, perhaps to the point where his body couldn't recover. Besides, his magic might not even work when he was already so frail. That wasn't the only reason I didn't want him to hear Melville, however. I suspected I was an integral part of Melville's plan, and Gabe would try to forbid me from being involved. I'd be forced to go against his wishes, and I didn't want that between us.

Melville pointed at my notebook. "May I borrow a blank page?"

Willie pointed the gun at him again. "So you can slice my throat open? I ain't stupid."

With a roll of his eyes, Alex forced her to lower the weapon again.

Melville sat beside me and accepted the blank page. "I found Thurlow—"

"Where?" Alex asked. "Tell us and we'll send the police."

Melville shook his head. "I don't know where he lives. When I say I found him, I mean I got word to him via a network."

"Of thieves and thugs."

"And worse." Melville began to draw what appeared to be a map on the paper. "He doesn't know who I am to you, Sylvia, or that I'm a magician. I told our mutual contact that I'd heard Thurlow tried to abduct you but failed. Given my previous encounter with the Glass family, I said I realized abducting you would upset Gabriel, which would upset his parents. I suggested it would be a perfect revenge for me and I wanted to be involved. I offered to help him lure Gabriel so he can study or use his magic."

"I didn't say anything about Gabe being a magician," I said. "I told you Thurlow abducted me to lure Gabe, but I didn't mention why."

"I've read the newspaper articles about him. It wasn't difficult to guess the reason. *Is* he a magician?"

"No," all three of us said.

Melville shrugged. "It's irrelevant anyway. What matters is that Thurlow and others believe he can magically manipulate time. They won't leave him alone until their theories are proved false, and that means they won't leave *you* alone, Sylvia. As your father, I have to protect you."

I rubbed my temples. "You don't need to. I have capable friends."

He concentrated on his sketch again. "I told our mutual acquaintance that I'll trick you into going with me to the meeting place, where Thurlow can swoop in and capture you."

I put up a hand to halt him. "Wait. Slow down. What reason did you give for knowing Thurlow's interest in Gabe? Only we know."

"I'm sure others do."

"Why would he believe I could be tricked into trusting you?"

"I didn't give a reason. I only said enough to pique his interest and meet me." He turned his drawing around so I could see it properly then stabbed the pencil in the middle of a blank area between streets whose names I didn't recognize. "Epping Forest at two this afternoon."

Alex peered over my shoulder. "Why so far away?"

"It's quieter than London parks and offers a lot more seclusion."

Willie snorted. "For Thurlow's men to hide, then capture Sylvia?"

"No. For both of *you* to hide and capture *Thurlow*." He pointed his pencil at Alex and Willie, then set about drawing lines through the park. "There are a number of paths, but I've given directions for him to meet us here, near the King's Oak Hotel. There are a lot of trees in this area with trunks thick enough for you to hide behind." He marked the hotel's location on the map and indicated the trees.

"No," Alex said. "It's too dangerous, and it probably won't work."

Willie disagreed. She indicated her gun. "I take this, you take yours, Alex, and we stand where we get a good view of the path."

"I can't believe you of all people are considering the plan." Alex lowered his voice. "I thought you didn't trust him."

Melville's back stiffened. "I'm not going to place my own daughter in harm's way. And whatever you may think of my past crimes, it wasn't anything personal against either of you, or against the Glass family. I was under Coyle's influence. I had to do as he said or suffer the consequences."

Alex still didn't look convinced, but Willie had warmed to

the plan. Once she set her mind to something, she rarely backed down. "We need to do *something*," she said to Alex. "Using Sylvia as bait to draw Thurlow out is at least a plan. You got another one?"

Alex huffed a breath. "Gabe would murder us if he knew."

"Don't tell him until it's over. It'll be fine, Alex. If we get in place well before the meeting time, Thurlow won't know we're there."

"He'll bring his own men."

"He's too arrogant to hide them. He'll have them at his back, like he always does." She tucked her gun into her waistband with a decisive shove. "This'll work."

Melville gave Alex an annoyed look, as if he were being deliberately disagreeable. "Sylvia's life cannot continue to be shadowed by this man. He needs to be arrested or he'll keep trying. You know that."

Hands on hips, Alex stared up at the ceiling. "Bloody hell," he muttered. "All right. Willie and I will be armed, but you two can't be."

"Thank you, Alex," I said. "We can't do this without you. But you can't tell your father, either. Not until it's over."

Now that his mind was made up, Alex took on the role of commander. "You and Hendry can't take guns, but you can still have weapons. Thurlow doesn't know Hendry's a paper magician, but even so, he won't want to see any paper near you, Sylvia. He has seen what you can do with it. You'll need to conceal some paper without trapping it somehow."

Melville picked up the map he'd drawn. "I know a way." He folded the paper into a square with a triangle on top, without using a spell, then tucked it into his jacket pocket leaving the triangle visible. It almost looked like a handkerchief, except part of the sketch clearly showed. "Have you got nicer paper? I can use one and Sylvia can tuck another up her sleeve."

"That won't work against a gun," Willie said.

"They won't have their guns in their hands. They'll need to

draw them faster than this paper moves." Quicker than a blink, the paper handkerchief flew out of Melville's pocket and circled Alex's head.

Alex ducked but it was too late. If Melville had directed it to cut him, Alex wouldn't have got out of the way in time.

"I didn't see your lips move," I said. "How did you make the paper fly without speaking the spell?"

"I thought it." Melville flew the paper back into his outstretched palm and scrunched it into a ball. "Some magicians are strong enough that they don't need to say the spell, they can just think it. If your magic is strong, Sylvia, then after a little practice, you'll be able to speak a spell in your head, too."

But not in time for today's meeting. "I haven't learned to control the magic yet. The paper could fly in any direction, including toward me."

Melville grasped my hand between both of his. "Don't worry. I'll be there to help you."

Willie went in search of some quality paper while Alex fetched his gun. Once she returned, Melville showed me how to fold the paper to make it look like a white handkerchief in a gentleman's pocket. It was easy.

Alex returned, tucking his gun into the waistband of his trousers. "Dodson is bringing the Vauxhall around. Willie and I will leave in that immediately, so we're in place well before two o'clock. You two leave in thirty minutes in a taxi."

I peered through the library window and watched Alex and Willie drive off. I couldn't believe we were going ahead with the rash scheme. It was not only very hastily planned, but it was also concocted by someone I wasn't yet sure possessed all his marbles. There was an air of madness about Melville, like a racing driver who can see the finish line and knows he has to take extreme risks to reach it first.

Thirty minutes later, the taxi that Murray had gone to fetch pulled up at the neighboring house. Bristow offered to tell the driver to reverse a little to meet us, but I told him not to bother. I hurried toward it alongside Melville, my attention on our surroundings, although I didn't expect Thurlow to be so brazen as to attempt to abduct me off an upscale street in Mayfair.

I was wrong.

As Melville and I reached the taxi, we could see the front passenger seat was occupied as well as the driver's seat. I registered the sleek dark hair of the female passenger at the same time I saw the gun pointed at her temple, and Thurlow turn to look at us through the window aperture. He sported cuts on his face and neck. He smiled that ugly smile of his with the crowded teeth fighting each other for space in the rat-like mouth.

I noticed everything all at once, too fast for me to think clearly, let alone act. I simply stood there and stared.

Beside me, Melville swore. "Are you Thurlow? You shouldn't be here."

Thurlow shrugged nonchalantly. "I know who you are to the Glass family, but I don't know why you'd help them to capture me, and I don't care. I suspected it was a trick and decided to find out for myself. I saw those two monkeys leave and waited around the corner for the footman to seek out a taxi. Ah, there it is now," he said as a taxicab pulled up behind us.

Bristow watched on from the top of the front steps. He was probably confused since he couldn't see what we could see.

Thurlow pressed the gun barrel into the passenger's temple. She had her back to us, but I recognized the sleek hair and the regal stiffness to the shoulders.

"Ivy, are you all right?" I wasn't sure if she deserved my consideration, after the role she'd played in my kidnap, but she was clearly not helping him now or Thurlow wouldn't be holding her at gunpoint.

"No," she said on a whimper. "My mother is dead."

"The Hobson bitch was going to blame me for everything," Thurlow snarled. "She thought I didn't know she was planning to turn herself in and tell the police I'd forced her to help me. No one takes me for a fool. If they do..." He cocked the gun.

Ivy's shoulders shook.

"Tell the taxi driver to leave, Hendry," he said. "And you, my pretty little Sylvia, empty your purse and roll up your sleeves. If I see a single slip of paper flying at me, I *will* shoot her."

Melville waved the taxi off while I tipped everything out of my purse onto the back seat of the motorcar. Then I unbuttoned the cuffs of my blouse and rolled them up. The hidden pieces of paper fell out.

Thurlow grunted. "Give them to Ivy."

I did as directed, then Ivy handed them to Thurlow. He sat on them.

At least Melville still had his paper handkerchief, although he couldn't use it without distracting Thurlow first. With his gun already drawn and cocked, Thurlow would shoot Ivy before the paper reached him.

It occurred to me that Melville might think it an acceptable risk to sacrifice Ivy to save me.

"Hendry, fetch Glass," Thurlow said, his voice oozing with confidence. He was aware he had the upper hand. "I'll keep the two women he loves most here with me as insurance. If he tries anything, I will shoot."

He continued to point the gun at Ivy's temple, so clearly she and Mrs. Hobson hadn't told him that Gabe no longer cared for her. I wondered if Ivy now regretted keeping up the pretense. Or perhaps Thurlow knew Gabe was the sort of man who wouldn't place anyone's life in danger to save himself, not even the life of someone who'd conspired to kidnap me.

I glanced over my shoulder and saw Melville speak to Bristow, still standing on the porch. Then Bristow disappeared inside.

"This is madness," I said to Thurlow. "Why do you still believe Gabe can perform magic?"

"The one good trait Mrs. Hobson possessed was her clever mind. After your little escape the other day, she and I reassessed what we knew. We went through every newspaper article, and pieced together everything we'd witnessed ourselves, and it became clear that Glass did *something* magical to save himself and his loved ones. She came up with the theory that he can't control it. The magic only works when his life is in danger, or that of a select few."

I scoffed. "That's absurd."

"Is it? Glass saved himself and his friends in the war. He saved you, my dear little Sylvia, at the racetrack when someone shot at you. Just as he untangled the boy from the fishing net off the Isle of Wight then helped him to the surface, all of which took time."

"The father drowned," I said.

"Because Glass didn't care about him. He didn't care about the lad, either. Both were strangers to him. I'm sure Glass would have saved the father if he could. He likes to be the hero. But he *couldn't* save him. Once the boy was saved and Glass returned to the net, it was too late for the father. Mrs. Hobson concluded that time only altered because *Glass himself* was in danger of drowning if he spent too long underwater. The boy and his father were irrelevant."

He was right about it all. I would never admit it to him, however. "If that's the case, and Gabe can't control the magic, why are you trying to capture him and use it for yourself? By your own theory, you can't harness it to use at will."

"I didn't say it was my theory. I said it was Mrs. Hobson's. It's why she gave up on our idea to lure Glass. But I haven't given up. I want to test it myself, before I make a decision." He adjusted his grip on the gun handle. "Imagine if shooting Ivy doesn't trigger his magic and she dies. It would prove her mother's theory wrong. I rather like the poetic justice of it, don't you, Ivy?"

I couldn't see her face, but Ivy sounded like she stifled a sob. "He doesn't love me," she choked out. "He loves *her*. Shoot *her*!"

"Oh, I *will* repeat the experiment with Sylvia, although it would be a gross pity if she died. I do like her better than you, which is why you're first. You may be pretty, too, but you're a snob and a cold bitch. Imagine, though, if I shoot you first and he *saves* you. What an unexpected twist in the plot that would be!"

Thurlow must know he'd not get away with it. He would become the most hunted man in the city.

Yet Hendry had proved that hiding for decades was possible. All he had to do was lay low until everyone had forgotten him, then live a life that didn't attract attention. With his underworld contacts, Thurlow could easily disappear.

Ivy sniffed. "You say I'm a bitch, but I'm not the one who stole another woman's fiancé." Her voice was a guttural growl, coming from the very depths of her. "I am not the one who *bewitched* him. Kill her first, so I can watch his face when she dies."

Thurlow smacked his lips together. Then he turned the gun on me. "Your idea has a certain appeal to it. I owe Glass for sending my girl away. It would be fitting to take his girl away from him."

Now that the gun was no longer aimed at her, Ivy turned in the seat to look at me. A gash on her forehead and another on her jaw from the paper I'd wielded with my magic didn't look too bad. Her eyes were red and swollen from crying, but there was a gleam of pure hatred in them as she glared at me. The polished façade had fallen away completely, revealing the rotten foundations underneath.

I didn't care about Ivy's reaction. She was trying to save her own life. What I cared about now was that Melville couldn't use his magic on the paper handkerchief in his pocket to attack Thurlow before he fired. With the gun already in Thurlow's hand, cocked and ready, the paper simply wouldn't reach him in time, no matter how fast Melville managed to work. Thurlow would shoot the moment he realized he was under attack.

Melville stood beside me again. In a moment, Gabe would emerge from the house. When he did, Thurlow would shoot.

Either Gabe's magic would activate as it had done in the past, taxing his strength, perhaps even to the point where his weakened body couldn't cope. Or it wouldn't activate at all because the magic knew it would draw on more energy than Gabe could afford to spend.

"Don't," I told Thurlow. "Gabe has been very ill these last few days."

Ivy gasped. "What's wrong with him? How bad is it?"

"He lost a lot of blood and is very weak. His magic won't work."

Thurlow huffed a laugh. "You don't know that, my dearest little pet."

"Don't call her that," Melville spat. "She is no man's pet, and certainly not yours."

Thurlow frowned. "What *is* she to you? No, don't bother to explain. I don't care. Ah. The door opens. Get ready for the show."

"No!" Gabe's voice was louder than I expected, stronger. It was a good sign and filled me with hope.

My hope dashed when I glanced at him. He wore only pajama pants. His chest and feet were bare. He'd not taken the time to throw even a dressing gown on. It was his physical weakness that worried me, however. He clung to the rail alongside the steps as he descended. The frail, aged butler behind him looked like a man in his prime by comparison.

"No, Gabe," I said. "Stay there. You can't do anything to help."

He was close enough that I could see the panic in his eyes. He didn't trust his magic to work either.

"Please," I begged Thurlow. "Don't do this. Whatever is in my power to give you, I will."

Ivy barked a laugh. "My God, did you hear that, Gabe? It seems my mother was right after all and the librarian is a whore."

"I meant—"

I cut myself off as Melville spoke the words of the paper moving spell. He spoke them loudly and clearly, not even whispered. Why? Why attract Thurlow's attention like that? Even more confounding, the handkerchief didn't fly out of his pocket. It simply lifted up, slowly, as if peeping out of the pocket to tentatively look about.

Melville's magic was strong. He didn't need to hesitate. At such a slow pace, the paper wouldn't strike Thurlow before he fired the gun. So why did Melville do it at all?

Then the reason became horribly, sickeningly clear.

He managed a tender smile for me before Thurlow turned the gun on him and fired.

CHAPTER 17

"No!" I caught Melville as he crumpled to his knees. "No, no, no!"

"Sylvia!" Gabe's voice was closer now, but not close enough. I wanted to touch him. He might be physically weak, but he had an inner strength that I needed as I cradled my dying father in my arms.

"So there *is* a connection between you two," Thurlow drawled. "Is he your father?" He snorted. "Pathetic. His magic isn't nearly as strong as yours."

Melville tried to reach up to me, but his hand fell back to his side. "Daughter."

"Shhh. Don't talk." I cradled his head in my lap, my hand pressing down on his stomach wound. But I couldn't stem the blood flow. It soaked his clothing and mine, and dampened the pavement. Unlike Gabe, medical help wouldn't arrive in time. Even if it did, a bullet wound in the stomach couldn't be fixed.

"The handkerchief." Melville's voice came out a whisper that I had to lean closer to hear.

"I know what you did," I whispered back. "I owe you my life. Thank you."

Unlike Thurlow, I'd realized Melville had controlled his

magic, deliberately keeping the paper's movements slow and unthreatening. Melville's actions had lured Thurlow's attention away from me and onto him. Fast movements would have made Thurlow panic and fire. With the gun pointed at me, I would be shot. But slow movements gave Thurlow time to react less rashly and shoot the man wielding the weapon instead.

Gabe's bare feet came into my view. He crouched beside me, a hand cupping my face. His thumb stroked my cheek, and I realized I was crying. I never thought I would cry for Melville Hendry. I should hate him. My mother had taught me to hate him. She certainly had, and had feared him, too. Even now, I didn't doubt that she had a reason to fear him. But I would never learn the specific incidents behind her reason, and a large part of me was glad about that.

I would remember Melville as the man I saw now, his head on my lap as the life bled out of him. He was multi-faceted, as most of us are. He was neither all good nor all bad. He was terribly flawed and deeply troubled. Circumstance had brought the worst out of him, suppressing the best. For some of that, he only had himself to blame, but not all.

"Sylvia..." His voice was so weak I could barely hear it. "Moving spell." He wanted me to use the handkerchief, the only piece of paper in our possession, to cut Thurlow. But it was useless against a gun.

Even so, I nodded. "I understand."

His fingers inched toward mine, still covering his wound. I stopped putting pressure on it and took his hand. I raised it to my lips."

"Father."

Melville's lips twitched with a whisper of a smile.

Then it slipped away, as did his life. He was gone.

I lowered his hand and silently looked at the handkerchief. One piece of paper against a gun was useless.

Gabe touched my cheek to get me to look at him. "It'll be all right." He was too pale to be out of bed. He crouched at my side and pressed his fingertips into the pavement to act as a crutch for balance. But they wouldn't hold him up forever. Sweat beaded his forehead with the effort of simply getting out of bed.

"Get back, Glass." Thurlow was still seated in the vehicle. "Or you'll be shot, too."

Gabe didn't move. I doubted he could. He was too weak.

"Gabe, do as he says and move away!" Ivy cried.

Gabe's ragged breaths quickened. Exhaustion, fear, or perhaps both, shadowed his eyes. "Sylvia…" he murmured.

Thurlow climbed out of the motorcar and rounded its bonnet. He stepped onto the pavement, his back to the row of houses, so that he could get a clear shot of me without Gabe in the way.

Gabe closed his eyes, squeezing them. Was he in pain? Or was it worry that he was too weak to save me? "Let her go," Gabe said. "It's me you want. I'll perform magic for you. I'll slow time whenever you want. You can change the odds of a race or get away from the police…you decide. Just let Sylvia go. Ivy, too."

Ivy sniffed. "Thank you for remembering I exist."

Thurlow huffed. "Doesn't it only work when your life is in danger or that of someone you care about?"

Gabe shook his head. "I *can* alter time at will."

"Forgive me if I don't take your word for it. I think I'll test it first." He cocked the gun.

"No!" I cried. "You can see he's ill. His magic might not activate if he's this weak."

Thurlow shrugged. "It's time to find out."

He pulled the trigger.

I lay on the ground, on my side, not far from where I'd been sitting with Melville's body. My ear hurt from the impact with the pavement, and Gabe's body, lying over me, was heavy. But he breathed. I could hear it coming in short, sharp bursts, and feel the rapid beat of his heart. He was alive, but not at all well.

"Have you been shot?" I asked, thinking that perhaps his

magic had engaged, but been too slow to ensure we both missed the bullet.

"I'm fine," he said, rolling off me.

Thurlow stood over us, his face blending with the gray clouds in the sky above. "Remarkable. I didn't realize time stopped for even a moment. I'm now convinced. Ivy, your mother would be pleased to know she was right. Smug bitch."

I couldn't see Ivy, but I could hear her crying. It sounded like she was still in the motorcar.

All I could see from where I lay was Thurlow, the sky, and the top floors of the houses. The curtains fluttered with the breeze. No, not the breeze, and not all of the curtains, just half a dozen at number sixteen.

How strange.

I registered the fluttering curtains, the appearance of Gabe's servants' faces at the windows, and the gun now pointed at Gabe, gripped by Thurlow.

"You were strong enough for your magic to save her," Thurlow said. "Are you strong enough for it save yourself, too?"

Before anyone could respond, he fired.

The next moment, the gun was nowhere in sight and Thurlow was holding his arm. Gabe was on his feet, bent over with his hands on his knees, his body heaving as he sucked in each breath. His magic had engaged again, but he wasn't strong enough to attack Thurlow. He'd only managed to knock the gun out of Thurlow's hand as he dodged the bullet. There was a small hole in the wall of the house behind Gabe.

I spotted the gun at the base of the steps of number sixteen. Gabe could never reach it before Thurlow did. He was too weak. It was up to me.

But before I could even get to my feet, Gabe fell to his knees, clutching his upper arm. The glint of a blade flashed in Thurlow's hand. He could have struck the knife at Gabe again, but he didn't. He simply watched him, smiling, as blood seeped from between Gabe's fingers.

I jumped to my feet. "Gabe!"

"Get back." Thurlow pointed the knife at me. "I'm in the middle of an experiment, my pet. You see, there might be a flaw with the magic. It activates to save him in an instant, but what if his death is slow? We'll know the answer soon enough. Either his magic will activate when he is still able to get medical help to stop the bleeding, or it won't, and he will bleed to death here. I can't wait to see the results of my experiment. Isn't science riveting?"

"He has already suffered a terrible loss of blood. This will be too much."

Ivy tried to rush past Thurlow to reach Gabe, but he grabbed her arm and hauled her back.

She screamed in frustration. "Let me go! You madman!"

Her timing was perfect. Her screeching covered the fluttering sound of loose papers being thrown out of several windows. It wasn't until the first sheets floated into his view that Thurlow realized what had happened. By then it was too late. I'd already spoken the spell in my mind. I almost cast a glance at Melville's body, since I'd only learned the trick of spell casting in silence while we'd waited for the taxi, but I didn't dare take my gaze off the papers and Thurlow. All my concentration was required now if I was going to control the direction of my weapons.

Dozens upon dozens of weapons.

They sliced through the air, swooping and dipping before rising again, just as they had done at the house where I'd been held captive. But this time, they surrounded Thurlow, and Ivy too, since she was with him. This time, I concentrated on just the two of them until I saw them, and only them. It was as if they stood on a theatrical stage beneath a spotlight while their surroundings remained in the dark.

Ivy screamed in terror.

Thurlow shouted. He swatted at the paper, but for every one he batted away, ten more attacked. Soon, the paper circling them completely hid them from view.

The knife clattered onto the pavement.

Murray ducked low and grabbed it. I hadn't seen him emerge from the house. In his other hand, he held Thurlow's gun. "You can stop it now, Miss Ashe. I'll take over from here until the police arrive."

I stopped my silent chants and the paper gently fluttered to the pavement, no more dangerous than feathers, revealing Thurlow and Ivy crouching, arms over their heads for protection. Scratches striped the backs of their hands, and their clothing had been slashed.

When he realized the danger had passed, Thurlow tried to get up, but Murray ordered him onto his knees. "Don't do anything rash, or I'll shoot you."

Thurlow obliged, but let out a string of expletives that would have made even Willie blush. Murray ordered him to be quiet, but Thurlow ignored him.

So Murray pistol-whipped him. "Don't speak like that in front of the ladies."

"Thank you," Ivy said. She'd rallied now that the paper storm had ended. No doubt she was thinking of a way to get out of her predicament using legal arguments.

"I didn't mean you, Miss Hobson."

"Excuse me? What did I do to you?"

"You and your parents were rude to the staff, as well as to Mr. Bailey and Miss Ashe. Not to mention your involvement in her abduction." His lips puckered in thought. "Maybe I should just shoot you to save the government paying for your prison accommodation."

That silenced her.

I turned away from them and knelt beside Gabe, who was lying on his back. On his other side, Mrs. Bristow tied a tourniquet around his upper arm above the wound while Mrs. Ling pressed down on it.

"Gabe," I said, my voice trembling. "Gabe, can you hear me?"

His eyes cracked open. "Sylvia. Well done."

I smiled, not because of his praise but because he sounded stronger than I expected. He must be taxed to his physical limit, yet he wasn't going to die. I stroked his hair back and kissed his brow. "And you," I managed to say through my tight throat.

Bristow gave orders to carry Gabe inside. He took over holding the gun so that Dodson and Murray could help Gabe. I worried about leaving a frail man in charge of the prisoners, but he looked more than capable. The butler's hands had never been steadier, his gaze never fiercer than now, with the gun pointed at Thurlow.

Thurlow and Ivy knelt side by side, their hands on their heads. Ivy sobbed, declaring her innocence and blaming Thurlow and her mother. Bristow ignored her. It was Thurlow who told her to shut up.

"Bloody women," he snarled.

I wanted to follow Gabe inside, but I couldn't leave the body of Melville lying there on the pavement. So, I knelt beside it and plucked off a piece of paper that had fallen against his face. I blinked at it, not quite believing what I saw. It was a blank letterhead with *my* name on it. The paper held magic in it. Peterson magic, if I wasn't mistaken. It would be strong, then. No wonder Ivy and Thurlow sported even more cuts now than they had before. Some looked quite deep. They'd leave scars.

Sally approached carrying a bedsheet. She gave Melville's body a wide berth, and handed the sheet to me. "Mrs. Bristow says to cover him with this so you can come inside to be with Mr. Glass."

I laid the sheet over Melville. Before I lowered it over his face, I touched his cheek. He looked peaceful and rather ageless, as if all his cares disappeared at the moment of death. It was the way I wanted to remember him. "Goodbye," I whispered. Then I covered him completely and went inside.

I found Gabe in his bedroom, Mrs. Bristow fussing around him. She made him drink a glass of water then settle back into the pillows. His face was ashen again, but the smile he gave her was robust.

"Thank you, Mrs. Bristow. I'll be all right now. Sylvia is here."

She patted his hand and turned away. She looked close to tears, so I embraced her. Since I was still feeling quite fragile, I began to cry. Her arms tightened around me.

"There, now, Miss Ashe, he'll be all right. He just needs to rest. The doctor is on his way to check him, but I'm sure he'll be fine."

I wiped my damp cheeks and sat on the bed. Before I knew it, Gabe drew me into an embrace. We clung to one another. Neither of us spoke. No words were necessary. The silence meant I could hear his breathing, more regular now, and the throb of his pulse. They were the best sounds I'd ever heard.

When I drew away, I was surprised to see Mrs. Bristow still in the room. "How did you know about the paper?" I asked her.

"When Mr. Hendry came to the door to ask my husband to fetch Mr. Glass, he also told him to gather as much paper as we could find and to throw it out of the windows when the time was right, and you could use your magic on it. We all gathered up a stack and took a position by a window. Murray signaled for us to throw out our stacks when Miss Hobson screamed. It worked well, didn't it?"

"Very well," I said.

"Perfectly," Gabe added.

Mrs. Bristow's eyes crinkled at the corners with her cheeky smile. She turned to go, only to stop and address us again. "He did an admirable thing today, did Mr. Hendry. I was here all those years ago, when he attacked Mrs. Glass, as she was still called then, before she became Lady Rycroft. I wouldn't say I knew him at all, but looking back, I remember a vacancy in his eyes. It was as if he wasn't there, inside the shell of his body." She gave me a flat smile. "He wasn't a nice man then, but he wasn't born mean. The world in general and Lord Coyle in particular made him like that. If he was born mean, he couldn't have fathered such a wonderful and kind young woman." She bobbed a brief curtsy, turned away quickly, and walked out of the room, closing the door behind her.

I lay down beside Gabe and rested my head on his chest.

He removed the pins and combs from my hair and stroked his fingers through it. If it wasn't for the languid motion of his fingers, I'd have thought he'd fallen asleep. His breathing finally steadied, and his body relaxed against mine.

"Sylvia," he murmured.

"Hmmm?"

"I love you."

I pushed myself up on my elbow to see him better. There was a little more color in his cheeks, thankfully, and his eyes were alert as they searched my face. I smiled. "I love you, too."

Our kiss was achingly soft. It was tinged with the relief we felt to be alive after coming so close to death. I'd suffered a loss today, but Gabe's kiss reassured me that he would be by my side while I digested that loss. He wasn't going anywhere. I hoped he understood that I would always be there for him, too, from the way I kissed him back.

When I was once again snuggled into his side, his good arm circling me, I teased the hairs on his bare chest. "Why did you have so much letterhead with my name on it?"

He laughed softly. "I ordered it from the Petersons after I learned you were a paper magician. I was going to gift it to you for your birthday. The surprise is ruined now."

"Nevertheless, it's much appreciated." I kissed him lightly. "You know me well."

He put a finger to his lips in mock thought. "Hmmm, so gifts of paper in some form or other for the next fifty birthdays. Noted."

"Fifty?"

"Hopefully more." His heated gaze met mine. "Many more."

* * *

THE DOCTOR CAME and stitched Gabe's wound, then Tilda arrived. She told us that Mrs. Bristow had telephoned her and asked her to come. After checking the stitching, she said she'd return later.

"You may stay with him, Sylvia, but he must rest."

I didn't think I was tired, but I fell asleep in Gabe's arms as he slept. We both awoke some time later to Willie demanding to be let in. While her tone was hushed, it was still loud enough to be heard through the door. I couldn't hear the response, or who gave it, but Willie's next words had me climbing off the bed in a hurry.

"If you don't let me in to see him, then you and me are finished, Tilda."

I had to let her in before she ruined a perfectly good relationship.

I opened the door to see Tilda sitting on a chair, her back to me, blocking the doorway. Willie stood in front of her, arms over her chest, a fierce glare in place. The glare vanished when I invited her inside.

Tilda moved the chair and entered after Willie. "Don't crush him," she chided as Willie threw herself on Gabe.

Alex must have been hovering nearby because he entered, too. He drew me into a hug. "The servants told us everything. Are you all right?"

"Thank you, yes. Gabe is, too. Like last time, he just needs rest."

Alex squeezed my hands. "Your father did a noble thing."

I nodded. It was all I could manage, otherwise the tears would spill again, and I didn't want to cry anymore.

Alex joined Willie at Gabe's side. "You've got to stop worrying us like this," he said. "Willie's nerves can't take it, and my nerves can't take any more of her fretting." He grinned and shook Gabe's hand warmly.

Willie poked Alex in the chest. "I don't fret."

"Have you been back long?" I asked, glancing at the clock. It was ten minutes past three.

"We arrived a few minutes ago," Willie said.

"When no one turned up at the meeting place in Epping Forest, we knew something was wrong," Alex added. "We drove back as fast as we could."

Willie *humphed*. "We missed it all. Even the police have gone, although Cyclops waited until we got back before he left for Scotland Yard."

"He's going to interrogate Ivy and Thurlow immediately," Alex said. "There were many witnesses, so there's no way Thurlow can weasel his way out of it in court this time."

"And Ivy?" Gabe asked.

"She's saying she was coerced by her mother and Thurlow, but Thurlow is claiming she was willing and even contributed ideas of her own to ensure you suffered. Given Thurlow's reputation, it's likely the jury will believe her over him. Or they might tar her with the same brush used to tar the Hobson and Son company once their fraud is made public. She didn't murder anyone, unlike Thurlow, so she won't hang if found guilty of aiding and abetting."

Willie looked smug. "So, either she'll spend a very long and uncomfortable time in prison, or she'll endure a humiliating trial at the end of which none of her former friends will speak to her. She'll be ruined." She wagged a finger at Gabe. "Don't you dare feel sorry for her."

He took my hand in his. "I stopped feeling a sense of responsibility for Ivy altogether when she helped Thurlow kidnap Sylvia."

I rubbed my thumb over his knuckles. "What about Mrs. Hobson?" I asked Alex. "Ivy says she's dead."

"My father sent men to the house where Ivy claimed they'd been hiding these last few days. The sergeant telephoned to say he'd found Mrs. Hobson's body. She'd been shot, most likely this morning."

I spared a thought for the woman who'd been set against me from the moment we met. It was as if she'd known even then that I would be the catalyst for Gabe ending his relationship with Ivy. She had also blamed me for Gabe refusing to use his family's reputation to support the Hobsons when they tried to claim all the boots made for the army held magic. That was entirely Gabe's decision, however. I hadn't bewitched him on that score, nor did I believe I'd been the entire reason he'd stepped away from Ivy. While my presence may have sped things along, he would have seen her for what she truly was eventually. All he'd needed was time for her true colors to reveal themselves, and his parents had given him that by leaving for America. Their absence meant he kept putting the wedding off.

Parents *should* protect their families to the best of their abilities. My mother had, and so had my father, in the end. Their methods were very different, with my mother avoiding conflict by running away while Melville thought it best to bring it to a head. Neither method was completely right or wrong. In their own ways, they'd loved James and me, and that's what mattered.

Gabe must have sensed the direction of my thoughts. He squeezed my hand to get my attention and arched his brows in question.

I nodded and offered a smile. I still felt somewhat on edge, but with Thurlow and the Hobsons out of our lives, the future was looking easier. As long as Cyclops found Stanley, all would be well.

Willie clicked her fingers. "How did the prophecy in the Hendry family journal go, Sylv?"

"'A magician from the line of Hendreau will save time,'" I recited.

She pointed at Gabe. "Time." She pointed at me. "A member

of the Hendreau family. You saved Gabe's life by creating the paper storm."

Alex, Tilda and I all looked at Gabe.

He rolled his eyes. "I am not time. I don't even know what that means."

"For the purposes of the prophecy you *are* time," Willie shot back.

"Prophecies aren't real."

Alex agreed. "They're deliberately vague to fit the agenda of any moron who believes them."

Willie bristled. "You calling me a moron?"

Alex merely smiled, which annoyed Willie more.

Tilda put an arm around Willie's waist and drew her to her side. "You are many things, but a moron isn't one of them. Now, we need to let the Master of Time get his rest."

Gabe groaned, but Willie giggled rather girlishly before pecking Tilda's cheek. "I might be a moron, but I'm your moron."

Alex snorted as he followed them out of the room. "That's not the sweet talk you think it is."

I placed my hands on the pillow on either side of Gabe's head then kissed him lightly. "I'll keep your circus quiet while you rest."

* * *

THE FOLLOWING MORNING, I was in the middle of showing Gabe the advertisement Huon had placed in *The Times* praising the graphite magic in Petra's pencils when Bristow entered the sitting room and handed Gabe a sealed envelope.

"I paid the lad who delivered it," Bristow said. "He says the man who gave it to him pressed upon him the need for urgency."

Willie sprang to her feet and approached Gabe. I thought she'd snatch it out of his hand, but she waited for him to open it, albeit impatiently. Without Tilda there to keep her calm, Willie had been anxious all morning, biting her fingernails to the quick. Like the rest of us, she expected Stanley to make a move.

She was right.

"He wants to meet me," Gabe read.

"No," Willie snapped. "Absolutely not."

I agreed with her. I didn't want him to go anywhere near Stanley.

"What else does he say?" Alex asked.

Gabe passed the note to him. "He apologizes for placing me in danger by taking too much of my blood."

Willie grunted. "Apology *not* accepted."

"He then goes on to say he now believes my magic is triggered only when I need to save myself and those I care about." His gaze met mine. "And he doubts I love him like I used to after what he did. In wartime, we were brothers-in-arms, and depended on one another for our mental and physical wellbeing. He knows he destroyed that relationship with his act of 'selfish desperation' as he calls it. He claims he only wanted to learn more about my magic so he could recreate it, not kill me."

"'Meet me at midday,'" Alex read, "'and I will right my wrongs by ensuring the world never discovers your magic secret so you can live in peace, without fear of others coming for you to study your magic in the future.'" Alex lowered the letter. "How can he manage that?"

Willie took the note. "We ain't going to find out. It's a trick. Stanley proved he can't be trusted. I'm going to telephone Cyclops so he can send men to…" She checked the note. "…to Farringdon Street at midday and arrest him." She went to leave, but Alex blocked her path.

"It's Gabe's decision." He looked to Gabe.

Gabe looked to me.

I stayed perfectly still. This was his decision to make, not mine. Besides, I was torn. I didn't trust Stanley, but I didn't know him as well as Gabe did. If Stanley spoke the truth and he knew of a way to end the speculation about Gabe's magic, then it was worth pursuing. Gabe was tired of the unwanted attention. He needed to be left alone to live in peace.

But if Stanley knew a way to end the constant speculation in the press, why hadn't he detailed his plan in his note? It would be easier to convince Gabe if the plan was a sensible one.

Gabe asked Willie for the note, then folded it in two. "I'm going, but you all have to stay here so he doesn't use you against me."

Alex scoffed. "Not a chance."

"Nope," Willie said.

I shook my head. "I'm coming, Gabe. But I'm going to be prepared."

CHAPTER 18

Holborn Viaduct hunkered over Farringdon Street in a glorious display of elegance and strength. Iron magicians had built it, so Gabe told me on the way, although no one had known they were magicians at the time of its construction in the 1860s.

Stanley's note asked Gabe to meet him under the viaduct, but Farringdon Street was a busy thoroughfare, so Alex parked the Vauxhall on a side street and we walked the rest of the way. I was conscious of not taxing Gabe too much, but he seemed well enough for a short walk after a thorough rest overnight. Anything more than a walk, however, would tire him.

It was fortunate that we did park on a side street as traffic banked up on Farringdon Street where it passed under the viaduct. Drivers shouted at each other to move, but it was no good. Something ahead had gained the attention of passersby, and they'd stopped to observe.

"I've never seen so many pedestrians here," Alex said. With his superior height, he was able to see over the heads of those in front. "I recognize one of the journalists who wrote an article about you, Gabe."

Willie stood on her toes in an attempt to see. "Where? I want to tell him to mind his own business."

"He isn't the only one with his notepad and pencil out. There are photographers, too."

I adjusted the weight of the paper stack in my arms. Gabe had offered to carry it, but I wanted the paper as close to me as possible. "Whatever Stanley has planned, he wants the press to bear witness."

"It doesn't make sense," Willie added. "He wrote that he wanted to fix things by ensuring the world never discovered Gabe's magic. So why invite the world here to witness whatever he's about to do?"

A train leaving the Holborn Viaduct Station blew its whistle, making my nerves jump. "Can you see Stanley, Alex?"

"No. I can see Jakes, though."

Willie swore. "That's all we need. A spy for the military."

"We'll ask him what he's doing here," Gabe said. "He might be able to shed some light on Stanley's intentions."

We carved our way through the crowd, but stopped before reaching Mr. Jakes when we saw Lady Stanhope. Dressed in black lace from head to toe, she looked like the dozens of other onlookers in the crowd, something which she probably would have hated. She liked to think herself above the masses, on a level just below the royal family. In truth, she was rather unremarkable. If anything, her sour, unsmiling face made people turn away, not look twice.

Gabe deployed his smooth charm, something he did only when he wanted answers. "What a surprise to see you, Lady Stanhope."

She gasped. "Gabriel! There you are. We've been waiting for you."

Heads turned toward him. Excited whispers rippled through the crowd.

Gabe's smile wavered. "Why is everyone here?"

"You don't know?"

"I received a letter—" He cut himself off as Mr. Jakes emerged through the throng. "Jakes. Can you shed some light on all this?"

Mr. Jakes plucked out a letter from his jacket pocket. "I received this from an anonymous source."

"I received one, too." Lady Stanhope withdrew a letter and a black silk fan from her purse. She handed the letter to Gabe and flapped the fan in front of her face.

Gabe lowered the letter so I could read it, too. It was written in the same handwriting as the one we'd received, but was unsigned. It invited Lady Stanhope to Farringdon Street at the Holborn Viaduct to witness Gabe's magic for herself.

"He ain't a magician," Willie made sure to say when she read that part.

Lady Stanhope turned her back to Willie and tried to hustle Gabe away from us. He stood his ground.

"Jakes, you need to stop this," Willie said. "Someone's trying to kill Gabe."

"Who?" Mr. Jakes asked.

Gabe glowered at Willie. She kept her mouth shut.

Mr. Jakes showed his letter to Gabe. "Mine is identical. According to the members of the press I spoke to, they received letters, too. The rest of this crowd is made up of passersby who realized something of interest was about to happen so have stayed to watch."

Gabe looked around at the faces turned toward him with curious expressions. As more in the crowd realized who he was, a hush fell over them. The only sounds came from the rumble of a train pulling away from the nearby station and the traffic trying to pass under the viaduct.

Lady Stanhope reached up a hand gloved in black lace and raked Gabe's cheek. "You look pale, dearest Gabriel. Are you ill? Why haven't you done something about it?"

"I've been resting."

"Let's not play this game anymore. You know that I know

about your…" She leaned closer and lowered her voice. "… magic."

"You know nothing!" Willie spat.

Lady Stanhope flapped her fan at her face, ignoring Willie. "Heal yourself, Gabriel. Do it where no one can see, obviously. Not here. At home, in private. Oh, I have an idea! Come to the countryside with me. I leave next week. I have a large manor with lovely gardens. It's so peaceful." She struck his arm with her fan as a thought struck her. "I can introduce you to some very eligible ladies."

Gabe's lips tightened in pain. She'd tapped the knife wound inflicted by Thurlow. "I don't need an eligible lady. I already have—"

"Pish posh. I know a very pretty, very *worthy* girl." As if anyone were in any doubt that she was implying I was *unworthy*, she deliberately angled herself between Gabe and me, presenting me with her back. "I'll make sure no one disturbs you while you heal yourself with your magic."

The muscle in his jaw bunched as he clenched his back teeth. "You are quite wrong, Lady Stanhope. I can't heal myself with magic. The doctor has prescribed rest."

She struck him again with her fan. "Gabriel, dear, I am not a fool. I know you can heal yourself. It's the only explanation for your miraculous survival."

"A lot of luck is the explanation. I'm sorry to disappoint you."

She went to tap him again with her fan, but he caught it. "I have stitches there."

She eyed him carefully, if somewhat skeptically, before laughing like a schoolgirl. "Surely you joke. You wouldn't need stitches. Your magic—"

"Is non-existent. I would remove my shirt right here and show you if I thought Jakes wouldn't add a note to my file that I was mad. He's from Military Intelligence," he clarified.

Now that he'd been brought into the discussion, Mr. Jakes

stepped forward. "Madam, I have studied Mr. Glass far deeper than you, and I can assure you, he *can't* heal himself."

She froze. Only her throat worked with her hard swallow.

I was rather looking forward to seeing how she responded, but a flurry of activity and whispers drew everyone's attention to the viaduct itself. Above us, Stanley Greville stood on the iron railing, an arm around the central lamppost for support. Rather fittingly, the bronze statues on either side of him depicted Fine Art holding what appeared to be a sketchbook, and Science with her scientific equipment.

"Don't come any closer!" Stanley shouted to the small crowd of pedestrians on the viaduct with him.

A constable stood among them and, realizing what was happening, tried to halt the traffic and urge the pedestrians to give Stanley space. Stanley ordered them further away. He didn't want anyone stopping him.

One of the journalists near us called up to him. "Sir, did *you* send us the letters?"

"What do you know about Mr. Glass's magic?" another asked.

"Can he heal himself? Or does he travel through time?"

"Bloody hell," Alex muttered. "This has gone too far. I'll stop him."

"Wait."

As Gabe said it, Stanley's gaze fell on our little group. Heads turned our way again as questions were thrown at Gabe.

"Did he invite you, too?"

"Will you display your magic for us, Mr. Glass?"

"I asked you here to bear witness," Stanley said, his voice rising above the traffic noise. "In a moment, I'm going to throw myself off this bridge."

Gasps burst from the crowd. One woman screamed. The constable called for everyone to calm down, then edged forward. He appeared to be trying to talk Stanley out of his decision, but we were too far away to hear what he was saying.

We pushed through the retreating crowd, moving against the tide. I shifted the stack of letterhead from one hip to the other as it grew heavy. None of us spoke. We didn't need to speculate about his sincerity or reason, or whether he would actually go through with it. We knew Stanley was deadly serious.

"You want us to witness your suicide?" one of the journalists called up. "There are ladies present!"

Several voices rose in accord, some pleading with Stanley not to take his own life.

"I'm going to throw myself off this bridge, but I won't die. My friend Gabriel Glass will save me with his magic, just like he saved me countless times in the war."

The gasps turned to murmurs of speculation and wonder. I overheard more than one onlooker say they thought as much all along. Others, however, suggested Stanley shouldn't put his life in peril to prove such a wild theory.

Gabe was one of them. "Stanley, don't!" he called up. "I *can't* save you."

Stanley's foot slipped off the rail. The crowd gasped again, but he managed to regain his balance. "If my theory is correct, and you are able to save your life and the lives of your friends by altering time, then this will work. We're friends. You saved my life before and I believe you will do so again. Your magic is special, Gabe. The world should know how special so that it can be examined and understood."

This time, even more voices chimed in for him not to test his theory in such a dangerous way.

But Gabe's wasn't one of them. Nor was Willie's, Alex's or mine. We all knew that Stanley was prepared to die. Indeed, he planned on it. By announcing his theory about Gabe's magic in front of witnesses and telling them that Gabe had saved lives by using his magic in the war, he'd put into everyone's minds that Gabe would repeat the incredible feat here and now. Yet Stanley knew that he'd lost Gabe's high regard after the abduction, a fact he was deliberately leaving out. Gabe's magic wouldn't engage to save Stanley, and Stanley wanted the world to witness that failure. The journalists and onlookers would see for themselves that Gabe couldn't alter time after all, or he would have done it to save a friend. With the theory disproved, the press would lose interest in Gabe and leave him alone.

And Stanley would be dead.

He was sacrificing his life to give Gabe his freedom.

That's why he hadn't described his plan in the letter. He knew Gabe wouldn't show if he did, because simply being here would lead to Stanley's death.

The surrounding noises seemed to close in. Engines of passing vehicles revved, a train pulled into the station in a squeal of brakes and hiss of steam. Above it all rose the voices. Members of the crowd shouted, pleading with Stanley or begging Gabe to act. The constable on the viaduct nearest Stanley blew his whistle, trying to keep the onlookers back. Motorcars and lorries on the viaduct had stopped altogether. Another constable cleared an area on Farringdon Street below, which only caused the traffic problems to worsen.

Amidst it all, Gabe's pleas to Stanley got lost.

There was only one thing in his power to do. He pushed through the throng, heading for the stairs. Willie and Alex followed, ever protective. I remained where I was, the stack of papers weighing heavily in my hands. I had thought I might need them to protect Gabe, but it seemed not. He was safe in this crowd.

From his vantage point on the railing, Stanley watched Gabe until he disappeared into the pavilion housing the stairwell. He readjusted his grip on the lamppost and kept his gaze on the stairwell exit on the viaduct itself. I couldn't see it, but I knew the moment Gabe emerged. The crowd on the viaduct stirred as it spat him out.

Stanley squared his shoulders. If he harbored any doubt about his plan, I couldn't detect it from where I stood, some sixty feet below. I got as close as the constable allowed.

But being closer wouldn't be of any use. I needed to be quick. I needed to speak faster than I ever had. And I needed to focus.

Stanley lifted a hand in a half-hearted wave. It was that simple motion that saved him.

It gave me precious seconds. As if it were a signal, I threw the sheets in the air and chanted the flying paper spell.

Stanley stepped off the viaduct rail.

Onlookers screamed. Gabe rushed forward.

My sheets of letterhead coalesced into a carpet of paper above Farringdon Street. It slid into place under the falling figure of Stanley. To my utter relief, the structure held. The spell I'd spoken into the stack before we left the house had strengthened every sheet even more. They held both the Petersons' magic and mine.

Under my direction, the paper carpet lowered Stanley gently to the ground.

Members of the crowd rushed in to assist him to his feet. Others stared at me, mouths agape, and several applauded.

I looked up to see Gabe, Alex, Willie and the onlookers on the viaduct peering over the railing. Applause sprinkled down from there, too. I received pats on the back and offers to shake my hand. I overheard someone say they didn't know paper could be that strong. I was asked where I manufactured it, and I gave them the name of the Petersons' factory.

I watched it all as if I was not a part of it, as if I was riding on the carpet of paper above the scene, observing. It wasn't until one of the constables ordered me to clear the paper from the road that my mind refocused.

I spotted another constable arresting Stanley and forged my way to him. I reached him at the same time as Gabe.

Stanley sat on the pavement, his hands cuffed, his wide eyes staring at those closing in around him. Journalists peppered him with questions, despite the constable ordering them to leave. Photographers' bulbs flashed like bursts of sunlight. One went off near Stanley's face, snapping him out of his trance-like state.

"You saw," Stanley told them. "You all saw. He didn't save me."

"Glass really is artless," one of the journalists said as he scribbled notes. "I always thought so."

"Pity," another journalist chimed in. "It's been a good story for my paper."

"If that lady hadn't been here..." said a third man with a shake of his head.

One of the journalists realized I was that lady. "Your name, Miss?"

I opened my arms as the papers came to rest on them in a neat pile. I finished chanting the spell once the last one floated into place. "I'd rather remain anonymous."

Gabe appeared at my side, accompanied by Juan. He must have received a letter from Stanley, too. Alex asked the constables to give Stanley a few moments to speak to his friends. He then suggested they report the incident to Detective Inspector Bailey at Scotland Yard.

With space cleared around us, Gabe crouched before Stanley. "I know this is hard," Gabe said. "But you're not alone."

Juan sat beside Stanley and put his arm around his friend's shoulders. "We are here. Me, Gabe, and the others. Do not do that again."

Stanley lowered his head further. "It wasn't supposed to end this way. I'm not supposed to..."

"We know how it was supposed to end," Juan said. "But we do not like that ending. It was good luck that Sylvia was here to rewrite it." He gave Stanley's shoulders a shake. "I know you are sad now, but you will not always be. You will get better."

"We'll get you the help you need," Gabe added.

"No one can help." Stanley didn't snap or sneer. He sounded empty, as if exhaustion had drained every last drop of his essence. "I tried the medication they gave me, but I felt strange when I was on it, not like myself. I couldn't think straight. It made me angry, resentful."

"There are other medications," Gabe said. "And if none work, we'll try other methods. The way to treat shell shock may not exist yet, but new treatments are being trialed all the time. One of them will work for you, Stanley. Just as long as you don't give up."

Stanley peered at Gabe and Juan, then Alex. "It's almost two years since the war ended, and everyone is moving on. Everyone except me. I *want* to move on…but I can't."

Gabe clutched Stanley's arm. "Not giving up is the first step. It's the hardest and most important. The other steps will come, in time. But no more stunts like this. Understand?"

"I had to do it. I had to make it up to you somehow."

"Not like this."

"What I did to you… You have every right to hate me." His gaze shifted to Willie and Alex again, then fell on me. "You all do."

I crouched down, too, and set the papers aside. I didn't know what to say to make his pain go away, so I simply hugged him.

When I drew back, Alex did the same.

Stanley began to cry. "I'm sorry. I'm sorry, Gabe."

Gabe drew him into a hug, too. "I forgive you."

By the time one of the constables led Stanley away, the crowd had thinned. All the journalists and photographers had departed, eager to be the first to go to print. Mr. Jakes was still there, watching on, as was Lady Stanhope. She was deep in conversation with Huon, of all people.

When they spotted us, she bustled over. She grasped me by the elbows. "My dear girl! You were magnificent! Why didn't you tell me you were a paper magician? Everything would have been different."

"You mean you wouldn't have been as rude to me?"

Her smile froze. Then she tittered with laughter. "Such an amusing girl, and so very pretty, too. It's no wonder you've captured Gabriel's heart. It's a shame he isn't a magician, after all, but finding you, Sylvia…what good fortune!" She looped her arm through mine. "What strong magic you possess. Now, you must be careful. Unscrupulous people will try to manipulate you. You must allow me to guide you. We'll have such fun. I'm very well connected, you know, and my friends will enjoy meeting you. You *must* come to my country house. We'll have fabulous parties, and I'll let you play with as much paper as you like."

Willie snorted. "You told Gabe your house is quiet."

Lady Stanhope ignored her. "You will make so many new friends, Sylvia. Friends worthy of a powerful magician such as yourself."

I jerked my arm free. "I have a gift for you, Lady Stanhope."

She pressed a hand to her chest. "How marvelous!" She licked her lips. "What is it?"

I asked Willie to hold the stack of papers for me. I removed the top one and folded it into the shape of a Sopwith Camel, using a spell to assist me to get it as close to a miniature version of the plane as possible. Then I sent it flying away. Far away, past the viaduct and over some buildings.

"Oh, dear," I said dramatically. "I do hope nobody tramples it before you find it, Lady Stanhope."

She picked up her skirts and hurried off in the direction it had flown.

Willie grinned. "Can you make me one of those, Sylvia?"

"I'll make you an entire squadron."

Her grin widened.

Beside me, Gabe rested a hand on my shoulder. I felt the weight of his exhaustion, the rapid throb of his pulse.

I circled my arm around his waist. "Let's get you home."

Alex left to bring the Vauxhall around, so Gabe didn't have to walk to it. Huon joined us while we waited and congratulated me on the rescue.

"Why are you here?" Willie asked him.

"I was meeting someone in the area, saw the crowd, and decided to see what was going on."

"Lady Stanhope?" I asked.

"No." His gaze flitted to Mr. Jakes, lounging against a lamppost, smoking a cigarette.

Most people would think he was simply casually lingering, but those who knew him would see the sharp gaze that missed nothing. Huon was far less devious. Going by his enthusiasm and the frequent glances in Mr. Jakes's direction, it wasn't difficult to work out that he'd struck a deal with Military Intelligence for his invisible ink business.

"Then why were you talking to Lady Stanhope?" I pressed.

"I've been meaning to speak to her for a few days and seeing her here gave me the opportunity. You see, I recalled that her husband is an important fellow at the Royal Academy of Arts and knowing how she loves to think of herself as some sort of mentor to young magicians who have yet to discover their talent, I simply mentioned how I'd recently come across an amazing artist who uses magic graphite in her exquisite sketches. Naturally, this young woman has never dreamed of exhibiting her work and is ripe for discovery by someone with an eye for quality." He smiled wickedly. "It was enough to pique her interest in Petra's sketches. I negotiated an enormous price for one she has hanging in her shop."

I laughed. "I do hope Petra appreciates your efforts."

His eyes flashed. "So do I."

* * *

By the time we returned home, exhaustion had turned Gabe's face ashen and made his steps plodding. Alex helped him up the stairs to his bedroom while I trailed behind with Willie. A short while later, Murray brought in tea and a meal of roast beef with buttered potatoes and beans. Tilda had gone to work, so I took over nursing duties. The first thing I did when Gabe finished eating was send everyone else out.

Willie refused to leave, however. "Someone should stay and watch over him."

"Sylvia will stay," Gabe told her.

"No! Your parents are returning the day after tomorrow and you're my responsibility. If Matt and India see you looking like this, they'll blame me. They won't care about all the times I saved your life, they'll just see you looking as weak as a ghost and think it's my fault. Don't know why, but everyone always blames me when you get into trouble."

"That's because it usually is your fault," Alex said. For my benefit, he added, "Almost every story from Gabe's wild and impulsive years features Willie."

"I'd like to hear them one day."

Willie thrust a hand on her hip and *humphed*. "They feature you, too, Alex. Just wait until I tell Daisy all about them."

His eyes clouded, and he sighed heavily.

"When did you save my life?" Gabe teased Willie. "Strange that I don't recall a single incident."

I tried to get Alex's attention, but he wouldn't look at me. It seemed he'd made up his mind and didn't want me to try and make him change it. He was giving Daisy up so she could reconcile with her family. It was a grand sacrifice on his part, but it was the wrong one. No amount of telling him that would make him realize it, however.

Alex took Willie by the shoulders and steered her toward the door. "He's not going to relax with you here."

"He will!"

"Willie, you are a distraction."

"But I'm the best kind of distraction."

I waited until Alex closed the door behind them, then climbed onto the bed beside Gabe. His chest was bare, since he seemed to only wear pajama pants when in bed, and I made the most of it, admiring his smooth skin with the sprinkling of dark hair. He was warm, and despite the hard planes of his muscles, I felt comfortable and relaxed, more relaxed than I had in a very long time. I closed my eyes and listened to the rhythm of his heart, still a little erratic after the events of the day.

His yawn was a sign that I should leave, too. I tried to pull away, but he refused to release me.

"Stay," he murmured drowsily. "I sleep better when you're near."

"I'll sit here awhile. Lie down." I adjusted the pillow then stroked his hair back as he sank into it.

His eyes fluttered closed, revealing eyelids darkened from exhaustion. He drew in a deep breath and released it slowly. I felt his body relax against mine, felt the twitch of his muscles as he gave in to the exhaustion. I suspected he would sleep soundly with the knowledge that not only was Thurlow behind bars, but the threat of abduction had come to an end. Stanley Greville had made sure of that.

I leaned down and kissed his cheek. "Rest now, Gabe," I whispered. "It's over."

CHAPTER 19

Returning to work in the Glass Library felt like going home. Everything was familiar to me, from knowing which step creaked, to where every book was shelved. I hadn't realized how much I'd missed it over the last few days until I entered the morning after Stanley's attempted suicide.

I placed my bag on the front desk and was about to call out to Professor Nash when a clock chimed. It wasn't a chime I'd heard before. It was musical, yet quite loud. It would have been heard even in the furthest nooks of the library.

I entered the main part of the library through the marble columns and studied the large clock above the fireplace. It was nine o'clock according to the brass hands, which kept perfect time thanks to Lady Rycroft's horology magic, but I'd never heard the clock make a sound before.

Professor Nash came down the stairs. "Sylvia? What was that?"

"The clock. Has it chimed before?"

"No. Never. How odd. I wonder what it means."

"Should it mean something?"

"Knowing India, yes." He smiled.

It was a genuine smile that lifted my heart. Lately, his smiles had been wan and fleeting, or missing altogether. He was lonely. The loss of his friend, Oscar Barratt, seemed to weigh heavier than ever on him. I'd heard that growing older made some people melancholy, and I supposed that was happening to the professor. I wished I knew how to improve his mood, but I suspected nothing I could do would make him better. What he needed was beyond my power to give. Hopefully the return of Gabe's parents would lift him out of the doldrums. What he needed now was old friends.

The clock chimed again, with the same musical notes. It wasn't quite like any clock chime I'd heard before. It rose in scale, each note a little higher than the last. "Do you think it's announcing something?" I asked.

The sound of the library's front door opening couldn't have been more perfectly timed. The professor and I exchanged knowing smiles.

He pushed his glasses up his nose. "It seems India has put a spell into it to announce her return, although they're a day early. And why would they come here to the library and not return to their house?"

We both turned as footsteps approached.

We were wrong. The man standing between the black marble columns holding his hat against his chest wasn't Gabe's father, Lord Rycroft. I'd seen photographs of Matt, and he looked a lot like Gabe. This man was about Lord Rycroft's age, with a little more weathering of his features. I'd seen photographs of him, too, but it took me a moment to realize that I'd seen those photographs here in this very library, and in the professor's adjoining flat. Indeed, it was Professor Nash's reaction that confirmed the man's identity for me.

He fainted.

I managed to catch him and lower him to the floor. He regained consciousness as Oscar Barratt crouched beside him.

"You're not usually this dramatic, Gavin." Oscar grinned. It made his interesting face rather handsome. He opened his arms to receive a hug. "It's good to see you."

The professor sat up, blinked at his old friend, then did something I'd never seen him do before. He punched Oscar. It was only in the arm, and it seemed to hurt the professor's hand more than Oscar, but it was still a surprising reaction from the gentle-natured librarian.

Oscar rubbed his arm. "I thought you'd be pleased to see me." He sounded hurt. He turned a worried frown onto me. "Are you his assistant? Do you know what's made him so aggressive? Is it the war?"

"I think it's the fact that he thought you were dead."

Oscar's brows shot up. "Why would you think that?"

The professor drew his legs in and I thought he was going to stand, but he remained seated on the floor. Perhaps he didn't trust his balance yet after receiving such a shock. I couldn't fathom the emotions swirling within him. "You never wrote to me to tell me otherwise! I received *no* word for *years*. Of course I thought you were dead! Why wouldn't I?"

"I did write to you." Oscar scoffed as if he suspected he was the victim of the professor's joke.

But the professor wasn't laughing. Indeed, he still looked furious.

"I wrote to you just after we parted ways, when war broke out," Oscar said. "I told you where to write to me. You didn't receive it?"

"No."

"I suppose we can blame the abysmal north African mail service and the chaos of war for correspondence going missing."

"Can we?" the professor growled.

Oscar twirled his hat in his hand. "I wondered why you never responded."

"Your brother didn't receive a letter either."

Oscar scoffed. "You know Isaac and I don't get along. I didn't write to him."

"And Huon? Why didn't you write to your nephew? He looked up to you. He could have done with his favorite uncle's guidance, by the way."

Oscar winced. "That's why I came home. One of the reasons. The other was to see you. I missed you."

The professor's lips pinched so tightly they turned white. I thought he was going to punch Oscar again, but Oscar knew him better than I did. He drew his friend into a hug and patted him firmly on the back.

I got up to leave them in peace. "I'll make some coffee."

Oscar broke free of the professor and put out a hand to me. "Strong coffee, if you have it, Miss…"

"Ashe. Sylvia Ashe." I shook his hand and headed to the staircase to make the coffee in the professor's flat.

"She's pretty," I heard Oscar say. "Huon would like her."

The professor's chuckle drifted up to me. "Gabe likes her more. Besides, Huon has his eye on someone else. You'll like her." A moment later, he said, "Is everything all right, Oscar? How is—?"

"Fine," Oscar said, a smile in his voice. "Everything is fine. I have a lot to tell you."

* * *

Oscar Barratt's return from the dead drew everyone to the library. Huon's reaction was similar to the professor's, but without the punch in the arm. He did scold his uncle, however, telling him that he should have written more than once, especially when he received no reply from either of them.

Huon introduced Petra as the woman he planned to marry, which caused Petra to blush fiercely and stumble over her words. Huon couldn't take his eyes off her. He was utterly besotted as she chatted to his uncle about his travels.

Later, when Daisy and I got Petra alone, I asked her how she felt about Huon now. "Has your opinion of him changed?"

"It has changed quite dramatically," she said, watching him from beneath her lashes. "He is cleverer than he seems at first, and funny, brave, and kind. He's quite perfect. I don't even mind that he's an ink magician."

"And your mother?" Daisy asked. "Does she mind?"

"She said she will accept him because he makes me happy. That's good enough for me."

Daisy, Petra and I sat on the sofa in the first-floor reading nook. Alex, Gabe, Willie, Cyclops, Catherine and their eldest daughter stood at the desk, listening to Oscar repeat a story that I'd heard him tell the professor earlier. Professor Nash was making tea with the two younger Bailey girls. It was a comforting scene of long-lost friends getting to know one another again, but I sensed all wasn't well with Alex.

He'd barely looked at Daisy since her arrival, and merely nodded a greeting. Catherine had spoken to him, but from what I'd seen of the exchange he'd disagreed with whatever she'd said. It was clear to everyone that he was miserable.

As was Daisy.

I was about to urge her to talk to him, again, but it turned out I didn't need to. After Petra declared that her mother would accept a rival into the family, Daisy got to her feet.

"You're very fortunate to have such a wonderful mother," she said.

Before Petra could answer, Daisy marched off. She strode up to Alex, grasped his face in both her hands and pulled him down to her level so she could kiss him thoroughly.

Willie and Ella both let out a *whoop* of delight. "It's about time," Willie declared.

Alex broke the kiss and stepped back. He ran a hand over his hair. "Daisy…no. We can't… Your parents… That's not what I want for you."

"That's unfortunate, because it's what I want for myself. You can argue all you want, Alex, but it's an argument I'm going to win." She stepped forward, but he stepped back again. "I love you, Alexander

Bailey. I love you, and nothing will change that. Not my parents' attitudes, nor the world's. It's time you accepted that I'm not giving up. You're the man for me, and you always will be. Only you."

She once more stepped toward him, but he moved away again. He butted up against a shelf, trapped. He swallowed.

"So, either you accept that we're going to be together, Alex, or you leave me no choice."

"I don't?" he choked out.

"If we can't be together, I declare here and now, in front of witnesses, that I will never be with another man but you. If you don't agree, then you condemn me to live the life of a spinster with no family of my own."

"But—"

"No buts." She inched closer. "I won't have a family because my parents are no longer a part of it, with or without you. So it might as well be with." She took another step until she was toe to toe with him. "So you see, Alex, either we create a family of our own with two loving grandparents and three sweet aunts, or I'll be a lonely old maid."

Alex peered down at her. His jaw firmed. Then he threw his arms around her. His words were lost in her hair, but I suspected she heard them. I suspected no one else was meant to.

Catherine snuggled into Cyclops's side, smiling. "She has his measure. I like her."

He circled his arm around his wife's waist. "I'd like it known that I predicted this from the moment I met her."

Willie snorted. "You did not. I did. Tell 'em, Gabe."

Gabe sat on the arm of the sofa beside me and twirled a loose strand of my hair around his finger. "I don't remember that conversation."

"Traitor," Willie muttered. "If your father were here, he'd take my side over Cyclops's."

"Would I?"

We all turned toward the deep, droll voice to see Gabe's

parents climbing the stairs. Even if I hadn't seen photographs of Matt and India, I would have known who they were. Matt was an older version of Gabe, except for the eyes. Gabe's green eyes were a match for India's.

He embraced his parents, albeit *after* Willie, who'd thrown herself at her cousin and his wife. When Gabe drew back, his mother continued to watch him, as if she'd been starved of the sight of him for too long and needed to get her fill.

While Cyclops, Catherine, Alex and Ella greeted them heartily and welcomed them home, Gabe took my hand. "Don't be nervous," he said, his voice as warm as his smile.

"I'm not nervous."

"You are. The vein in your neck below your ear throbs when you're nervous."

"It does not."

He kissed the vein, but because it was in a ticklish spot, I giggled. I felt his smile against my skin.

"That's better," he said, tugging me toward his parents. "Mum, Dad, this is Sylvia."

At the last moment, I remembered these two were a lord and lady, and I didn't know the protocol. Should I curtsy?

India must have realized why I hesitated. She drew me into a hug. "I am so glad to meet you, Sylvia."

Matt shook my hand. "I feel as though we already know you. Gabe told us all about you in his letters."

"Oh," I said, on a breath.

"Six months' worth of letters," India added. "It was clear from the first one that you were special." She smiled gently as she clasped both my hands. "I can already tell I'm going to like you. Are these your friends?"

I introduced Petra. They already knew Huon, and Alex introduced Daisy. He couldn't stop smiling as he did so.

India, still holding my hand, squeezed it. "So much has happened in the last six months. I'm sorry to have missed it, but

I'm not sorry we went away when we did." She exchanged a knowing glance with Catherine, her dear friend.

"It turned out to be the right decision," Catherine said. "Ivy is—" She stopped herself with a shake of her head. "We'll talk about it later. Today is not the day."

Matt looked past me. "Oscar? You don't look very dead."

Oscar shook Matt's hand vigorously. "Surprise." He embraced India. When he drew back, he clasped her hands lightly. "You look very well."

"So do you, for a dead man," she said with a scowl. "Seeing you here is quite a shock. Is Gavin all right?"

Oscar rubbed his arm where Professor Nash had punched him. "I believe he's feeling better after venting his frustration."

"He has been rather down these last few years, you know. You'd better make it up to him."

On cue, the professor arrived, carrying a tray with tea things, Mae and Lulu behind him, also carrying trays. He beamed. It was the happiest I'd ever seen him. "Matt! India! We thought you weren't coming until tomorrow."

"Our ship docked early," Matt said. "We decided to surprise Gabe and caught the midday train to London, but he wasn't at home. Bristow said you were all here. Did the clock downstairs chime?"

"Yes, as it happens. Did you make it chime, India?"

"I practiced a new spell I created on the voyage home," she said. "Did it chime at nine o'clock precisely?"

The professor pushed his glasses up his nose. "Yes. Is nine AM significant?"

"It's when our ship docked. My spell was designed to announce our arrival on English soil. I'm so pleased it worked, although it is a rather pointless spell."

Matt put his arm around her. "Not at all. In future, you'll have all the clocks chiming your arrival, so Willie knows when she needs to start behaving."

Cyclops snorted. "That's not going to make her behave."

Willie nodded, all seriousness. "Very true. So, how's Duke?"

"He and his family are well," Matt said. "He misses you."

"Naturally."

"So he's visiting us in the autumn."

Willie tried to hide her happiness, but failed spectacularly. She burst into tears.

We moved to various sofas and chairs to talk. I poured tea while the professor served the cake. It was to magic that the conversation turned. It began with Cyclops asking after their traveling companions, Dr. and Mrs. Seaford.

"They're both well," India said. "He was very interested to learn that your mother was a silver magician, Sylvia."

I glanced at Gabe. Clearly his letters had kept his parents informed of events here in London. "She was, although I didn't know it until after she died."

Gabe took my hand in his and offered me an encouraging smile.

"Gabriel—Dr. Seaford, that is—was adopted by a silver magician," India went on.

"He was?" Gabe asked. "I didn't know that. His name wasn't in the magician files. Marianne Folgate was the only one."

"Gabriel asked us to leave it out to maintain privacy. His adopted father had no natural children, so we assumed silver magic no longer existed. Perhaps you're distantly related to him, Sylvia, but as far as we know, he had no other family except his adopted son. We're sorry there are no family members for you to connect with."

"It's quite all right," I said. "I've recently discovered aunts and cousins on my father's side that I never knew existed." I looked to Gabe, not wanting to mention my father's name to them. I didn't want his parents to regard me with disappointment, perhaps even dislike.

India allayed my fears, however. She leaned forward and touched my knee. "Melville Hendry is your father, isn't he? When Gabe wrote to us about your paper magic, Matt and I considered the possibility that you're Hendry's daughter. We didn't know for sure, of course. We've been on a ship for several days without any news, but rest assured, it doesn't matter to us."

"Don't let Willie try to tell you otherwise," Matt said wryly.

Willie sank into a chair. "He's dead anyway," she muttered.

India and Matt offered me their condolences. It seemed strange to receive them. I'd never come to terms with having a father, so losing Melville so soon after meeting him didn't feel as painful as it should.

"We met your mother, Sylvia," Matt went on. "Marianne was a strong, capable woman. We both liked her."

To think they'd met her all those years ago, and now here I was, seated in the library they funded, their son's hand warming mine. My mother hadn't liked men. She'd feared them and raised me to fear them too, except for James. Yet, I think she would have liked that I'd found my soulmate in the son of the couple who'd helped free magicians from persecution. Like my mother, India seemed to have a strength about her that wasn't obvious at first glance, and Matt was clearly in love with his wife. Anyone who saw the way he looked at her could see it.

Matt and India wanted to know everything that had happened since the last telegram they'd received before boarding the ship to come home, so I left Gabe, Alex, Willie and Cyclops to talk to them. I smiled at Professor Nash as I passed him chatting to Huon, Petra and Oscar. Daisy had been cornered by the Bailey sisters, so I climbed the spiral staircase to the mezzanine level alone. I ran my fingers across the spines of the books shelved alongside the narrow mezzanine walkway, then looked out onto Crooked Lane through the large arched window. Dusk had settled over the city while we were talking. We all ought to be going our separate ways, but no one seemed to want to leave.

I stood in the wider section of the mezzanine, the window and cozy armchair behind me, and surveyed the scene below. I breathed in deeply, drawing the scent of old books and paper into my lungs. A wave of contentment washed over me. It was the paper, calling to my magic, telling me I was exactly where I should be, where I belonged.

Contentment turned to happiness when Gabe's arms circled my waist from behind. "Is it overwhelming?" he asked.

I leaned into him. The scent of him replaced the paper, but it was no less fulfilling. "Not at all. I like your circus."

His soft laughter ruffled my hair.

Matt's explanation about a man named Ponzi drifted up to us. The term sounded familiar, but it wasn't until he told Alex, Daisy and Oscar about an article in the *Boston Globe* that mentioned the complete collapse of the investment scheme that I recalled Hope, Lady Coyle, had told us her son had invested everything in it. They would be ruined now, even more than they already were.

I pushed thoughts of Valentine and his mother from my mind. I didn't want to think about them at this moment. I wanted to enjoy it.

"They're talking about you," Gabe said, nodding at Cyclops and Professor Nash.

Thanks to our vantage point, Cyclops's voice drifted up to us, but I doubted they were aware I was listening in. "She doesn't need a father. She already has a man in her life who thinks of her as a daughter."

Professor Nash lowered his teacup to his saucer. "Yes, I do think of her like that. It's perceptive of you to notice that I'm a father figure to her."

"I meant *I'm* a father figure for Sylvia."

"I think you'll find that she sees *me* that way. Sorry, Cyclops."

"You're very important to her, of course, but I already have three daughters, so I'm an expert at being a father to girls."

Ella, who'd been passing, stopped to scold Cyclops. "The fact you just called your three grown daughters girls, not women, proves you don't have a clue what makes us tick."

Cyclops pouted. "Lulu's still a girl."

Ella laughed. "It's a joke, Father. You're wonderful." She kissed his cheek, winked at Professor Nash, then threw herself onto the sofa beside Willie.

Willie, however, was also pouting. "I am not old," she said, stroppy.

Catherine rolled her eyes in exasperation. "That's not what I said. I said I liked Tilda for you, because she's mature, and perhaps she'll help you settle down now that you're *older*."

Willie crossed her arms, jutted out her jaw, and turned away.

Catherine appealed to India. India, however, had an impish look on her face. She winked at Catherine then, her face serious, made Willie look at her. "Don't you think it's time to age gracefully?"

Ella laughed. "I've known her all my life, and she's never done a single thing with grace. I doubt she'll start now."

"I can be graceful! I just choose not to be." Willie poked Ella in the shoulder. "So you can pipe down or I'll tell your mother what you got up to last Saturday night."

Catherine narrowed her gaze. "What did she get up to?"

Ella glared at Willie.

Willie smiled back, triumphant, then stood and walked off.

India followed her. "I'm looking forward to meeting Tilda. She sounds marvelous."

"She is."

India frowned. "You sound unhappy about that."

Willie shrugged a shoulder but gave no answer.

India turned Willie to face her fully then dipped her gaze to Willie's level. "You deserve contentment, too."

Willie sighed. "I don't know. There's no…thrill. No excitement."

"And yet you're drawn to her?"

Willie nodded. "I don't understand it. Why do I like her so much when she's so modest and sensible?"

"You like her because she makes you feel content when you're with her. It's something no one tells you about love, but love *is* contentment. You can't chase thrills forever. The highs you experience from temporary amusements are fun, exciting, but they're also fleeting. When they're over, you feel empty. If Tilda fills that emptiness, then she's worth having in your life."

"Thanks, India. I needed to hear that." Willie smiled. "I'm real glad you're back."

Gabe turned me around within the circle of his arms to face him. "It could be your circus, too."

I smiled, even though my insides had suddenly turned to jelly.

He removed a small box from his pocket and got down on one knee. "I wanted to do this somewhere special. Somewhere that has meaning for us. I couldn't think of a better place to ask you to be my wife than here, surrounded by paper and books." He glanced past me. "And our circus." He opened the ring box to reveal a sparkling diamond. "I love you, Sylvia. I love everything about you, but I mostly love the way I feel when I'm with you. More content, and happier than I've ever felt. Will you marry me?"

I got down on my knees too, because some things should be said face to face. "I already think of you as my family, Gabe. I love you, and yes, I want to marry you."

I hadn't realized the circus had gone quiet until Ella's cheer led a round of applause and well-wishes from below.

I laughed against Gabe's mouth.

He placed the ring on my finger then drew me up to stand beside him. I grinned and waved, pretending the wave was in gratitude but, really, I just wanted to see how the ring looked.

"Shall we go downstairs?" he asked.

I drew his arms around me again. "I want to savor this moment first."

He held me tightly, his chin resting on the top of my head. I could tell from the angle of his head that he looked at his friends and family below. I did, too, but not for long. I was drawn to the bookshelves filled to bursting with magical knowledge. Gabe was right to propose here. The most important phase of my life began the moment I set foot in the Glass Library. My happiest memories were made here. Our journey as a couple was deeply woven into the fabric of the library, and I knew in my bones that it would play an equally important role in the journeys we were yet to take—together.

THE END

Did you know the **Glass Library** series is a spin-off of the **Glass and Steele** series? Go back to where it all began with book 1, *The Watchmaker's Daughter* by C.J. Archer.

Want to read more of C.J.'s books? As well as historical romantic fantasy, C.J. also writes historical mysteries, light epic fantasy and has some older historical romances that might interest you. Check out her website for descriptions of other books and series and choose one you like.

A MESSAGE FROM THE AUTHOR

I hope you enjoyed reading THE JOURNAL OF A THOUSAND YEARS as much as I enjoyed writing it. As an independent author, getting the word out about my book is vital to its success, so if you liked this book please consider telling your friends and writing a review at the store where you purchased it. If you would like to be contacted when I release a new book, subscribe to my newsletter at http://cjarcher.com/contact-cj/newsletter/.

ALSO BY C.J. ARCHER

SERIES WITH 2 OR MORE BOOKS

The Glass Library

Cleopatra Fox Mysteries

After The Rift

Glass and Steele

The Ministry of Curiosities Series

The Emily Chambers Spirit Medium Trilogy

The 1st Freak House Trilogy

The 2nd Freak House Trilogy

The 3rd Freak House Trilogy

The Assassins Guild Series

Lord Hawkesbury's Players Series

Witch Born

SINGLE TITLES NOT IN A SERIES

Courting His Countess

Surrender

Redemption

The Mercenary's Price

ABOUT THE AUTHOR

C.J. Archer has loved history and books for as long as she can remember and feels fortunate that she found a way to combine the two. She spent her early childhood in the dramatic beauty of outback Queensland, Australia, but now lives in suburban Melbourne with her husband and two children.

Subscribe to C.J.'s newsletter through her website to be notified when she releases a new book, as well as get access to exclusive content and be the first to learn about discounts and giveaways. Her website also contains up to date details on all her books: http://cjarcher.com

Follow her on social media to get the latest updates on her books:

facebook.com/CJArcherAuthorPage
x.com/cj_archer
instagram.com/authorcjarcher

Made in the USA
Monee, IL
20 March 2025

14290450R00163